aunty lee's
chilled revenge

ALSO BY OVIDIA YU

Aunty Lee's Delights
Aunty Lee's Deadly Specials

aunty lee's chilled revenge

A SINGAPOREAN MYSTERY

OVIDIA YU

WILLIAM MORROW
An Imprint of HarperCollinsPublishers

P.S. is a trademark of HarperCollins Publishers.

HarperCollins books may be purchased for educational, business, or sales promotional use. For information please e-mail the Special Markets Department at SPsales@harpercollins.com.

FIRST EDITION

Library of Congress Cataloging-in-Publication Data has been applied for.

ISBN 978-0-06-241649-0

16 17 18 19 20 ov/rrd 10 9 8 7 6 5 4 3 2 1

Dedicated to Rajeev Doraswamy, Ram Doraswamy, and Aaron Mali, with thanks for the amount of time and attention your wonderful mothers devoted to the birthing of this book

aunty lee's
chilled revenge

Prologue

They had opened the clinic doors at nine as usual. Dr. Samantha Kang had just escorted an obese corgi with breathing difficulties and its worried owner into the examining room when she heard the crash and Lisette, the receptionist, shrieking.

The corridor was full of black smoke and the smell of kerosene when she opened the door and saw a fireball blazing in the reception area. Lisette stumbled into her, coughing and tearing. "I don't know what happened!"

"Get them out the back." Dr. Kang pushed Lisette and the corgi and its owner through the animal holding area to the goods entrance. They had three dogs, two cats, and a rabbit in the back room. Gino, the veterinary assistant, was already putting the second cat into a carrier, and Samantha started leashing the dogs. There was no point rescuing terrified dogs from a fire only to be run over.

Somehow they got all the animals out. Coughing and dizzy from smoke, the vet stumbled around to the front of the clinic and sat on the grassy patch that separated it from the main road. Normally she avoided even walking here, given that it was where many of her canine patients relieved themselves. She held a shivering Chihuahua on her lap, and a brown "Singapore Special" mutt laid a grateful, moist snout on her leg. A curious crowd had gathered but the fire was already out. Within ten minutes of the alarm, two Singapore Civil Defense Force fire bike riders with compressed foam backpacks had arrived and extinguished the blaze. Now two red rhinos and a full-sized generic fire engine arrived from the SCDF to find only sodden, black-streaked walls and smoky dampness.

"Dr. Samantha Kang? I am Emergency Response Officer Sarah Hisham. How are you feeling?"

"Yes, I'm Samantha Kang," Samantha said to the uniformed woman squatting in front of her. "I'm sorry." The Chihuahua gave a halfhearted yap but subsided when she put a comforting hand on its head.

"Sorry?"

Samantha indicated the main road, where a traffic officer was directing cars around the stationary fire engine. The rhinos had driven off the road to park on the grass slope, their flashing lights giving the place a festive air.

"We got you all over here for nothing. It was just a small fire. I don't know how it happened."

"Calling us was the right thing to do," Sarah Hisham said. "The best fire is no fire. Second best is small fire." It sounded like a standard joke, but Samantha could not smile.

"There should be some way of saying it's a small fire, just send one or two firemen. Don't waste resources. You shouldn't be wasting resources."

"Better safe than sorry. Now come with me so we can take a look and make sure you are all right." The emergency officer gestured to what looked like a white school bus with a red stripe, almost hidden by the fire engine. "That's the 'transformer' vehicle. It functions as a mobile hospital."

"I'm all right. I'll just sit here awhile."

"Can you walk?"

"Of course." But she couldn't seem to make herself stand up.

The uniformed woman gently lifted the dog off Samantha's lap, holding it competently in the crook of one arm as she held the other out to Samantha.

"Come. Let's get you to the trauma station and test you for smoke inhalation . . ."

But Samantha suddenly scrambled to her feet, squinting through smoke-stung eyes at someone among the curious bystanders who should not have been there.

1
Aunty Lee's Delights

"We should get a ladder for the kitchen," Aunty Lee said.

All the tables in Aunty Lee's Delights, the famous little Peranakan café just inside Binjai Park, were already full for the weekend's *nasi lemak* brunch to high tea buffet. It had the air of an extended family reunion as people offered to share table space with strangers who, though discerning enough to appreciate the best "homemade" Peranakan food in Singapore, had been impulsive enough to turn up on a weekend without reservations.

But Aunty Lee, who would normally be darting about supervising, seating, and recommending the fried prawns or spicy mutton with cheerful garrulousness, was sitting grumpily at a table by the entrance, barely smiling at the compliments or sympathy people stopped to give her.

Rosie "Aunty" Lee was seldom grumpy and even more

seldom found sitting still. But she had twisted an ankle falling off a stool balanced on an upside-down pail placed on
a coffee table, and Nina Balignasay, her Filipina domestic
helper and loyal friend, was angry with her. Nina came hur-
rying now as Aunty Lee started to stand up.

"What do you want to get from the kitchen, madame? I
will get it for you."

Aunty Lee knew Nina was angry because she was calling
her "madame" and making her obey doctor's orders to rest
her foot.

"I want to get a ladder. So next time I can get things for
myself without everybody making such a fuss."

"Next time you tell me what you want and I get for you. You
don't climb around like a monkey like that!" Nina put a little
basket of prawn crackers on Aunty Lee's table. "Madame,"
she added before walking away. The light fragrant crackers were crispy and savory, but did not make Aunty Lee feel
better. Neither did the fact that her partner, Cherril, seemed
to be managing fine with Nina and two extra helpers in the
kitchen. It was as though they didn't need Aunty Lee at all.
That hurt even more than her ankle.

At first glance Aunty Lee was a typical Singapore Peranakan *tai-tai*. She was fair skinned and plump cheeked
enough to please the most demanding in-laws, and short
enough not to embarrass the most average-sized man, and
the traditional *kerongsang* (brooch) she wore sported *intan*,
or rose-cut diamonds, set in handcrafted twenty-karat gold,
enough to impress the most snobbish customers. And as her
late husband had always said, she was *kaypoh, kiasu,* and *em*

zai si. Kaypoh or busybody enough to stick her nose shamelessly into everyone's business, *kiasu* or tenacious enough to follow through, and *em zai si* or "not scared to die" as she charged recklessly in search of answers—something which had led to her solving several murders.

Of course Aunty Lee had been famous throughout Singapore even before that—smiling from her jars of Aunty Lee's Shiok Sambal and Aunty Lee's Amazing Achar.

But a closer look revealed a pink Converse T-shirt beneath her intricately embroidered *kebaya* blouse. And instead of a traditional batik sarong and seed pearl slippers, Aunty Lee was wearing Kaffir-lime-green yoga pants and one pink-and-green Nike Hyperdunk basketball shoe—men's width, because her feet were small and wide like the rest of her—and one ankle immobilizer, which she was impatiently tapping against her walking stick.

As far as Aunty Lee was concerned, the worst side effect of her twisted ankle was that her stepson's wife, Silly-Nah (as Aunty Lee called the unfortunate Selina), had been coming in daily since Aunty Lee's fall, saying it was her duty to keep an eye on the family business. (It was not a family business, Aunty Lee thought sulkily, it was *her* business.) Nina's disapproval should have been penance enough for climbing up on any number of shaky coffee tables without having to listen day in and day out to Silly's orders and instructions. Selina seemed to think sampling dishes and criticizing "Too hot!" or "More salt!" was the way to run a café kitchen. Aunty Lee observed Selina had already taken on extra weight with her extra role.

This reminded her to hobble round to check the buffet. Aunty Lee liked buffets. The curious, content crowd of people roused memories of family feasts and celebrations, and the sheer abundance of food woke a purely animal joy that no written menu could equal. Three *batu lesong* or stone mortars containing homemade *sambals*—spicy sauces—held pride of place. As they ran down, Nina or one of her helpers added peanuts, chopped onions, chili peppers, and lemongrass to toasted *belachan* and pounded a fresh portion. As any Peranakan cook knew, it was the quality of your *sambals* that determined the quality of your kitchen. Aunty Lee was very proud of her *sambals*. Having no one to pass them on to was one of the few things that made her regret having no daughters of her own.

The rest of the buffet was equally impressive. The huge pot of coconut rice released a steamy fragrance of coconut and pandan—screw pine leaves grown in Aunty Lee's own garden—every time it was opened. And then there was the parade of fried fish, fried chicken, *otak-otak*, omelets, cucumber slices, peanuts, *sambal sotong*, and, of course, the *achar* Aunty Lee was so famous for. Desserts were on a separate, chilled counter next to the drinks station Cherril had set up. But where was Cherril? Cherril Lim-Peters (Aunty Lee's new business partner who was responsible for the drinks) had taken a half-day off and booked a table for herself and three other people, saying, "I have to meet them today. But this way I'll be around if anything comes up."

Aunty Lee looked through the crowd of eaters to the

corner table where Cherril looked as out of sorts as Aunty Lee felt. For some reason this immediately made Aunty Lee feel better and she perked up and paid more attention. One of Cherril's friends had just arrived . . .

Josephine DelaVega asked for a glass of water and pulled out a cigarette as she joined Cherril at the small corner table.

"You can't smoke in here," Cherril said automatically.

"I'm not smoking it. I'm just holding it."

Josephine was wearing a silky olive-green blouse over white tailored pants, her long hair loosely pulled back with a green-and-purple bandanna. Cherril, though as tall and slim as her friend, knew she faded into the background when beside her. She felt suddenly dowdy in her beige-and-yellow knit dress. Why hadn't she worn pants today?

Cherril looked tense and tired, Aunty Lee thought. So did her companion. To Aunty Lee's eye, both women had the semi-starved look of Japanese Occupation survivors and she ate a few more prawn crackers to comfort herself. Aunty Lee wondered whether Cherril's companion had also been an air stewardess. Cherril's training with Singapore's premier airline was as obvious to any Singaporean as any soldier's military training. It was in her professional posture and grooming, her welcoming but impersonal smile, and her ability to pacify cranky children and angry drunks without smudging her mascara. No, Aunty Lee decided, seeing clearly from the way she talked how upset the strange woman was. Aunty Lee wished she was close enough to hear what she was saying.

"We should have killed the bloody woman like she killed that dog!"

Aunty Lee, along with most of the café, had no trouble hearing that. As curious heads snapped round to the corner table, Aunty Lee was already hobbling her way across. And as Cherril smiled gamely at staring customers, Aunty Lee pulled out the chair beside her and eased down into it.

"I hope you don't mind. With my foot like that I cannot stand very long, must sit down."

Selina, full of righteous indignation, had also started in that direction. But seeing Aunty Lee establishing herself, she stopped and turned away.

Cherril had not seen Josephine DelaVega and Brian Wong for years, not since she stopped volunteering with the Animal ReHomers. She had not taken this threatened lawsuit as seriously as Josephine seemed to. In fact she had looked forward to catching up with Josie and Brian and telling them about her new career at Aunty Lee's Delights. She regretted that now. Josephine had been late, and Brian had texted twice saying he was almost there but there was still no sign of him. And there was no sign of Allison Fitzgerald—Allison Love, as she now called herself. Perhaps the woman wasn't going to show up?

"Maybe she isn't coming after all. Maybe she just wanted to scare us," she had suggested.

That was what had made Josephine flare up.

"Sorry," Cherril said to Aunty Lee.

Aunty Lee shook her head dismissively, beamed at Cherril's companion to show it was no problem, and clearly conveyed that she wanted the story behind the woman's outburst.

"Cherril, does your friend like my food? Have you tried my *sambal* quail eggs yet?"

"We're fine. Thanks," the Eurasian woman said with automatic, dismissive politeness.

But Cherril knew Aunty Lee would not be shaken off so easily. Still, hadn't she known that when she booked herself a table in the café? And wasn't part of her relieved to have her protective *kaypoh* friend around?

"Aunty Lee, you know Josephine DelaVega, don't you? Josie, this is Rosie Lee—the famous Aunty Lee who's also my new boss."

Josephine switched modes smoothly, automatically half straightening her knees while leaning forward into a respectful half-bow. "Hello, Aunty Lee, you may not remember me. I'm Constance and Joseph DelaVega's daughter. I used to visit you with my mum ages ago. I was so amazed when Cherril told me she's working with you here."

To young people two or three years could be "ages ago." Not surprising, Aunty Lee thought, given the pace at which things changed in Singapore.

"Of course I know Josephine!" Aunty Lee bobbed her head enthusiastically though she had not recognized the young woman till Cherril's introduction. "I've known Baby Josie since she was so small. That's what your dad used to call you, right? She's the famous one, our beautiful Miss Singapore! Josephine, I haven't seen your mother for so many years! How are Connie and Jojo? The last time I saw your mum she said she had diabetes and your father had gout and maybe dementia. How are they now? You must tell them to come here and see me!"

"I will, Aunty Lee." Josephine smiled. "My parents are doing okay. I must tell them I saw you today. I remember coming to see you at your house with my mum and you gave us curry puffs, hot out of the oven!"

"Out of the frying pan," Aunty Lee corrected. "Oh, I must give you something to bring back for them! *Wah lao,* today got Singapore beauty queen come to my shop! I must tell Nina to quick quick make a shelfie out of you!"

Aunty Lee's last remarks were addressed to the room at large as she hobbled at top speed toward the kitchen, clearing the way in front of her with her stick. People were staring curiously and whispering again. Josephine DelaVega, former Miss Singapore–Business Galaxy ("beauty, brains, and business") gamely returned the tentative smiles sent in her direction and pretended not to notice people snapping mobile phone shots without asking permission.

Cherril winced. Whyever had she thought meeting here was a good idea?

"She's telling someone to put me on the shelf? Who is Nina?"

"Nina's her helper. I think Aunty Lee just wants a photo of you in the café. She puts them on the shelf behind the counter so she calls them shelfies."

Josephine grimaced. "I look like shit."

"No. You look great." Cherril's reply came automatically.

"Hi, gorgeous." Brian Wong startled Cherril by kissing her on the cheek from behind. "Hi, Josie! My three favorite ladies in my favorite café!" Brian waved his fingers at Josephine across the table.

Three? Oh yes. Aunty Lee was back, with a grim-faced Selina at her heels.

"Hello, Aunty Lee, do you remember me? It's Brian, Brian Wong."

"Of course I remember you," Aunty Lee said with genuine pleasure as she waved him to a seat. Some cooks hated Brian Wong, the former animal activist who had been instrumental in getting shark fin and bear gall bladder banned in Singapore, but Aunty Lee (who was open-minded enough to have vegetarian friends) liked the young man.

"Selina, go and get water for them—wait, wait—take photo for us first then go and get the water."

Brian circled the table to put an arm around Aunty Lee for the photos and then gave her a quick hug before sitting down.

"How nice to see you again, Brian. It's been so long. You're looking good. Have you got a girlfriend yet?"

"Not too good I hope!" Brian neatly deflected her question. "Can you believe I just saw a man in the gents putting on lipstick?"

"In my toilet here?"

"No, in a hotel—anyway, how are you all?"

Brian Wong had been a journalist with the *Straits Times* when volunteering with the Animal ReHomers. Since then, Brian had been more in the news than behind it after developing the iGrow Organic app, which delivered personalized exercise, meal, and snack plans with hydration records and iPhone reminders and connected the user with any Organic Eats chill-vending machines in the vicinity. *Time* magazine had credited him with revolutionizing worldwide workplace health, and Singapore had given him an Innovation Excellence Award, but he still had the boyish, open smile Aunty Lee remembered.

"So are you all having my *nasi lemak* buffet? Brian?" Aunty Lee gestured toward the buffet spread. Even though other hands had prepared today's dishes, she had guided the process as both composer and conductor and she was very proud of it.

"It looks fantastic," Brian said with automatic, almost convincing politeness as his eyes scanned the people in the crowded room but missed the food. "Allison's not here yet? I was afraid I might be late."

"You are late. Very late," Josephine snapped, though she had arrived barely ten minutes earlier. She fumbled with her bag and pressed two Panadol capsules out of their foil casing, swallowing them with the last of her ice water. "God, I've got such a headache. Can I have more water?"

"Josephine only just arrived. Cherril was sitting here by herself for at least an hour!" Selina reached rudely across Josephine with a jug and filled Brian's glass first. "Are you here for the buffet too?"

"Only half an hour. Maybe forty-five minutes!" Cherril murmured.

Forgetting her ankle for a moment, Aunty Lee jumped up on seeing all the ice in Selina's water jug had melted, but sat down immediately, wincing.

Brian was the only one who noticed. "What's wrong? Aunty Lee, are you all right?"

"She has a sprained ankle," Selina said. "She fell. She's lucky she didn't break it—or something else! Old people are always falling down and breaking bones. Maybe now you'll take things easy!"

Aunty Lee refused to be distracted from the nugget of information that she had caught. "This Allison you are all waiting for is the bloody woman you wish you had killed like a dog?" she inquired with the air of a helpful child.

Cherril gasped and giggled. Josephine invoked fecal matter. Brian looked taken aback then laughed. "I'm with you there"—he pulled out his phone—"but I'm sure we'll be able to work things out without killing anybody. I'm just going to take this outside—better signal."

"Brian Wong is such a nice boy," Aunty Lee said as soon as the door closed behind Brian. She looked meaningfully at Josephine. "Why is he here today? Are you two . . ." She tapped her forefingers together before entwining them.

Josephine had closed her eyes and looked as though she was praying for her painkillers to work.

"Why are all of you here today? Are you having a business meeting?"

"Aunty Lee, you're so . . ." Cherril started, and stopped. Being called *kaypoh* was generally an insult but one Aunty Lee embraced cheerfully. After all, knowing everybody's business was necessary if she wanted to feed everybody good food, and surely there was nothing wrong with that. It surprised Aunty Lee that more people did not feel that way.

Josephine's eyes remained closed as she said, "Allison Fitzgerald is filing a lawsuit against the three of us for breaking up her marriage. She found an American lawyer who got his last client nine million U.S. dollars on a similar lawsuit. She's coming to meet us here."

2

Puppy Killer

"Alienation of affection? This Allison woman got divorced and wants to sue you all?" Aunty Lee's eyes darted between Cherril and Josephine before settling on Josephine. "She thinks you stole her husband? What did you do with him?"

"Aunty Lee! It's nothing like that!" Cherril did not give her friend a chance to answer. "This woman and her husband adopted a dog—a puppy—from us when we were running the Animal ReHomers. Now she claims that dealing with the Animal ReHomers stressed her into a nervous breakdown and led to the breakup of her marriage. Since the ReHomers organization doesn't exist anymore, she's suing the three of us because we're the ones she dealt with."

Aunty Lee looked puzzled. "She didn't like the dog?"

"She agreed to return it to us if she couldn't keep it. But

instead she had it put down and then lied that she had given it to a friend."

"I remember her now! The puppy killer!" Aunty Lee thumped her stick against Josephine's chair in delight at remembering the case. "The puppy killer! It was in the newspapers!"

It had also been all over social media and even international newspapers. After all, nothing unites Singaporeans like getting really angry at something or someone, especially when they can feel self-righteously patriotic about it.

"But I didn't know you all were involved. Tell me all about it!"

Josephine smiled and excused herself to make a call as Cherril began.

Five years ago, Allison and Mike Fitzgerald adopted a small mixed-breed puppy from the Animal ReHomers, a volunteer society dedicated to improving the lives of Singapore's abandoned and unwanted dogs. In Singapore only one dog of an approved (small) breed is permitted per Housing and Development Board (HDB) flat under threat of a S$4,000 fine. Given the tendency of new puppies to appear and dogs to grow, and the fact that 80 percent of Singapore's population lives in HDB flats, finding new homes for dogs is a constant process. The adoption agreement signed by the Fitzgeralds for the puppy, Lola, stipulated it would be returned to the Animal ReHomers should the adoption not work out.

Allison Fitzgerald would later say to reporters, "I thought that was just to make sure they would take the dog back. I don't know what I signed. Who reads all those damned papers they make you sign?"

Allison called the ReHomers two months later.

"I was the on-duty that day and I took her call. She said she wanted to return the puppy she'd taken. I looked up the records and said sure, but asked if she would be willing to keep Lola a few more days or help with boarding costs till we found another home for her. It's the standard response we were supposed to give. They were always short of money and space at the shelter. And quite often people changed their minds. I mean, you get fuming mad when a puppy pees on your Persian carpet or chews the heels off your Louboutins, but given time to cool down you realize it never meant to, right? I mean, would you give away a child who scratched your car or something? Anyway, Allison said she would get back to us.

"That was just after Josie was crowned Miss Singapore–Business Galaxy. The Animal ReHomers was one of the charities she had to support as titleholder. She wasn't on the volunteer schedule, but she would come and be photographed with the dogs that were up for adoption and say how cute they were and how much she wished she could bring them all home. She was very good about it. I was impressed."

"Impressed?"

Cherril laughed. "Because she actually didn't like touching the dogs, didn't like getting fur on her clothes and doggy smells on her hands. But for the pictures she would cuddle and kiss them and let them lick her face—she was very professional. She was my role model, you know.

"Anyway, Josie was in the office two days later when I called Allison back to arrange to collect the puppy, Lola. Allison said not to bother because a friend had taken it. That was good news but I was surprised. I asked for the friend's address because we always kept records on the dogs we found homes for, but Allison hung up on me. I asked Brian Wong what to do. Brian wasn't just a volunteer; he was one of the founders of the ReHomers. And I think he had a bit of a crush on Josie, so he asked if she wanted to come with us to the Fitzgeralds' Clementi Crescent house to get details of the people who had taken Lola. So Josie and her photographer came—she usually brought a photographer when she came to help.

"Allison refused to tell us who had taken Lola. We were outside her gate saying all we needed was a phone number or an address. Brian thought she had probably passed Lola to one of her neighbors, so if we knew where she was we could check up on her. But Allison started shouting at us for harassing her. She even called the police and said she was being attacked! But when the police came we showed them a copy of the agreement Allison had signed and they also asked her where the dog was. So then Allison started shouting and swearing at them, and she even slapped herself and said she would report them for police brutality. It was like she was crazy! By then quite a few neighbors had come out to see what the shouting was all about, and a reporter friend of Josephine's showed up and interviewed them about the dog, and Allison's husband came home . . . and then Allison finally admitted she had lied. The puppy was not with a friend—it was dead. The day she called me, right after she hung up, Allison had taken Lola to the vet across the road and had her put down."

Cherril was silent for a moment, remembering. "Poor Lola. She was such a sweet, goofy puppy and she never had a chance. Josephine found some old photos of herself with Lola and posted them with pictures of her crying after finding out Lola was dead. And there were photos of Allison shouting at the police and giving them the finger. Even then things might have died down, but Allison sent a seven-page letter to the press saying she had a right to euthanize what she called a savage dog, and accusing us and the police of harassing her, and complaining that despite all her calls the British High Commission had not done anything to defend British citizens, and what a shitty place Singapore was. Josie wrote back of course. So did Brian, and the story went viral online with about fifty thousand comments, most of them telling Allison that if she hated Singapore so much she should leave and stop killing our dogs."

"Mathilda was back in Singapore on vacation," Aunty Lee said, remembering how upset her stepdaughter had been. "She and her friends all got so worked up. I made dog-shaped cookies and Mattie sold them online to raise money for the campaign to make the puppy killer apologize to the Animal ReHomers. She called them Lola Cookies. They were chocolate and ginger flavored and had raisin noses." Aunty Lee herself had not fully understood what all the commotion was about. In the old Singapore Aunty Lee had grown up in, there had always been several dogs keeping wild pigs out of the vegetable garden and barking warnings of snakes and strangers, and fed on leftovers from the outside kitchen behind the main house. As a girl, Aunty Lee had paid no more attention to the working dogs outside her father's house than to the servants working inside it. Now Nina's friendship had changed her thinking on domestic helpers, just as Anne Peters's Tammy was changing her attitude toward dogs.

Cherril stared at Aunty Lee. "How can you remember something like that?"

"I remember the Lola Cookies," Josephine said, coming back to the table. "I didn't realize you'd made them. People said they were too cute to eat but they were delicious."

Aunty Lee glowed with satisfaction. "I thought the puppy killer and her family had left Singapore."

"They did," Josephine snapped, "swearing never to return. But she's back."

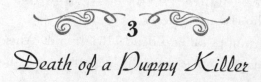

3

Death of a Puppy Killer

The door chimes jangled and they looked around and saw a large Caucasian woman with curly dark hair. She wore a billowing blue-and-green batik sundress and stopped in the doorway to look around the room. Aunty Lee saw Cherril nudge Josephine, *Is that her?* Josephine barely glanced at the woman before shaking her head.

Brian pushed rudely past the woman without seeming to notice her. "Allison Fitzgerald isn't coming. She's dead." He stood by the table, looking at Josephine as though waiting for instructions.

Cherril's laugh was an automatic reflex. "That's crazy. You called the number she gave you? Who answered? What did they tell you?"

"I called the hotel. The police are there. They just found her dead in her room. They're looking for her sister, who came with her. Apparently she booked a taxi to bring her here."

"Here?"

"Aunty Lee's Delights in Binjai Park. Here."

"Who is dead? The puppy killer?" Aunty Lee wanted to know. "Who is coming here?"

"Yes, the puppy killer is dead," Brian said. "Allison Fitzgerald, or Allison Love as she calls herself now—called herself, I mean."

They had forgotten about the new arrival. Selina approached the woman with, "Do you have a reservation?" but was flicked away like a mosquito. Now the woman approached their table.

"Excuse me. Are you Brian Wong?"

Brian rose to his feet. "Yes. I am. And you are—are you Allison Fitzgerald's sister?"

"I'm Allison Love's sister." The woman looked around their table. "Allison Love, not Fitzgerald. My name is Vallerie. Allison isn't feeling very well. She doesn't want to leave the hotel, but if you all come over to the hotel with me she'll talk to you there."

They stared at her. Even Aunty Lee was speechless.

"It's the Victoria Crest Hotel. I've written down the address and room number for you. Just get the reception to phone up to Allison when you get there."

"She doesn't know!" Cherril started laughing hysterically. "She doesn't know! She doesn't know! She doesn't know!"

"Allison Love is dead," Josephine told the woman, speaking for the first time since hearing Brian's news. "I'm sorry."

Vallerie stared at her with a loathing that made Josephine wonder how this stranger could tell she was lying.

Fortunately the door jangles sounded again.

"Aunty Lee, I could have phoned from the station but I thought I better come round," Inspector Salim said. Aunty Lee felt a huge flood of relief on seeing him.

Inspector Salim Mawar was the officer in charge of the nearby Bukit Tinggi Neighborhood Police Hub. A quiet, upper-middle-class residential area in a good school zone, Bukit Tinggi seemed the ideal preretirement posting for an older officer who could keep wealthy residents happy. But not only was Inspector Salim far from retirement, he had solved several murder cases in his time there. Salim was very aware how much having a busybody like Aunty Lee on the side of the law had helped him. He was also very aware of her cooking (which he considered second only to his mother's) and of her assistant, foreign domestic worker Nina Balignasay. There was something about Nina that made Salim feel contentedly stupid when she was around. Salim told himself it was important to get to understand and bond with "outsiders" like her. Singapore had been home to Salim's family for many generations, but he was aware his country's strength and dynamism came from its ability to attract the best and brightest of foreign talent. Like he had learned as a boy breeding guppies, for the best colors you had to constantly add specimens caught in different canals to vary the gene pool.

"Salim, you are just in time," Aunty Lee said. "Somebody's dead! Only we don't know what's happened yet. But you look hot. Tell Nina to get you a cold drink."

"I'm here on official business." Salim paused and looked around at the people still in the restaurant. By now, most of the brunch crowd had finished and left, and Nina and the temporary servers were sorting leftovers and tablecloths and folding napkins for the tea/dinner guests under a barrage of instructions from Selina. The few stragglers deep in their own conversations paid them no attention.

"You're not here to accuse me of poisoning somebody again, are you?" Aunty Lee meant it as a joke but he didn't laugh.

"A woman tourist was found dead in her hotel room."

"No!" Nina, who sometimes seemed to have supernatural hearing, held a drying cloth up to her mouth and looked round to see if any customers had heard him. A young couple was staring and she flew into action. "You want bill? So sorry! Coming right away!" Nina would get the remaining customers out—probably with free takeaway desserts to keep them happy. Aunty Lee turned her attention back to Salim.

"The response team said the dead woman's sister told hotel staff she was coming here. Our station is the nearest so they called and asked us to come around to find her and make sure she's all right. Her name is Vallerie Love."

Aunty Lee nodded to where Cherril had pulled a chair from the next table for Vallerie. Aunty Lee was careful to keep her voice low. "That's Vallerie, the sister. She just heard the news. What happened?"

"Ms. Allison Love was found dead in her hotel room. That's all we know." Salim looked back to the entrance clearly expecting to see someone, but there was no one there.

Right on cue, Staff Sergeant Neha Panchal appeared through the kitchen area. "The back entrance is secure, sir," she announced, ignoring Selina's "only staff allowed here" protests. SS Panchal always followed proper procedure when she could.

Inspector Salim and most of his colleagues from the Bukit Tinggi Neighborhood Police Post were great favorites at Aunty Lee's Delights, though lately they seemed to turn up as often to interrogate her customers as to enjoy her cooking. But that didn't matter to Aunty Lee. She thought of them as nephews and nieces who went off to other countries to study or work (or who just went off to do their own thing and never had time to call). No matter how long ago was the last time they came home for dinner, you still remembered their favorite foods, and if you had advance notice those dishes would be ready on the table. That was why even if they only ordered drinks (and hardly touched them), Aunty Lee knew Nina would already have Salim's favorite flaky mushroom and (halal) chicken pastry squares in the oven and Staff Sergeant Panchal's favorite juicy shrimp wontons in the steamer. They would be presented later, as takeaways "on the house."

"Come, she's here," Inspector Salim said. He would have

preferred to break the news on his own, but regulations strongly recommended the presence of a female officer, as that female officer had reminded him. He went over to the plump Caucasian woman.

"You are Vallerie Love, sister of Allison Love?"

Vallerie nodded.

"You've just learned that your sister is dead?"

"They're lying." Vallerie looked from Salim and Panchal to the table where Josephine and Brian were sitting. As Cherril moved back to join them she added, "They told me she's dead but it's not true. I just left her at the hotel."

It was the shock, Aunty Lee thought. Despite the dramatic reactions portrayed in the media, she had observed that the most common response to bad news was denial. Even now she could tell Vallerie knew her sister was dead—she just didn't want to believe it.

"If you'll just come down to the station with us, we would like to ask you some questions—"

But Vallerie shook her head and said loudly, "If Allison's dead that ex-husband of hers must have followed her here and killed her—or these damned animal activists!" She turned on Josephine and Brian, with Cherril standing frozen between them. "You threatened her and she didn't take it seriously and you killed her! Oh sweet Jesus, I knew we shouldn't have come! She told me you were out to get her and I didn't believe her! Oh no! Oh no!"

Nina had cleared the last of their lunch guests out just in time, Aunty Lee thought.

Vallerie was having a hysterical breakdown every bit as dramatic as the breakdowns Aunty Lee had seen on television. She laughed and cried and flung everything she could reach (plate, water glass, chopsticks, spoon, fork, and knife) in all directions. Aunty Lee tried to remember whether the correct response was to throw a warm blanket or cold water over the woman. She would have liked to offer some hot soup, but it didn't seem appropriate, especially as Vallerie seemed quite capable of throwing that too.

"Excuse me. Let me handle this. I am a trained emergency medical technician."

Staff Sergeant Panchal came forward and laid firm, authoritative hands on Vallerie's flailing arms.

"Who are you? Don't touch me! How dare you!" Vallerie screamed at her. "I'm calling the embassy! I'm going to sue you! Police abuse!"

"I am a licensed medical professional trained to provide pre-hospital medical/trauma basic life support," Panchal recited as she maneuvered Vallerie onto a chair. "Qualified to carry out semi-invasive procedures such as clearing oropharyngeal airways to maintain basic life support. If the rest of you would just move back—thank you. Miss, I would like you to focus on breathing. Are you feeling any dizziness or nausea? Any cramping in your fingers?"

"No. No, I'm fine. It's all right." Vallerie tried to wave her away. "Don't touch me!"

"Do you have any underlying medical or heart conditions? Any history of seizures? Do you need to be taken to hospital to see a doctor?"

"No, no. I'm fine. Really. I don't need a doctor. I need the police, the real police, not Singapore police. I know what it's like here—you'll try to blame me for what happened to my sister and frame me for it!"

It was difficult to tell whether her fears were based on hysteria or misinformation.

"I assure you we are real police," Salim said. "Do you want to call someone to come to the station with you?"

"I don't know anybody here. My sister's dead—how can I trust anybody here?"

"You can talk to her here," Aunty Lee suggested. "We can close the café so nobody else comes in. You know you are quite safe here, right?" This last to Vallerie, who hesitated, then nodded.

"I'll talk to you here. But you have to question them too." She nodded toward Brian, Josephine, and Cherril. "They're the ones she was filing a lawsuit against."

"Lawsuit?"

"For breaking up her marriage. They are the ones responsible for her death."

4
Questions

"Somebody killed the puppy killer!" Aunty Lee announced, coming into the back kitchen where Nina and the helpers were packing food into bento-style meal packs. There were seldom many customers in the lull between brunch and high tea, but if anyone did come, Nina had a selection of "specials" for them to buy.

Nina had worked for Aunty Lee and her late husband for years. Back in the days when Aunty Lee sold yam cakes and pineapple tarts and *achar* out of her Binjai Park house, it was thanks to Nina she had not given away more than she sold. Now it was still the business-minded Nina who managed the shop accounts. Thanks to careful investments of her pay, Nina was already one of the largest landowners in her village back in the Philippines. On her last visit home it had seemed that every friend and neighbor had a potential husband for her to settle down with. They could not understand why, if she no longer needed the foreign money, Nina wanted to go back to Singapore.

"What happened to her?" Nina had not understood the Singaporean rage over the case. With people in the world struggling to afford food and medicine, it was difficult to get worked up over a dog that had been humanely put down. Even now she had more important things on her mind than what had happened to the woman. "Why are you walking around? What are you looking for?"

"Salim didn't say yet. But I'm sure she was murdered or why would they send him here to question the sister, right? I want to give them something to drink. For the shock, you know."

"I'll get it. You go and sit down." Nina did not call her "madame," and Aunty Lee, pleased, sat where she was.

While waiting for the kettle to boil, Nina put a mug of homemade soy milk in the microwave to heat for Aunty Lee. She was tired of being angry with Aunty Lee, but the old woman was like a puppy that had to be disciplined for its own safety.

"Why did your sister arrange this meeting and then not come?" Aunty Lee heard Salim asking as she hobbled back into the café followed by Nina pushing a trolley of drinks. "Did someone contact her? Was she threatened?"

"If she thought this is a dangerous place she would not send her sister here, right?" Aunty Lee asked. She paused by the two tables they had pushed together, with Panchal and

Salim sitting on either side of Vallerie. Brian pulled out a chair and seated Aunty Lee between himself and Salim.

"But we are not dangerous here. What would you like to drink? Must rehydrate to stay alert, you know. There's hot coffee, tea, and barley, and cold barley, soy, and sour plum water." Aunty Lee pointed at Nina's trolley, which looked like a cross between a posh in-flight drinks service and a roadside *kopitiam* stall.

"No. We're on duty." Panchal rejected the blatant attempt to corrupt a police officer. Salim accepted a black coffee politely enough, and then apparently forgot about it.

"You were telling us who changed your sister's mind about coming here today," Salim prompted Vallerie, who was stirring a third spoonful of sugar into her tea. "Was she meeting someone else?"

"No. She didn't know anyone else here. She wanted to come. But then after she heard about the fire at the clinic this morning—the clinic where the dog was put down—she got scared. If the crazy animal activists attacked the vet clinic, she was afraid they would be out to get her next and she was afraid to leave the hotel."

"Rubbish!" Josephine said to nobody in particular.

"What fire?" Cherril asked Brian, who shrugged.

"Can you tell us how your sister learned about the fire at the Sunset Healthy Pet Clinic?" Panchal interrupted, speaking clearly for her phone recorder.

"I don't know—the radio or people talking or something—I can't remember. After hearing that, she was afraid to come and meet with the crazy animal activists here in case they kidnapped her or something. I didn't believe her and now she's dead!" Vallerie wailed.

"The crazy animal activists meaning Josephine DelaVega and Brian Wong?" Inspector Salim tried to draw Vallerie back to the subject. "And Cherril Peters? Why did your sister think they wanted to hurt her?"

Vallerie just wailed wordlessly.

Brian Wong spoke up. "No one wanted to hurt Allison Fitzgerald—"

"Allison Love," Vallerie stopped in mid-wail to snap.

"Nobody wanted to hurt her," Brian continued. "The Fitzgeralds left Singapore, the Animal ReHomers closed down, Allison was out of sight and out of mind until she wrote to Josie and told her she was suing the three of us for breaking up her marriage. She cited some American case where a woman got nine million dollars from an alienation of affection lawsuit. We didn't think it would come to anything but we agreed to meet her here today. We were all here waiting for her but she never showed up."

"She got a threat saying 'you're next' from these people!" Vallerie pointed at Josephine and Cherril. "They were sending her threats. When she heard about the clinic fire, she knew she was next!"

They both spoke up denying this, but Salim held up a hand to quiet them. "What threats? Did you keep any of them?"

"They were threatening phone calls," Vallerie said. "Nobody other than these people knew she was here or where we were staying. It had to be them."

"What happened at the vet clinic?" Aunty Lee asked.

"The Sunset Healthy Pet Clinic was attacked," Vallerie said with some impatience. "Don't you people know anything? That's the vet clinic Allison brought that blasted dog to—"

"There was a fire there this morning," Cherril said. "It was on the news. They said they got all the animals out safely."

"I also heard about the vet clinic fire." Aunty Lee had listened to Nina read details off her newsfeed. "I thought they said cause of fire unknown."

"Pure coincidence," Brian Wong said firmly. "The clinic fire was probably an accident and nobody was hurt. What probably happened today is somebody broke into your hotel room expecting to find it empty. Your sister was in the wrong place at the wrong time."

"Allison was scared. She thought she would be safer in the hotel—that's why I came to ask you people to meet her there. She should have known there was nowhere in Singapore she would be safe!"

"Are you sure she was killed?" Aunty Lee asked. "Maybe a heart attack or something . . . Vallerie, when you came in you said your sister wasn't feeling very well, right? Could she have come down with one of those viruses that are always killing National Servicemen training in the sun? Or could she have picked up Ebola on the plane? Salim, how did she die?"

"I cannot say, madame," Salim said. "But it was not a virus."

It must have been a violent death, Aunty Lee guessed, or the police would not be so certain of what had *not* been the cause of death before there was time for an autopsy. "Was anything taken from her room?"

"When Miss Vallerie is feeling up to it we would like her

to help us by looking around the hotel room and telling us if anything is missing." Salim looked at Vallerie. "I'm sorry for your loss, but we also need you to come and identify your sister's body."

Vallerie shook her head without answering. "I can't. Get somebody else to do it. I'm never going back there again. I can't bear to."

"Does she have to identify her sister?" Aunty Lee asked.

Salim nodded. "There is no one else here who knew her, I'm afraid."

"It's that damned ex-husband of hers," Vallerie said suddenly. "Mike Fitzgerald. If these psycho activists didn't kill her then he must have done it. I'll bet you he's been plotting with these people. He wants Allison dead so that he can marry again, and he wants to marry one of these sluts!"

There was a stunned silence after this.

"You should have called the police after the threatening phone call," Aunty Lee said thoughtfully. "They can trace the call and find out who threatened your sister. Here the police are very good at listening to phone calls and catching people. Maybe they can look at her phone and see who called her."

"They called the hotel. Allison didn't have a phone for Singapore and neither do I. Anyway, Allison didn't trust the Singapore police. She tried calling you a lot for help when trespassers were threatening her on her private property, and your so-called police took their side and called her a liar!"

"Your sister was a liar." Josephine was cold and precise. "And it wasn't her property. She even tried to blame the landlord, told the newspapers she had to get rid of the dog fast because the landlord insisted. But they interviewed the landlord who said it wasn't true. His previous tenants had had Rottweilers that dug up the fence, so he kept their deposit to fix it, but he was an animal lover and would never tell anybody to get rid of a dog. In fact he contributed to our campaign and said he would not renew their lease."

"And we weren't threatening your sister," Brian added. "We just wanted to contact the friend she said she gave Lola to."

"Another lie," Josephine interjected.

Brian ignored her, but Vallerie's eyes stayed on Josephine even as he continued. "The Animal ReHomers never threatened her. Some people said things online, but nobody took those seriously. Your sister made a lot of people very angry. They were just letting off steam."

He looked at Vallerie with the dispassionate calculation of a farmer debating whether a pig was ready for slaughter, and Aunty Lee felt suddenly afraid of him. Vallerie Love didn't seem to notice anything. In fact she seemed most comfortable talking to Brian, perhaps won over by his looks and manner. Or perhaps Vallerie Love considered other women and uniformed civil servants beneath her notice.

"Allison was happy in Singapore until the blasted dog business erupted. After that everything else in her life just fell apart. She came back hoping to find some kind of closure. Instead look what happened. She's dead and you lot are going to get away with it over again!"

Salim did not want to drag things out too long. Now that Vallerie seemed to have calmed down he nodded to Panchal, who said, "That will be all for now. We will be in touch with all of you for your statements. Miss Love, we will bring you back to the hotel now. They said they can arrange for another room for you to stay in."

"I don't want to go back to that hotel. I'm never going back to that hotel!"

"Would you like us to find you another hotel?" SS Panchal asked, tapping efficiently on her phone. "I can get you a list of hotels in a similar price range."

"Or you can stay with friends if you prefer," Inspector Salim suggested, "as long as we know how to contact you."

"I don't know anybody here!" Vallerie wailed, her hysterics threatening to return. "I only came because Allison wanted me to, and now she's dead! My knees hurt and I can't walk any more!"

As someone also having trouble walking, Aunty Lee felt a bond with Vallerie. Perhaps, despite her bung ankle, she could help her?

"Drink some more tea," Aunty Lee urged. "You just had a terrible shock. You must keep up your blood sugar." She signaled to Nina, who disappeared into the back kitchen. Aunty Lee thought Vallerie looked like a stress eater. So many people reacted to stress by abusing their bodies with cigarettes, alcohol, and jogging on treadmills, so why not food? It did good food a great disservice, but right then the poor woman deserved any comfort she could get. Losing a sister was bad enough; losing a sister in an alien country with no friends was much, much worse.

"We'll get you something to eat. You must keep up your strength, you know. You just had a terrible shock."

"I can't eat local food," Vallerie said mechanically. "Local restaurant food is so spicy, it makes me sick. There's a McDonald's near the hotel but I don't want to go back there. I never want to go back to that hotel!"

SS Panchal had left her seat to confer with Inspector Salim. "Nonemergency ambulance?"

Cherril, looking worried, was whispering to Brian and Josephine, who looked bored and was tapping on her mobile phone. Aunty Lee made up her mind before Nina returned from the kitchen to dissuade her.

"You must come and stay with me," Aunty Lee said firmly. "My house is just up the road and I have lots of space. Inspector Salim can tell you I can be trusted, and when you are feeling better he can come to talk to you in my house."

Aunty Lee knew Vallerie had no reason to trust her. But she had no one else to trust, and surely a plump middle-aged (or even elderly) widow with a twisted ankle must appear less threatening than a strange police station or the hotel one's sister had died in. She smiled at Vallerie and did her best to look old and harmless.

"My house is very comfortable and very safe. The police have my address so they will know where to reach you. Would you like that?"

Vallerie hesitated, then nodded damply. "Yes."

5

88 Binjai Park

Straits Financial Daily:

The woman who was found dead in the Victoria Crest Hotel yesterday has been identified as British citizen Allison Love. Formerly known as Allison Fitzgerald, Ms. Love was the focus of controversy in Singapore five years ago when she claimed she was justified in having an adopted puppy put down. The subsequent Web outrage led former Cabinet minister Cheng Yee to caution against extreme overreactions on the Internet and suggest Internet monitoring procedures. Mr. Cheng, who is the first Cabinet minister to lose a group representative constituency (GRC), could not comment on whether the two events were connected.

Seen on the Scene:

[Shots of a covered body on a stretcher being carried out of the hotel and old photographs of Allison Fitzgerald raising a middle finger to the press camera, Josephine posing with Lola the puppy, and blurred shots of Cherril and Brian covering their faces.]

Allison the Puppy Killer is back—and dead. Is this karma or overkill? Let us know what you think! We want to hear your comments!

The next morning found Aunty Lee, as usual, sitting at the antique marble-topped table on the sheltered side porch of 88 Binjai Park. Over the past fortnight, Aunty Lee had been grumpy with frustration at the sight of her garden and the many things an ankle stabilizer and crutch barred her from doing; her ripe mangoes had not been collected (reminding her of the excess waiting in her kitchen), lemongrass was invading the screw pine leaves, and giant kaffir limes had been left to ripen on the bushes instead of being plucked and pickled . . . but today when Nina placed a cup of hot tea on the table, her employer smiled at her and said, "Good morning. Going to be nice and sunny. Clothes will dry well."

Nina was less cheerful. She did not mind houseguests but preferred them to come without murderous connections.

Murder investigations disrupted opening hours at the café and sleep and housework cycles, and were bad for both business and health. Still, it was good to see Aunty Lee perked up, and hopefully the presence of a guest would prevent her from climbing onto things.

Vallerie had not appeared since being put to bed in Mathilda's old bedroom the day before.

"Have you heard any more news about the murder? Did Salim say anything?"

"Madame, this is not your business. Your business is to get better and look after your café." Aunty Lee's Delights was not opening till 11 A.M. for brunch, so Aunty Lee shrugged that off.

"Yesterday Josephine said they should have killed that woman—and now that woman is dead! She said it in my café so of course it's my business."

Nina was unimpressed. "I also say like that what. Last week I told the egg deliveryman if he is late again and I got to go one more time to buy eggs from 7-Eleven I will kill him. If he gets heart attack are you going to call police?"

"Did Allison Love die of a heart attack?"

Nina started back into the house without answering.

"Is our guest awake yet?"

"Just now she go to the bathroom but never come downstairs yet."

"Ah."

Nina left Aunty Lee to her newspapers. Today, in addition to her regular paper, the *Straits Times*, Aunty Lee had asked for the *Business Times*, the *New Paper*, and *Today*. Fortunately the nearby 7-Eleven was well stocked with papers (as well as fresh eggs).

Unfortunately for Aunty Lee the newspapers proved sadly disappointing.

There was nothing on the murder she did not already know. Aunty Lee studied a photo of the dead woman. Allison and Vallerie looked very alike, though it was not immediately obvious with Vallerie being so much larger in size.

"I wish I knew how to make those spy drones," Aunty Lee said in grumpy frustration. "I would make them small, like mosquitoes. And just make them fly around checking on people. I'm sure so many crimes could be prevented. And they could chase away mosquitoes so dengue fever also no more." But she was not really disheartened because there was still Vallerie Love asleep upstairs.

The reporters had not had a chance to speak to Vallerie. Aunty Lee had spent much of the previous day comforting and soothing the woman as she swung between furious, wild accusations and miserable wailing. Vallerie was not only in shock over her sister's death but clearly terrified for herself. Aunty Lee hoped she would be calm enough to answer questions today. Though Vallerie insisted no one other than the Animal ReHomers and Allison's ex-husband could have wanted to hurt her sister, she might remember someone Allison had met or mentioned. Despite her temporary handicap, Aunty Lee was sure she could do better than the police (certainly better than SS Panchal!) gathering information in this case.

Aunty Lee did not believe any of the former Animal Re-Homers could have killed Allison Love. Cherril had been in the café all morning, and surely neither Josephine (whom she had known as a child) nor Brian (so polite and so handsome) could have had anything to do with it. That left the unknown ex-husband.

Vallerie rolled on her bed and stretched out on the clean sheets. Despite the shock and horror of the past twenty-four hours and her resolution not to let her guard down, sheer exhaustion had relaxed her, and though she had not expected to, the bereaved sister had slept well. She would have liked to stay in bed now. But she had to think about what she was going to do next.

The room they had given her looked like a room a child had grown up in and then moved out of. The books on the shelves ranged from childhood favorites to philosophical texts, and there were graduation photographs on the wall. Once alone she checked carefully for bedbugs, cockroaches, and other horrors she suspected Singaporeans of keeping in their homes. Fortunately it seemed clean enough, and once she locked herself in she felt safe for the first time in that terrible day. The windows looked down on the large back garden of the house and carefully placed trees concealed the other houses that surrounded them. There was an attached bathroom with a shower and toilet, the mattress was firm and the bedding clean, and all in all she knew taking the risk to stay here had been the right decision.

Vallerie knew Allison would have had reservations about

accepting the fat old café cook's invitation to stay with her. Allison would have preferred a decent hotel with standards of cleanliness to live up to, even if she didn't have the means to pay for it. But Allison was not around anymore, Vallerie reminded herself. She, Vallerie, had to make her own decisions now.

Allison might be gone, but she still had to think about what she could do for her.

And she was hungry.

Of course murder was a terrible thing. But when the victim was not somebody you had known personally it became like one of the crime shows on television—an interactive show that they had front row seats for. Which made it extra frustrating because Aunty Lee was right in the middle of the action but had no idea what was happening.

"Maybe you should phone Salim," Aunty Lee suggested when her helper came out with hot tea. "Just to find out what they've found out so far. For Vallerie's sake, of course. The killer must have attacked her sister while she was in the taxi coming to our place yesterday, can you believe it? If only her sister had come with her she might be alive now!"

"Or maybe the killer would have followed them to the shop and killed them both there," Nina suggested. "And all of us too. Or taken us hostage. Again." Nina had not enjoyed her firsthand experience of being taken hostage, which she blamed on Aunty Lee's meddling and interfering.

"I'm sure Salim will want to talk to Vallerie again. You should call and tell him he can talk to her here. It will be less stressful for her. If you heard her in the toilet just now she must be awake. She'll probably be hungry. Can you make her a breakfast that will put her in a good mood?"

"What are you going to do with this woman, madame?"

What Aunty Lee wanted to do was find out why Vallerie's sister had blamed Josephine, Brian, and Cherril for the breakdown of her marriage. There might be nothing in it, of course. Aunty Lee felt sorry for the late Allison Fitzgerald. Losing a husband, whether to death or divorce, was difficult. And people in crisis often created and clung to a personal view of reality, however warped. It was a matter of survival, when the only stable thing in your life was an object you could focus your hatred on. But why had she blamed the former Animal ReHomers?

But intrigued as Aunty Lee might be by Allison's death, at the moment her immediate concern was Vallerie. Vallerie Love was terrified and traumatized and a guest in her house, and Aunty Lee was first and foremost a good hostess.

"I'm going to take care of her while she's here."

Having a guest to occupy Aunty Lee while her ankle recovered was a good idea, Nina thought. She only wished Aunty Lee had guests who were interested in batik and orchids rather than murder and lawsuits.

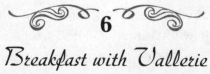

6

Breakfast with Vallerie

By the time Vallerie came downstairs wearing a red hibiscus-patterned housedress of Aunty Lee's that Nina had unearthed, Aunty Lee was finishing her oatmeal porridge with fresh mango chunks.

"Ah, Vallerie. Good morning. How are you feeling? Do you think you can manage to eat some breakfast? Come and sit down."

Aunty Lee indicated a chair and put a cushion over her stack of newspapers.

"Thank you, Mrs. Lee." Vallerie sat down. "I don't know if I can eat anything. I know I should try, for Allison's sake. But it's so difficult."

"*Yah hor.*" The sound Aunty Lee made managed to convey agreement, sympathy, and encouragement to move on. "But you must try to eat something. Our mangoes are very sweet.

Just ripe this morning. Ripe on the tree is always more tasty than when they cut down green to transport here to sell in supermarket. And you mustn't call me Mrs. Lee. No need to be so formal. Every time you call me Mrs. Lee I am scared somebody is catching me for traffic offense. Everybody calls me Aunty Lee. Even my stepson and stepdaughter."

"I can't call you 'Aunty,'" Vallerie said after a pause. "What's your name?"

"Rosie."

"I'll call you Rose," Vallerie said.

Vallerie might have been a good-looking woman when not in the grip of sisterly bereavement. She had an ample bosom and an even more ample midsection and a lot of very black hair. Large, healthy people had a beauty that was all their own. Often they were happy, relaxed, and knew how to enjoy life and good food. They could be very good company too, radiating contented appreciation. Of course there were also some unhappy fat people who stuffed themselves with food they did not enjoy, and these gave off a very different vibe. To Aunty Lee's experienced eye, Vallerie Love looked like an unhappy eater. For Aunty Lee this covered people who ate when they were unhappy as well as people who were unhappy about what they ate.

Aunty Lee believed the right kind of food could comfort the mind as well as the body. And providing that food was Aunty Lee's territory.

I'm going to take care of her and feed her up and make her happy, that's all, Aunty Lee thought, starting with breakfast and then, perhaps, solving her sister's murder.

"Black coffee," Vallerie told Nina without looking at her.

Watching happy people eat was always a pleasant distraction, but this cross and miserable-looking woman had all the allure of a reality show crisis. However, Aunty Lee was not one to approach a juicy crisis unprepared.

"Egg and bacon?" Aunty Lee suggested.

"All imported from goodness knows where I suppose."

"My bacon comes from organic Australia, my eggs come from free range, so more delicious and more healthy than normal breakfast."

Vallerie snorted but did not say no.

Nina headed to the kitchen.

"I'm not surprised my sister couldn't stand it here," Vallerie said. "Singapore, I mean."

For a moment Aunty Lee wondered whether Vallerie was deliberately trying to provoke a fight. Drunken tourists had a reputation for using insults in bars and taxis to start fights, which resulted in their getting thrown out without having to pay. But Vallerie was neither drunk nor expecting to pay. Looking at her, Aunty Lee realized Vallerie was barely aware of her audience and was literally speaking her mind—or rather her thoughts—unfiltered. Like water in a clogged sink filter, her anger and grievances and spite swirled round and round in her head, occasionally flooding over and spilling out in words.

Aunty Lee tried to open a new drainage channel. "What made your sister come back to Singapore?"

"She didn't want to, she had to. It was unfinished business," Vallerie said.

Nina returned to set the table. She placed a *keropok* basket by Vallerie who took one, then another and another of the crispy prawn crackers. She had seemed to like them yesterday and Nina had obviously noticed and remembered.

"But why now, five years later?" Aunty Lee was like a persistent dog, refusing to be distracted by tidbits or games when she could sniff a rat trapped in a drainpipe.

"Why does it matter? She's dead now!"

Nina added a little dish of fragrantly crispy savory anchovies and peanuts. Vallerie Love was clearly very hungry, but Aunty Lee hoped she would not fill herself with fried snacks before a good, nourishing meal was put before her.

"But why now? Was it her idea or did somebody tell her to come? Did anybody else know when she was coming to Singapore?"

"You mean did someone get her to come over just to kill her?"

Aunty Lee nodded. "Who else knew she was coming here? Oh, and if you need to get in touch with anybody back home to tell them you are all right you can use the computer in my late husband's office. Nina can show you where it is and how to use it."

Vallerie shook her head. "Nobody's going to bother. Nobody gives a shit. Do you have Wi-Fi?"

"Of course! Nina, what's the password again?"

Nina, reappearing with fried bacon, pork sausages, and eggs, only just managed not to look surprised and said, "Password is the house address, madame," as she put the food down in front of Vallerie, along with a small dish of cut mango which the guest ignored.

Aunty Lee returned to the subject that interested her more. "You will probably have to go to the hospital morgue to identify your sister's body."

"That's crazy. Who else would it be? I don't want to go to some creepy morgue and look at poor Allison's body." The aroma of crisp, fried bacon drew Vallerie's attention to her plate.

Aunty Lee did not like morgues any more than anyone else. But there was no reason for Vallerie Love to upset herself and her health until it was confirmed that the dead woman in the morgue was Allison Love.

"Anyway, until you identify the body as your sister there's no point in getting upset. It might all be a mistake."

"You're mad! Who else would it be?" Vallerie flared up. "That's so bloody stupid."

"Strangers are always getting hotel rooms mixed up," Aunty Lee said vaguely. "Of course they can use DNA and all that to test, but it is faster and cheaper if a family member can ID."

"There isn't any toast. Why isn't there any toast?" Vallerie turned to look around for Nina. "This is ridiculous. How am I supposed to eat this?"

"Do you know why your sister picked that hotel to stay in? Did she know somebody there or had she stayed there before?"

Vallerie shrugged *no idea* over a mouthful of bacon.

"The police said they need you to make a statement when you are feeling better. And I will be happy for you to go on staying here, but I'm sure you will want to collect your clothes and things from the hotel. You can look over the room at the same time to see whether anything is missing."

"I suppose so." Vallerie looked glum. She was probably thinking of her sister, dead in the hotel room, Aunty Lee thought.

"You mustn't think of it as the place where your sister got killed," she said helpfully. "Just try to spot something that will help the police find out who killed her."

This mention of her sister made Vallerie close her eyes and wrinkle up her face. Fortunately Nina arrived with hot buttered toast before she could break down.

"And after your poor sister's body is taken care of, what will you do then?"

"That's none of your business," Vallerie snapped automatically. She seemed unfamiliar with letting people be nice to her. Then, as Aunty Lee continued to look on her with steady kindness, Vallerie seemed to accept the woman was only trying to help. "I really don't know. All Allison wanted was what was due to her. Those animal people started a vendetta against her. They hounded and harassed her, they went after her husband and kids . . . they drove her to a nervous breakdown and she ended up losing her husband and children and now she's dead. Actually what I want to do now is make sure they pay for what they did to her!"

There was a controlled, over-the-top note to her voice that suggested Vallerie was acting a part and made Aunty Lee wonder whether she really believed this. Most people might have thought Vallerie was in shock, but Aunty Lee could tell the woman was afraid of something, hiding from something—or someone—in fact. But who could that be, given she had never been to Singapore before and knew no one on the island?

"And now they're all going to gang up against me—those animal people, the police, even you! You're going to believe whatever they tell you!"

"So tell me your version," Aunty Lee suggested. She liked to hear all sides of a story. It was the same way she always approached a new dish. The more recipes you started with, the easier it was to get to the essence of a dish and put together a version that worked for you.

"That stupid, lying, loudmouth slut started everything—"

"Josephine DelaVega?"

"Yes, exactly. She put her lies about Allison online—all absurd, ridiculous slander—and it even got into the papers back home, and our ma was calling her and saying, 'What have you done? Why are you killing people's pets again?'"

"Again?" Aunty Lee said involuntarily, though she had fully intended to let Vallerie run on unchecked, just to see how long it took her to start repeating herself. "Your sister killed animals before?" Her comment only stopped Vallerie for a moment.

"Our mother was always picking on Allison, blaming her for everything. It was very hard for her."

Vallerie was very devoted to her sister, Aunty Lee thought. Most people were only really interested in talking about themselves, but Vallerie Love only wanted to talk about her sister.

Vallerie leaned across the table and said confidentially, "You pretty much saved my life yesterday. I didn't think I'd find anyone here willing to show a little Christian decency. Thank you. And thank god your food's not like the rest of Singaporean food. Allison told me about the food here. It's already so bloody hot but all the people insist on eating so much spicy stuff on top of it!"

Aunty Lee waved off the thanks as well as the "Christian" decency. "You can stay here as long as you have to. We can cook you nonspicy food. We can cook anything. But you know, here with the weather like this, spicy food can give people better appetite. That's why most of the hot countries all have spicy foods. Not only Singapore—look at India and Mexico."

Vallerie shuddered at the mention of India and Mexico.

"You were very fond of your sister. It must be so hard for you."

"Oh yes, it is. Allison was always the leader, the one with the ideas and the energy. She was always going out and doing things. She was our parents' favorite, you know."

"That can't have been easy for you."

"It's just how it was. Allison was always the popular one. Guys were always falling for her, starting from when she was still in school. She could have done so much better for herself if she hadn't married Mike Fitzgerald with his sweet talk. She had a degree for chrissakes. And she followed him out here and ended up working as some low-down receptionist and having to kowtow and say thank you to your tin-pot government here for allowing her to work. It was all a huge joke."

Vallerie grabbed a piece of toast off the plate Nina had just put down beside her and smeared jam thickly and furiously on it. She paid no attention to Nina. "Thank you," Aunty Lee mouthed. Nina acknowledged her with a token twitch of the lips, not quite a smile.

Nina and Aunty Lee might live in the same country in the same house, but as a foreign domestic worker Nina was exposed to a lot more of the hidden underside of people. Nina had observed people were generally worse than they appeared socially; if this was Vallerie's social side, Nina was not looking forward to encountering her dark side. And though as a "foreign worker" rather than a "foreign talent" Nina's experiences of Singapore were far worse than anything Vallerie or her sister could have encountered, Singapore had made it possible for her to keep her family alive, and Aunty Lee had become family to her. As far as Nina was concerned, this crazy woman could mouth off at Singapore all she liked, but Nina was going to keep a sharp eye on Aunty Lee and Aunty Lee's property while this unwelcome guest was around.

7
Sunday Morning Café

Cherril had been the first to arrive at Aunty Lee's Delights that morning. She had arrived just after nine and now, at almost ten, she was still the only one there. Sundays at the café didn't start till eleven, but Aunty Lee generally liked to get in early. Even after her fall, she would often have her breakfast at one of the café tables while watching Nina set up for the day. Of course she had that woman staying with her now—Cherril grimaced at the thought. Mechanically she checked the cordials and glasses and the rest of the drinks preparation. While she didn't feel at all like talking, she badly wanted to figure out what had happened—not just to Allison Love but to all of them.

Cherril was tired. Vallerie Love had gone home with Aunty Lee after talking to Salim and Panchal at the café, but she, Josephine, and Brian had been taken to the Bukit Tinggi

Police Hub to answer questions and give their statements. Vallerie was a bereaved relative but they were suspects, Cherril realized. Allison Love was dead and her sister had accused them of killing her. Cherril had thought they were being questioned to placate Vallerie Love, who had alternated sobbing with shouting hysterical accusations at them. But at the station they had printouts of some of the comments from the "Puppy Killer" forums of five years ago, and Cherril was shocked by how vicious their comments sounded now. "We were young and angry," was all she could say. "We weren't the only ones angry with her."

It had been late by the time she was finally allowed to leave the police station the night before, and that was only after Mycroft came to get her and pulled all the strings of influence he could reach. Apparently several other customers had heard Josephine say they should have killed Allison. Giving their statements had been a long, laborious procedure with much repetition and waiting in between sessions. As Brian had joked, it almost made you want to confess to something, just to get it over with. But Cherril often stayed back later than that at the café and had not thought to call home. She had been surprised when her husband showed up at the police station.

"Why didn't you call me? I would have come earlier."

"How did you know we were here?"

"Josephine called."

"Josephine? She didn't tell me she was calling you."

"I think she probably called every lawyer contact she had in her phone. She probably forgot we're married."

"And you came because Josephine needed a lawyer."

"I came because she told me you were here at the station with her."

"Did you get them to let her go too?" Cherril had not seen Josephine again after a desk sergeant had come to tell her that her husband was waiting for her outside.

"I don't know. They probably did." Mycroft didn't seem interested in Josephine's fate.

It was unlike Mycroft, who was normally punctilious about seeing things through. But Cherril had to admit a nugget of satisfaction. She could not help wondering at Josephine calling Mycroft for help without mentioning it to her. Why hadn't she just asked Cherril to call her husband? Even as she wondered Cherril knew the answer: Josephine believed she had more insight and influence (especially with men).

Josephine had told the police she and Cherril had arrived at the café around the same time, with Brian joining them soon after.

"It's less complicated," Josephine had explained in the ladies'. "The police aren't good at dealing with complicated things."

When Mycroft asked her why she hadn't told him about the threatened lawsuit, Cherril could only say that Josephine had been so certain they would easily talk Allison out of it, that she was only trying to get money out of them. But going over the police printouts of their forum posts made her see that if any of the enraged commenters on the Animal ReHomers website had killed Allison Love, they were all responsible for inciting her death.

Her phone was flashing with updates. Aunty Lee (or more likely Nina) had sent a message telling Cherril they could manage without her if she didn't feel up to coming in. But that day Cherril far preferred being in the shop than back home where they were so sensible and reasonable. Right now Cherril needed someone to be irrational with, like Aunty Lee.

If Cherril had said, "If she hadn't come here just to make trouble for us, she would still be alive now, but I can't help thinking that if we hadn't made such a fuss over the dog years ago none of this would have happened, which means it's sort of our fault she's dead, not that we shouldn't have called her out for killing the dog, but maybe we shouldn't have let her have the dog in the first place," Aunty Lee would have agreed without correcting her grammar (Anne) or logic (Mycroft).

And though Cherril dreaded the questions Aunty Lee was certain to ask (Aunty Lee had no qualms about being impolite), now she was feeling let down that Aunty Lee was not there to ask them. Instead, Cherril supposed she was looking after Allison's sister and felt a twinge of jealousy. Just as she was wondering whether she should call Aunty Lee to see when she was coming in, Nina arrived and said that Aunty Lee was still talking with Vallerie back at the house.

"Yesterday's two helpers coming in again today so it will be okay," Nina assured her. "If you got to go and talk to the police some more I can stay here and supervise."

"Thanks. I'll manage. You can go back to the house to help with Vallerie."

Mark and Selina also turned up at the café right after church. They had been spending less time at the café since Mark handed over the drinks business to Cherril, but Aunty Lee's twisted ankle had brought them back. Selina considered it her Christian duty to help the weak and incapacitated—whether or not they wanted her help—especially when there might be profits involved.

"We read about the murder in the papers and saw your names and Aunty Lee's Delights mentioned, so we thought we better stop by just to make sure this place hasn't been closed down—again!" Selina said brightly. There was nothing Selina loved so much as poking (helpfully, of course) through other people's dirty laundry. This morning she was radiant in anticipation of a good gossip. "Where's Aunty Lee? They haven't arrested her, I hope! Ha ha! Isn't it terrible how dead bodies seem to show up in Aunty Lee's vicinity? Everybody was talking about it during post-service fellowship. They asked me, 'Isn't that Mark's stepmum's place?' and I looked and couldn't believe it, so Mark insisted we rush over right away and find out what's happening, didn't you, Mark?"

Mark smiled at Cherril. "Are you okay, Cherry? You look tired."

"Oh yes. I'm fine. Just a bit tired, thanks."

"Look, sit down and I'll get you a coffee."

Cherril felt certain it was Selina rather than Mark who had rushed over for news, just as it had probably been Selina who directed any lurid post-service discussion.

"She works here, why are you offering to get her coffee in her own kitchen? Anyway, tell us what happened! And where's Aunty Lee? Is she at the police station? What did that woman die of? The newspapers didn't say. Was she poisoned? Here?"

"She wasn't poisoned here." Cherril's previous airline training gave her an edge in dealing with difficult people, but she still found Selina Lee a challenge. "She never came anywhere near here."

"Selina almost had the whole church taking bets on whether the woman was poisoned, stabbed, or pushed out the window," Mark said genially, "with heavy odds on poisoning."

It seemed to Cherril that since Mark had saved Aunty Lee's life last year he had become much nicer to everyone at the café. He seemed more comfortable in the role of generous benefactor than supplicant—and it suited him better too.

Selina ignored Mark's attempt at diversion. "According to the papers you were one of the people the dead woman was coming here to meet. So, tell all!"

But Cherril didn't have anything to tell, except that she, Josephine, and Brian had been at the police station answering questions till late.

"It's nothing to do with us and the café at all. We just happened to arrange the meeting here—in fact the meeting didn't even take place here, so really we're not involved at all."

"But you were in the papers, Cherril," Selina insisted. She looked at Cherril, who had moved to sit by the drinks counter while Mark warmed up a cup for her coffee. True, the café did not officially open for over an hour, but normally Nina would be rushing around and Cherril would be sorting out fruits and vegetables and syrups for her drinks. Instead Cherril was sitting motionless, staring into space.

Selina continued. "I recognized you at once even though your hair was so funny in the photo. I told Mark there's a jinx on this place. Everybody who works here gets involved in all kinds of funny business. Luckily he got out in time, ha ha." But her banter was wasted. Cherril did not seem upset. Indeed she barely seemed to be listening to Selina. Neither, it seemed, was Mark.

"Try my new health cocktail mix?" Mark broke into Cherril's thoughts. "I think it will do you more good than a coffee. Come on. Just try it. Don't worry, I made it according to your recipe. I just added a dash of vodka and Tabasco, like a Bloody Mary. And don't worry about what happened to that woman. Nobody thinks you people had anything to do with it. And I don't think anybody is really sorry she's dead."

Mark would have made a good nanny, Cherril thought, or a good father. A cool, soothing swallow of the sweet, sharp blend of celery, carrot, and lemongrass made her feel better. Mark's innovation worked too—she made a note to try introducing mildly alcoholic cocktails at weekend brunch buffets. She was glad she had come in to work instead of staying at home. She was even glad Mark and Silly-Nah had shown up. Thinking of Aunty Lee's name for Selina made her smile and Mark took this as a good sign.

"You knew the dead woman years ago, didn't you? It must have been a shock for you."

"Even if you weren't friends," Selina put in. "Were you? If

you didn't know her then, why were you meeting her here? Why did the police have to question you for so long?"

"I only met Allison once, when I went with Josephine and Brian to find out where she had sent the puppy, and she called the police. Everything else was by phone and e-mail. I was handling most of the secretarial stuff so my name was on the mailers; I suppose that's why she wanted me here. The police interviews last night took so long because they didn't have enough staff on duty to take our statements and because they wanted to go over the online stuff. The sister kept saying we had threatened her sister so we must have killed her, and I think they can't ignore accusations, so every time she accused us they had to record what she said."

"Anyway, it's over," Mark said firmly. "And it's nothing to do with us or Selina's old friend Josephine."

"You know Josephine DelaVega?" Cherril was surprised.

"We were in the same school," Selina said primly. "I would say I knew *of* Josephine. But then everybody did. She was what people called 'havoc.'"

No one would ever have called Selina Lee "havoc."

8

Back at the House

"Inspector Salim on the phone," Nina announced, bringing the phone out to the patio where Aunty Lee and Vallerie still sat over the remnants of breakfast. Once Vallerie had been persuaded to try to eat just a little, to keep her strength up, she had managed to put away quite a bit, and Aunty Lee was pleased with both of them. Vallerie was looking more relaxed—almost ready to talk, in fact. Without seeing her (or supplying breakfast), Salim was clearly hoping the same thing.

"What does he want?"

"He wanted to find out how Miss Vallerie is this morning. He wants to ask her some questions if she is feeling better. Also he needs her to identify her sister's body and tell them if anything is missing from the hotel room."

Vallerie's sullen look returned. "I already answered all

his questions yesterday. They should be questioning those animal people and Mike Fitzgerald."

"Vallerie isn't comfortable going to the morgue or going back to the hotel alone." Aunty Lee started her side of the conversation even as she reached out for the phone. "Even a policeman should understand her being afraid of that hotel. Hello, Salim? Have you had breakfast yet? Look, if I had a sister and she was killed in a hotel in England I also would be scared to go back to that hotel alone. And how can you ask her to go to the morgue when she doesn't even know what happened to her sister? She has to prepare herself first, right?" She lowered her voice. "What happened to Allison Love?"

Inspector Salim swept past her questions. "We need her to officially identify her sister's body. How long before she feels better?"

"I don't know how long. How long do you take to solve a case? She is still in shock. Later I will make her some soup—my soup is very good for people in shock. Anyway, I have lots of room in my house; she can stay here until she is feeling better."

As Salim's silence conveyed his exasperation and amusement she added, "I can invite who I want to come and stay at my house, I suppose. This is a free country."

"Nothing is free in this country. But yes, of course you can invite Miss Vallerie to stay with you. She will be much more comfortable staying with you than in the hotel, given that she doesn't know anybody here. But I need her to make a formal identification of Allison Love's body and sign the autopsy agreement."

"Bloody stupid cops," Vallerie said when Aunty Lee conveyed the request. "Who else would it be? What would they do if I wasn't here then—label her 'Jane Doe'?"

"They would ask England to send DNA and dental records," Nina said, stung out of deferential silence (reserved for visitors she didn't like) by the insult to local police.

Vallerie stared at her.

Aunty Lee looked cautiously in Nina's direction before addressing Vallerie. "Shall I tell him you will go to the morgue this afternoon just to get it out of the way?" She took Vallerie's shrug as assent.

Aunty Lee returned the phone to Nina after switching it off. "Salim's application for a sabbatical to study law will probably be approved soon," she commented. "He's very smart, that one. Shouldn't have any problem if he works hard. That young man will go far."

"Crazy! With people getting murdered on his watch he wants to run away to study?" Vallerie shook her head.

"Singapore has too many lawyers already," Nina said. "Not enough policemen to do the real work. Who is going to look after the police post when he is away studying?" It was the first agreement Aunty Lee had heard between Nina and Vallerie.

"People will always be dying, Nina. If Salim waits until nobody is dying that may be because everybody is already dead."

Vallerie wasn't interested in Salim's career path. "The police don't care. The bloody police don't care what crimes are going on in front of them as long as they get their bloody salaries. You won't believe the times I've called the police only to have them tell me there's nothing they can do. There's nothing they can be bothered to do, that's what they really mean!"

Getting very worked up very fast seemed to be something the two Love sisters had in common, Aunty Lee thought, remembering some of the outbursts attributed to Allison Love years ago. Was this due to something in their shared upbringing or a personality trait inherited from an excitable parent? It would have been interesting to see them all getting worked up at the same time.

In the Lee family Mathilda was the excitable one, though fortunately she remained sweet natured when she got worked up. By contrast Mark grew more quiet and withdrawn under pressure. Had Mark married a talkative woman to restore some natural balance? Selina was very different from Mathilda, but they had the same energy and ebullience. Somewhere in this was an important point, Aunty Lee felt, but she could not put her finger on what it was. Allison and Vallerie Love had not been close as sisters until Allison needed help. Vallerie had left her own life behind and come to the other side of the world with her. Did Aunty Lee's mind keep going back to this point only because she did not have a sister who would do the same for her, or was there something more there?

And was her own lack of a sister the reason Aunty Lee

felt a growing responsibility toward this stranger? Vallerie Love was not at all the kind of woman Aunty Lee would have chosen for a sister-confidante. Of course, if they had actually been sisters they would have adapted to each other growing up. No, for Aunty Lee, taking Vallerie into her home was an extension of her feeding and fussing over people in her café. People as disparate as psychiatrists, librarians, and urban social landscape planners saw their professional craft as an art shaped by vocation, and like them Aunty Lee found it difficult to draw a line between feeding people as customers and nurturing them as family.

Admittedly, Aunty Lee had been no more than curious about Vallerie on first seeing her at the café with Cherril and her friends. But on hearing the news of her sister's death, this curiosity was superseded by concern. What a terrible thing to happen to somebody in an unfamiliar place! Of course it must have been far worse for Allison, who had been killed. But at least that was done and over, and there was nothing Aunty Lee could do for Allison Love except perhaps nose out what had happened to her. Vallerie, on the other hand, was still adrift in Singapore. The police clearly had further questions for her, which meant she was staying on for a while at least.

"And Inspector Salim wants to talk to you when you're ready. Shall I tell him that we'll meet him at the café at twelve for lunch? It's so much easier to talk when there's food around, don't you think? Or would you prefer to talk to him here, in private?"

Vallerie had already put away a substantial breakfast, but

she nodded. "Lunch at the café would be best. I think it's safer to stay in a public place. Is your servant getting the car out or do we have to walk all the way?"

They had not been in the café long (Nina driving them over) when the bells over the café door jangled, announcing Salim's arrival. Aunty Lee rose from her seat and waved her stick happily in his direction. "Salim! How nice to see you. I thought you were coming over later, to join us for lunch?"

"Please sit down, Aunty Lee. I was hoping I could speak to Miss Vallerie before lunch?"

"Vallerie is going to be having lunch here first so you may as well join us. Just to make her feel comfortable. She's in the toilet now." Aunty Lee felt quite sure Salim already knew that Vallerie had headed for the ladies' as soon as her mobile phone buzzed. Though no one would have accused the Singapore police of listening in on phone conversations, people generally assumed that they had every access to all information. "Vallerie doesn't know anybody else in Singapore so maybe I better stay with her today. What do you want to speak to her about? Yesterday she already told you everything she knows, right?"

"I just want to ask her more about the threats she said her sister received. And then we need the identification."

"Come here, better eat lunch." As Aunty Lee spoke Nina put a large platter of seafood noodles in the center of the table. "I made your favorite lemongrass and garlic sauce. If you eat with us you can talk to Vallerie and ask her questions without frightening her."

Nina set another place for Inspector Salim Mawar without saying anything. She did not approve of policemen eating with people they were supposed to be questioning. In fact Nina did not approve of policemen in general, though she had come to appreciate that police in Singapore generally were not bullies and did not accept bribes unless they were steamed, baked, or deep-fried. But still she worried—both for them at the shop and for this policeman who ought to have been treating them as suspects.

"Madame, Salim should pay you for asking all his questions for him!" Nina said. But she made a point of picking out several of the largest prawns and juiciest bamboo clams and setting them aside on his plate. She knew Salim was fond of their flat rice noodles fried with seafood—what aficionados knew as Aunty Lee's Super Seafood Hor Fun.

"If you are questioning us," Aunty Lee said, "sit down and do it properly. You should put us at our ease, which means you should come and eat with us. Do you know yet exactly when that woman was killed? Do you want pickled green chilies?" She was dying to know what else he had learned but did not forget her hostess duties. "And how?"

"Yesterday morning between nine and eleven A.M.," Inspector Salim told Aunty Lee. "When the sister left, Allison was lying down with a headache. Then later the receptionist put through an outside call and Allison answered, so we know she was alive then."

He stopped as Vallerie emerged. She had clearly thought about what she wanted to say. "The Animal ReHomers are the only people who had any reason to attack Allison. Allison was filing charges against them because their campaign of cyberbullying and harassment gave her a nervous breakdown and destroyed her marriage. Her ex-husband was working with them to destroy her so that he won't have to pay alimony. You should check up on him too. I wouldn't be surprised if he's also in Singapore plotting with them against her."

"But her encounter with the Animal ReHomers happened five years ago," Salim said. "Do you have any idea what made your sister decide to come back to Singapore to file the lawsuit now?"

"All that Allison wanted was to get what these people owed her for what they had done to her. They wrecked her life and got away with it. She had rights. And that husband of hers was on their side. I'm sure he followed her to Singapore. He was probably stalking her. Isn't there any way you can check? Passport or flight records or something?"

"Of course we can check," Salim said. "Now, about the identification—"

"I'm hungry," said Vallerie. "Why are all of you just sitting here? I don't know about you but I haven't had any lunch. How do you eat this stuff? Don't you have any normal food like a steak or a pie or fish and chips?"

It might be escapism through eating, but it was better than those people who tried to solve their problems by starving themselves, Aunty Lee thought. "After lunch," she told Salim. "We eat first."

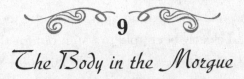

9

The Body in the Morgue

It was a good thing Aunty Lee's ankle injury had shown her that Nina and Cherril could be trusted to run Aunty Lee's Delights in her absence, even with Selina's well-meant interference. But if she hadn't had anyone to leave in charge, Aunty Lee would likely have put up a CLOSED DUE TO SUDDEN DEATH sign rather than miss accompanying Vallerie Love to the morgue at the Singapore General Hospital. This was a matter of national pride as well as curiosity. How long would Singapore remain a number one tourist destination if visitors like Vallerie were left to find their own way around dead bodies?

There was little reason to think the dead woman in the hotel room could be anyone other than Allison Love, but Aunty Lee approved of having systems in place to make sure of this. No matter how much she trusted her suppliers, Aunty

Lee always sniffed and tasted her ingredients before using them.

The identification at the morgue of the Singapore General Hospital turned out to be a mere formality. It being a Sunday (Salim having had a word with Commissioner Raja), there was no one else around apart from the technician on duty who had clearly been told to watch out for them.

Vallerie Love glanced at the body laid out on a trolley under a sheet and wailed. For a moment the hysterics of the previous day threatened to return. Fortunately Aunty Lee had come equipped with a bottle of her strongest Chinese medicinal oil and waved it under Vallerie's nose. The whiff of camphor, menthol, and eucalyptus shocked Vallerie into silence, and when the morgue attendant briefly pulled back the sheet from the head of the corpse she nodded and said, "That's her," and signed the identification form without further drama. Indeed there was not much of her face left to be identified. It looked as though someone had tried to smash the woman's face in, and Aunty Lee felt an irrational urge to straighten the nose that now lay on one cheekbone.

When Aunty Lee asked, "How was she killed?" she was making morgue small talk, without expecting to hear anything beyond "blunt force trauma to the head." Instead the morgue technician looked awkwardly at Salim and said, "Sorry, I cannot discuss that." That made Aunty Lee perk up and she also looked at Salim but got nothing more. She asked about the clothes the dead woman had been wearing, whether she had been in bed, et cetera, without learning anything more useful. It was enough to make anyone suspicious, she thought. Usually when there was nothing interesting the technicians were only too happy to relate pointless details at great length. If this young woman was saying nothing it was either because she was not feeling well or because she had been told not to say something . . . Aunty Lee studied the morgue attendant, who was the picture of health, apart from a slight fragrance of formaldehyde. Her eyes were bright with secrets kept and her mouth stayed firmly closed.

"Can you lift the cloth farther?" This was clearly not for the benefit of the bereaved Vallerie, who had already headed for the exit.

After a glance at Salim, who shrugged, the technician obliged, lifting from the bottom. A towel discreetly shielded the torso and private parts. Aunty Lee observed that despite superficial differences (Allison's corpse showed the woman had clearly been toned and fit compared with Vallerie's heavier and flabbier body), the sisters were of similar build and coloring. It reinforced her feeling that Vallerie was a stress binge eater—and her sister's death would not do her any good!

And though she was no expert, the discoloration around the neck suggested the woman had been strangled. But why the official reluctance to say so? Was it purely to spare Vallerie's feelings? Probably not, given the technician was explaining that they would be running the standard tests even if it was obvious how she had died. Standard autopsies were probably exercises for new doctors, Aunty Lee thought.

Inspector Salim had arranged to speak with Vallerie Love in the little waiting room after the identification viewing.

"We haven't been able to contact your sister's ex-husband yet," Inspector Salim said. "He doesn't answer any of the numbers you gave us. We'll go on trying, of course. Our contacts in the UK are also trying to get in touch with him. But in the meantime you can sign these documents—they are just to say that we have taken your sister's body and effects, which will be returned to you after you decide what you want to have done—"

"No!" Vallerie's voice rose. "Haven't you heard anything I said? I'm not responsible for Allison. I signed your identification papers but I'm not going to sign for anything else. I can't make any decisions about her. You have to get that husband of hers to decide. That's what she would have wanted. Allison wouldn't want me to decide anything. She would have left it to him. Allison always let him take care of everything. That's how we were brought up. Leave it to the man to take care of everything. The separation wasn't her idea. She believed in marriage forever as long as you both shall live and she was right! The least that man can do is take care of her now for the last time!" She sat down so hard on the dirty lounge sofa that its back creaked away from the seat.

"Oh my god. Even the furniture here is out to get me. I hate this goddamn place!"

Vallerie got up with some difficulty and whacked the offending sofa hard with her purse. She was laughing and crying and swearing. Salim wondered whether she was having a breakdown. He should have had a female officer present. But the officer who was supposed to have accompanied him, SS Panchal, had called in sick at the last minute. Salim suspected Panchal was sussing out a change of job. That was why it had not taken much to persuade him to accept Aunty Lee's pressing offer to come with Vallerie Love, somewhat to her delight and surprise. But Staff Sergeant Neha Panchal was not his immediate problem right now. Right now his problem was the large, plump woman with pinkish-white skin and a lot of very black hair that was popping out of the huge knot she had tied on the back of her head with many small decorative pins. Perhaps Aunty Lee could say something—

"I like your hairpins," Aunty Lee said. "Where you buy them from?"

Vallerie stopped in mid-wail. "What?"

"Your hairpins are very nice," Aunty Lee repeated in the low, slow, authoritative voice she had heard Anne Peters use on Tammy when the young dog got overexcited. Anne had picked it up from a television dog trainer who taught people to manage their dogs by directing focus and often said she wished she had known of this method when her children were young. Aunty Lee did not see why something that could effectively calm and distract an intelligent dog like Tammy should not work on a not too intelligent human. "Peranakan women like to use special hairpins when putting their hair up, but I haven't seen any like yours. Where did you buy them?"

"Online, I think," Vallerie said, raising a hand to touch her hair. "I don't usually buy things online, but they were nice and cheap so I thought why not . . ." Her voice was still tense and defensive, but at least she was talking rather than wailing. Salim looked at Aunty Lee with surprised appreciation.

"Best to get cheap things for everyday use." Aunty Lee nodded approvingly. "Here in the old days you had to wear expensive hairpins to show people your family had money. I remember my mother had diamond-encrusted sets. You know *intan* diamonds, those rough-cut diamonds from Kalimantan. That was before they started bringing in faceted diamonds from Europe and then those became all the rage. But do you know, nowadays the old *intan* jewelry is so rare it has become more valuable. But then after my father died my mother could not wear her diamond hairpins during the mourning period. He was the only son of an eldest son, so the mourning period was three years. She could only wear jade and emeralds and pearls. And then she died just before the three years were up so she never wore her diamond hairpins again. I can show them to you one day, if you like?"

Vallerie Love hesitated, then nodded. She was playing with a couple of hairpins she had pulled from her head and looked slightly mesmerized by Aunty Lee's jewel talk.

"People don't wear mourning nowadays," Vallerie said. "At least normal people don't. But I would like to, I think. I should get some more of these hairpins here as souvenirs, to remember my sister by."

She tried to reattach the hairpins and straighten another, but succeeded in detaching it and a clump of hair that pulled several other pins out of place. "And I was meaning to get my hair done here. It's all grown out, I know. Hairstyling and manicures and massages are all so much cheaper here than at home. But then after all this I can't just go and get my hair done. It wouldn't feel right after what happened to poor Allison, you know what I mean?"

"Of course you must get your hair done," Aunty Lee said. "As soon as you have answered Inspector Salim's questions we will go and collect all your things from the hotel and then I will bring you to see my hairdresser. Salim, that's all right, right?"

Salim understood the need to stress normality and normal concerns after a traumatic event and nodded.

"I just have a few more questions. I won't keep you long. Did your sister have any other family—other than you and her ex-husband, who we are still trying to reach?"

"Apart from me, Mike and the children are the only family Allison had left. No matter how badly he treated her, she was still the mother of his children and he owes her something for that. Once you have children together you are a family forever. Divorce papers and restraining orders are all a load of rubbish. You have children together, you are a family forever. If you're looking for someone to take responsibility now, Mike Fitzgerald is the one you should be looking at. I wasn't even in England for years. I hadn't even seen her for years until she turned up and asked me to come to Asia with her."

Salim nodded, wondering whether it was her religious or social beliefs that made it so difficult for Vallerie Love to accept the breakup of her sister's marriage. He knew from his reports that Vallerie was unmarried and had not been back to the United Kingdom since moving to Long Beach, California, in the United States. Was it just sisterly love that made it so difficult for her to accept her sister's divorce? But Salim remembered that Vallerie's sister was just over twenty-four hours dead. As for her sister, the confidential personnel records on Allison Fitzgerald (as she had been then) which he had of course looked up warned that she was highly volatile and always ready to make calls to the police about noisy neighbors, over crying babies, maids who stopped by her gate to chat with her maid, and the cars that crowded their cul-de-sac during a neighbor's funeral wake. The Fitzgeralds had been equally ready to complain about the ineffectiveness of the Singapore police to the British High Commission in Singapore.

"So you didn't keep in close contact with your sister?"

"We were close without being in touch, if you know what I mean. I grew up in England but I've been living in America for years now, since before Allison got married. I didn't even go back for her wedding though I know I should have. I didn't know Allison wanted to file that lawsuit until we got here. I thought we were just coming over here for a holiday together, for her to get some closure on what happened, she said. I thought coming to Singapore sounded like a good idea because I've never been here and Allison always said she had liked Singapore until all that terrible business came up."

"And the threats your sister received. Did she say who they came from?"

"It's obvious, isn't it? The only people who knew she was coming are those Animal ReHomers people. They sent threats to scare her away, and when it didn't work they killed her. Unless it was Mike. Oh god, it was probably Mike working with them. He's connected with them, you know. He's hooked up with one of those sluts. Oh god—that was probably her plan right from the start. And that slut didn't just want to steal herself a husband. She got that bastard husband of Allison's to follow her here and kill her!"

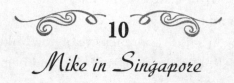

10
Mike in Singapore

Once given a name, pointed in the right direction, and released, nothing can beat the Singapore system for efficiency. By Monday morning an airline booking, immigration and credit card records, and an observant hotel doorman placed Mike Fitzgerald in Singapore and proved he had been in Singapore the day his ex-wife was murdered.

"And now poor old Vallerie is stuck in Singapore staying with Aunty Lee." It was early morning in Singapore but she had no idea of the time where Mike was. Lying on her side in bed, Josephine carefully focused her carefully lined eyes on the camera on her iPad Air rather than looking at the image of Mike on its screen. She recorded all her Skype conversations with Mike so she could study his face and responses all she wanted to—later. But while online it was more important to give Mike the impression she was looking directly into his eyes. Josephine understood the importance of making people feel they were the single focus of your attention.

"And of course—poor Allison. I mean, I can't say I liked her, but nobody deserves to die like that . . . Still, I'm not sorry her stupid lawsuit is off."

She had been a little apprehensive of how Mike would take the news of Allison's death. His ex-wife had been an off-the-wall loony, but the man had once found her worth marrying. Now the woman was no longer a threat, so Josephine could afford to be gracious. Mike would be in Singapore soon, and part of her was very glad that what had happened to Allison had happened before his arrival.

Though Josephine had met Allison in person only a few times, she knew how vindictive the woman had been. That was why Josephine had been so adamant that she didn't want Mike's ex-wife to know they were engaged. Dreadful as it was, Allison's murder actually made things much easier for Josephine and Mike Fitzgerald. Now they could go ahead without being afraid that a crazy woman was going to come and wreck everything.

"I wish you could come over sooner," Josephine said. "I wish we could just move everything up or just go away together and forget about all these awful people!" She did not really mean that. Mike had booked a suite at the Shangri-La, where they would be staying while he was in Singapore. Their engagement party was going to be in the Shangri-La's Amethyst Room. It was not a very large room, but then they had planned to have a very, very small (but still classy) party.

But now their main reason for keeping things small and quiet was dead . . .

"We can probably get the Shangri-La to give us a bigger room, if they don't have any other bookings. Some of my old schoolmates married people it would be useful for you to know if we're going to be living part of the year in Singapore. I can invite them if we get a bigger room."

Mike did not answer immediately. Josephine had rolled onto her back as she talked, but now she sat up and her eyes flicked to the image of Mike on the iPad screen. Mike was better looking in person than on-screen and seemed to be staring at her left shoulder. Josephine knew this was because of the position of the camera on his MacBook and quickly redirected her own eyes to her device's tiny camera window.

"It probably won't cost much more."

"Maybe we should wait a bit," Mike said. "There are so many complications now." His out-of-focus hand blurred across the screen as he rubbed his eyes.

"Wait?" Josephine said sharply. "We've been waiting." She was about to remind him that the biggest and nastiest of their complications was dead, but she heard the shrill note in her voice and stopped herself in time. Allison was dead and Josephine was alive—she had already won. She just had to anchor down her prize before the complication inside her grew much larger.

Mike had always refused to discuss his ex-wife with her. He said there was no point dwelling on things that could not be changed. "Define the lesson and move on," she had heard him telling his children. Oh, those children. Of course Mike was probably thinking of those blasted children. It was because of them that Mike had been tied to his ex-wife even after their divorce. Josephine had done her best to win them over on her last visit to England, but what did you talk about to children? They seemed to adore their mother even after a restraining order was needed to prevent Allison from wrecking the house and attacking their babysitter. Josephine pulled her attention back to the screen and saw uncertainty in Mike's face. What had she said to trigger that? Oh . . . Josephine continued in the same urgent tone: "Can you imagine what it must be like for the poor kids, having to go to school, having to carry on with their—whatever—without knowing what's going to happen to them next?"

It worked. Thinking his sweet Josephine had united his children and herself as "we," a big load lifted in Mike Fitzgerald's mind. "We'll work something out," he promised with a warm smile. "We'll talk to them together and see how they feel about living in Singapore."

There was no way Josephine wanted Mike's children in Singapore with them. Allison had always turned to Mike when she got into trouble or ran out of money, but at least that could be handled with a call to a lawyer or a bank. Having two stepchildren underfoot all the time was a different matter. She would have to look into boarding schools . . . but that could wait till after they were married.

"How are the children taking it?" she asked, adding, "Poor things," to sound sympathetic rather than ghoulishly curious.

"I suppose I should talk to that sister of hers," Mike said

without answering her question. "Do you know what she plans to do?"

"About Allison, you mean?"

"No, about the bloody financial crisis. Or why don't I ask you what you plan to do about the financial crisis, huh?"

Josephine said nothing. She would get him to work on his anger management issues, but not till after they were safely married.

"So you're going to get all hurt and sensitive on me now?"

Josephine still did not say anything but looked away and gave a muffled little sniff. It worked.

"Look, sweets, I'm sorry. But you've got to understand the pressure I'm under. You don't know what the last few years with Allison were like and then all this. I wish she hadn't dragged Singapore into it. It's almost as though this is one of her manipulations."

"She's dead, Mike. No more manipulations."

"Yes. Of course. If her sister's already in Singapore she might want to take care of everything before I get there. But I'll send you something. Tell her I'll help with the expenses. Just make sure you see the receipts and make her sign for anything you give her."

"Okay." Though Josephine didn't think Vallerie would be up to handling anything. The woman had fallen apart, wailing that Allison's husband and children should be with her, but she was not going to tell Allison's ex-husband that.

"Do you know what happened to her? All they told me is she was alone in the hotel room and someone came in and killed her."

"That's all I know."

"Was she—did they do anything else to her?"

"I don't think she was raped," Josephine said. Though why should that be so important to him? "So are you coming over earlier then?"

"I suppose I should try to. At least there are compensations."

She knew he was trying to be nice, even trying to flirt a little. But Josephine was not sure that she wanted to be a compensation. And she had her own news for him. "Mike, I have something important to tell you."

"Hang on just a sec. I've got a call coming through. One of the kids—"

While she waited Josephine thought about what she was going to tell Mike, what she hoped he would say to her . . . and what he would probably say. "You must do whatever you think best" was one of Mike's favorite responses, which said exactly nothing. What she really wanted him to say was "That's wonderful, I'm so happy for us, let's get married right away!" but though this sounded good in her fantasies, she knew it was not likely to come out of the practical and systematic Mike Fitzgerald.

Then just as quickly he was back and already reaching out to break the connection as he said, "Sorry, sweet lips. Got to go." She heard someone at the door, knocking and calling out to him. She could not make out what they were saying but there was something strangely familiar—almost a Singaporean timbre—about their voices.

"Wait, Mikey—I didn't get my good-bye kiss—who's that calling you?"

But her screen went dead. Josephine waited for Mike to call back but he did not. That was the problem with long-distance communications. Was it Myanmar or Cambodia Mike Fitzgerald was in now? Josephine was not really interested enough to keep track of countries without designer malls. Besides, another call was coming in for her. It was a local number, so she took her time getting to it. There was no one in Singapore she wanted to speak to with any urgency. And she wanted to take a moment to enjoy the sensation of being in touch with Mike, even if only via Skype. They would not be separated for much longer now. And once they were married she would put an end to his traveling to places she was not interested in.

Josephine had no objections to marrying a divorcé. By the time a man had proved himself someone worth marrying, chances were he was already married—or unmarried for reasons that might surface disastrously later. But a dead first wife was much more respectable and far less trouble than a divorced one. So as far as Josephine was concerned, things were going very well with Mike. With Gucci, Lanvin, Moncler, and Stella McCartney now making clothes for children, Josephine would definitely have the edge over all the other mothers when it came to dressing a child, as long as its father could afford her. The biggest problem with winning a beauty title was how swiftly your year of glory passed in an exhausting crush of events. And how it dated you forever after. The first question most people asked was "What year did you win the title?" followed by "You still look quite young" or "You look exactly the same," which was both untrue and conde-scending. Winning beauty pageants had catapulted Oprah, Diane Sawyer, and Halle Berry into celebrity-status careers— why couldn't the same have happened for her? After years of waiting for success Josephine knew why: because she was trapped in Singapore. The ex–beauty queens Singapore con-sidered most successful were running companies and giving talks to graduates on how "looks are not enough" in between being photographed jogging with handsome husbands and teaching cute children the importance of recycling. In other words, no success at all as far as Josephine was concerned. She needed a husband who could get her out of Singapore.

"Madame, Madame Anne phoned to say if you want to sit in the chair she will push you one round while she is walking the dog. You can go out and come back before it rains. And Commissioner Raja said since the restaurant is closed today he will take you out to eat dinner. "

"Tell him he can bring me out for dessert. By the time that man is free to eat dinner I starve to death already!" The café might be closed, but there was always something to eat as they prepared for the coming week.

Vallerie looked curious but Aunty Lee shook her head ca-sually. "Old friends," she said. "Old people like us, we have to stay in touch."

Anne Peters was a longtime Binjai Park neighbor. Anne was also Cherril's mother-in-law, and she and Aunty Lee had grown closer since Aunty Lee helped resolve her daughter Marianne's death two years ago.

Of course Aunty Lee was still not able to go on their morning walks, but she had so missed their chats that one of her late husband ML's old wheelchairs (there were advantages to having a house with two storerooms) had been pressed into service.

"Even without the exercise it's nice to get outside and look at trees," Aunty Lee said. She was very fond of trees, especially the enormous old trees that had sheltered Singaporeans long before the days of air-conditioned walkways and shopping malls. Whatever people might say about Lee Kuan Yew these days now that the country, like a strictly raised teenager, was demanding more freedom, Aunty Lee would always appreciate Singapore's first prime minister for conceptualizing Singapore as a "garden city" and planning for trees as well as buildings. "Nina, will you bring the chair? Vallerie, do you want to come?"

She knew Vallerie would say no.

Anne Peters pushed Aunty Lee's wheelchair while Aunty Lee held on to Tammy's leash as the dog zigzagged among fascinating smells, other dogs, and the humans in her pack. Though Aunty Lee was quite able to hobble around with her stick indoors, she enjoyed the stately progress they made. It was a brief window of coolness, the sky gray with storm clouds announcing a coming shower.

"The last time I remember doing this was when I was pushing Marianne around in her little pram." Anne Peters laughed. Anne was a slim, gracious woman who seemed proud to those who did not know her well. Aunty Lee, who knew her very well, liked and loved the fragile woman protected by her shell of respectability.

As the women enjoyed their gentle promenade, admiring the plants and trees and criticizing renovations in progress, Aunty Lee filled in Anne Peters on all that had happened .

"So Cherril's not involved in anything?"

"Not at all."

As always, the mention of her daughter-in-law led to Anne lamenting her lack of children. "I know she is still young, but if they don't do something soon it will be too late before they know it. I thought I would have lots of time to have a third, maybe a fourth one. Two boys and two girls, I thought. And maybe one more just to spoil and play with. But then I blinked and now I'm waiting for my first grandchild."

"Have you asked Mycroft?"

"Mycroft?" Anne Peters laughed. "Mycroft doesn't tell me anything. I don't mean just work and confidential things. But you ask him 'How was your day, what did you have for lunch?' And it's like he has to swim up to the surface from a great depth and it takes him a while to remember who you are. Then finally he says 'fine' or something to that effect, and of course by that time you've forgotten what you asked him!

"I asked Cherril, 'Don't you find it irritating that he doesn't talk?' and the girl said, 'Better he's not good at talking than he talks too much.'" Anne Peters smiled as they walked. "I told her that her mother had brought her up to be happily married."

Aunty Lee knew her friend had been initially wary of her son's choice of wife. It was not Cherril being Chinese that she minded, but her having been an air stewardess. Some people, especially women, were prejudiced against air stewardesses, even though they were better equipped to deal with emergencies than most other women. Fortunately Anne seemed to have gotten over that after their marriage.

"After what happened to—what happened two years ago, it seems ridiculous to get upset at anything else. I wanted to die. Or to kill somebody. Just to see how it felt, just to show someone else how it felt to lose a child." The wheelchair slowed to a stop.

Aunty Lee shook her head. "But you didn't."

"No, because it wouldn't have brought my poor baby girl back. And it was destroying me. My husband and son, they keep things inside. It is their way of dealing with it."

Aunty Lee's way of dealing with her own loss when ML died had been to work. She had cooked and cleaned and organized till she was too tired to miss her husband—and she had still missed him. Though years had passed, now that she couldn't walk freely, the memory of the miserable lethargy of those early days of loss returned.

Tammy broke the mood by giving a sharp, inquiring bark and the women laughed. "Sorry, Tammy," Anne said, and started pushing the wheelchair again.

Tammy trotted purposefully ahead of them, reaching the end of her leash, then stopping to investigate something with her nose so the two women overtook her and she had to race to catch up, panting with satisfaction and giving

Aunty Lee a token lick before slobbering her affection on Anne.

"Has Cherril said anything to you about her parents? Parents can be so difficult," Anne Peters said. "There's so much unspoken social prejudice. My parents were educated and enlightened, and it was still difficult for them when I married Mycroft's father. I don't think Cherril's family was happy about her marrying an Indian man. It's not just Chinese people. Even among Indians there's all this internal prejudice against people with darker or lighter skins."

"You can't beat the Chinese. We have prejudices against different dialect groups, different accents, different times you left China, just against everybody who is different in any way. And then for people who are the same as ourselves we are prejudiced against people who are richer or poorer, who went to government schools or mission schools, who went to university abroad instead of locally . . . there is always some excuse to be prejudiced."

They laughed. At some level prejudice was a survival instinct. What was different might be dangerous.

"I wonder if Cherril's parents told her not to have children in case her half-Indian babies come out black."

"No way. Chinese mothers always want grandchildren no matter whether they come out black, white, blue, or green. And no matter what color they will love them and call them naughty to ward off bad luck. Don't worry."

By this time they had made their way back to the café. There was an unfamiliar man in uniformed overalls hesitating in front of the shop.

"Hello!" Aunty Lee called out as soon as she noticed him, leaning forward in the wheelchair as though she could urge it forward. "Who are you looking for?"

"Cooking oil delivery for Mrs. Rosie Lee?" the man said. "More in the truck." He was clearly not a regular supplier as his delivery truck was pulled up in front of the shop and all Aunty Lee's suppliers knew to use the back service lane, where they had direct access to the kitchen storeroom. Fortunately, Aunty Lee thought.

Anne Peters looked into the truck and saw more bottles, canisters, and even plastic buckets of viscous yellow fluid . . . and she also saw Aunty Lee looking guilty.

"You've been buying things online again?"

"I asked for samples only. I have to try out and taste before I can decide what to buy, right? I thought they would send one bottle each."

"They may have." Anne looked into the truck again. "Big bottles. Barrels, really."

"Bring him back to the house," Aunty Lee told Nina, who had appeared. "And tell him to put them with all the others. I will try them out at home, not in the shop."

"Cherril doesn't want to try out cooking oil in the shop?" Anne asked innocently. She got along well enough with her daughter-in-law. But that just made Cherril's possible skirmishes with Aunty Lee all the more interesting.

"Cherril thinks we should buy the cheapest cooking oil we can get," Aunty Lee explained. "She says my regular suppliers are overcharging me. She said there is no difference in taste whether I fry *keropok* in peanut oil or canola oil and I should focus on the bottom line. The bottom line is how does it taste! I must try out the samples first before I can serve them to customers. I will be frying prawn crackers and *taupok* at home once I get back on feet. Do you want?" Generally Aunty Lee was faithful to her regular suppliers, but since being immobilized she had discovered the world of online shopping.

"Cherril wants to make big profits for you," Anne said with a small smile. "And I think she wants to impress you. She looks up to you, you know."

"Sometimes we must pay more for better quality. Sometimes these young people just look at price and forget quality!"

Aunty Lee had told her friend (with much relish and only a little exaggeration) about Vallerie and her intention of following through with the threatened lawsuit. Now Anne peered through the window to see if she could catch a glimpse of the woman.

"What is the sister like?"

"I think she is still in shock," Aunty Lee said charitably. "She's full of guilt—keeps talking all the things she should have done for her sister but didn't do . . . and I think she's frightened."

"Frightened? Of what?"

Aunty Lee started to ease herself out of the wheelchair as Nina came out with her stick. "Her sister just got murdered and she is alone in a strange country—of course she's frightened." But she herself had also wondered.

But that could wait. Right now she had to sort out cooking oil by not only purity and quality but—sadly—price.

11
Monday Conversations

Lunchbox Live News & Interviews:

Interviewer: I'm at Victoria Street today, outside the hotel where the recent shocking murder of British tourist Allison Love took place. And our question today is: How safe is Singapore? Excuse me, madame. Would you tell our listeners how safe you feel in Singapore? As a tourist?

Man: Don't stop, Mom. Don't talk to her. She may have a gun.

Woman: She's just a reporter, Dad. Look, she has a microphone. He's just worried because of all your murders here. He's been living off beer and Lays Cheese and Onion in case of food poisoning, haven't you, Dad? What was that question again, miss?

Interviewer: Thank you, that's very interesting. Have a good stay—hey!

Man: Foreigners are being killed here all the time by the yakuza but people are too scared to talk. I watched *Japan Town* on the plane coming over and I know all about your professional killers and carotid arm locks and Tasers and—

Woman: That was a movie, Dad, and not as good as the book. And I keep telling you we're not in Japan.

Man: It's Asia. Japan, Singapore, it's the same thing.

Woman: Give me that microphone. Here you are, dear. We're having a lovely time.

It was a typical Monday morning at Aunty Lee's Delights. Open over the weekend, the little café was officially closed on Mondays, which was when Aunty Lee and Cherril planned the week's meals and Nina ordered ingredients and scrubbed out everything to her satisfaction.

Aunty Lee popped a little red *ang ku kueh* into her mouth. She was not as passionate about sweet cake desserts as about fiery *sambal* fry-ups, but she definitely had nothing against them and she enjoyed pleasing customers who expected them. These little turtle-shaped cakes were especially popular, given the Chinese significance of turtles and how easy it was to pack and bring home a little box of good luck and longevity. The little steamed cake's delicate yet chewy skin around grainy golden sweet potato filling proved Nina's *ang ku kuehs* were as good as Aunty Lee's own . . . or rather, that Nina had successfully followed Aunty Lee's instructions. Restaurant reviewers might joke about her special touch or secret recipe, but the fact was that there was always a system. As with making Western pancakes, the glutinous rice flour batter improved with overnight refrigeration—it was as simple as that. But then again the system was not everything. Cherril wanted to have their *kuehs* made by machines instead of by hand. There could be timers, she said, and thermometers to make sure the batter was left to stand long enough at the right temperature. But that was entirely too much system, Aunty Lee thought. Soon you would have a machine to taste your sweet potato filling for you and tell you if it was sweet enough or needed a bit more coconut milk. You would not need cooks to produce food anymore, and then who would take over all their other, undefined, nurturing functions?

"Try one?" Aunty Lee said to Vallerie, who shuddered and said, "Artificial coloring. Look at the red. It's probably going to give you all colon cancer!"

Aunty Lee looked at her partner, sitting silently at the table. Cherril was usually vehement on the subject of using only organic spices and natural coloring. They still had not sorted out the cooking oil issue, but this was probably not a good time given Cherril had a knife in her hand and a bowl heaped with washed fruit forgotten beside her.

Being involved in a murder had certainly distracted Cherril from her business expansion and automation plans. Even a cloud of murder had a silver lining, Aunty Lee thought. But she would not say that to Cherril of course—or to Vallerie.

Vallerie had come in to the shop with them. Though she was afraid of people as well as afraid to be left alone, she seemed to trust Aunty Lee. She did not, however, trust Inspector Salim, who came into the shop now.

"I've already answered all your questions over and over again. I don't know what else you want from me. Why aren't you out there going after whoever killed my sister?"

"Miss Vallerie, what I would like is for you to come and look around the hotel room you and your sister were staying in. If anything is missing or out of place or anything else looks wrong, you can tell me. My officers have already taken all the samples they need, so this is just one last informal look before everything is cleaned up. And then after that you can collect all your things."

Vallerie looked hesitantly at Aunty Lee.

"You need to get your things anyway," Aunty Lee said. "I'll come and help you to pack. Luckily we're not open today." She was sure Inspector Salim had factored that in.

"Can't you just send your servant to pack up everything and bring it over?"

The "servant" bristled, but discreetly. The police officer looked openly startled. Aunty Lee stepped in: "Nina wouldn't know what you want. And you are the only one who can tell if there's something funny there that didn't belong to you or your sister."

"It would really help us if you come and take a look around," Salim said. "Then you can sign the release form."

"More forms," Vallerie grumbled, but she seemed reassured by the mention of paperwork. "My sister is dead and you just want to make sure you don't get the blame if anything's missing or damaged. I'll sign your stupid forms."

"Good idea." Aunty Lee thumped her stick. "Where are the forms? Inspector, why don't you drive us to the hotel with you now?"

"Actually now is not a good time. I am on my way to Holland Village and just stopped by to speak to you."

"Why Holland Village?" Aunty Lee demanded. "Don't tell me it's another murder."

She had not been serious, but Salim's silence told her she had hit the mark.

"Another murder?" Nina said at the same time as Aunty Lee said, "Who?" since Vallerie was clearly alive.

Salim noticed that though Cherril threw him a shocked glance at the mention of murder, she resolutely returned to her pile of beetroots and said nothing.

"Are you talking about the girl vet?" Nina asked. "The one in Holland V?"

Aunty Lee remembered Nina had read her something that morning about the death of the young veterinarian who, with other veterinary clinic staff members, had recently been lauded as a hero for risking her life and saving all the animals during a clinic fire. She had been found dead in the second-floor toilet of the Holland Village Shopping Centre.

"There's nothing online about how she died. Was she murdered?"

"Why would you think so?"

"It's obvious, right?" Aunty Lee was fond of the inspector but had no patience with his bureaucratic nonsense. "She is a strong, healthy young woman, no mental problems, no health problems. Why would she suddenly go and drop dead, true or not? That only happens to young people when you make National Servicemen run around in the sun." Aunty Lee did not approve of people being made to run around in the sun. It was no use telling her it was necessary for national defense. These days nations were defended by brains behind computers controlling drones, not brawn in camouflage uniform.

"Unless she was murdered, what has that got to do with you? And even if it is your business, it is not our business." Nina knew from experience that murders were bad for workflow and business. "Somebody got murdered you straightaway come here and look for us. *Siao* ah you!" Nina said. "Maybe she killed herself because of the trauma of the fire. All the animals screaming and everything."

"But you said all the animals were saved, right?" Aunty Lee protested. "The papers called Dr. Kang a hero."

Inspector Salim was watching Vallerie. "That was the vet clinic your sister brought the dog to. Samantha Kang was the vet your sister went to."

"Was she?" Vallerie's face contorted, then she burst out at Inspector Salim. "That vet— Yes, she was the one. She was the vet that did the procedure. Samantha Kang, that's the name. If euthanizing that damned dog was so wrong she as a vet should have said so. She should have warned Allison. It was her fault more than Allison's, but Allison got blamed for everything. And now those crazy animal activists killed her too!"

"You don't know that. Maybe she was traumatized by the fire at the clinic," Nina repeated, keeping an eye on Vallerie. There were breakable things within reach of those arms should the woman decide to wail and flail again. "Like people getting traumatized after fighting in wars. Or you know what? Maybe she is the one that accidentally started the fire. Smoke cigarette, throw in dustbin . . . they said don't know what started the fire, right? Then maybe after that she got guilty nightmares and went and killed herself."

Though Aunty Lee objected automatically she was watching Salim closely. "They saved all the animals, what. They were all so brave; didn't you see that photo of them in the newspapers holding the dog with three legs? Why would she have nightmares? I think somehow she must have hit her head during the animal rescue—what is that word—coconut-custard her head—"

"You mean concussed, madame."

"Whatever. Anyway, like *kenah* hit on the head with coconut until brain like custard. And then got a dizzy spell at the bus stop and fell down in front of the bus." Aunty Lee came to a stop, struck by a new idea. "She was working at that clinic where the fire happened, right? Maybe someone started the fire to try to kill her. But she escaped, so later that someone had to kill her somewhere else. Did somebody purposely set the clinic on fire?" She looked hopefully at Salim. But Salim was used to Aunty Lee and his face showed nothing.

"Maybe there was a jealous husband or boyfriend," Nina suggested, who had a tendency to blame things on men.

"No *lah*. Her kind no boyfriends. Look at the photo: so skinny, hair so short. Don't know why they are all like that. No BA at all," Aunty Lee said decisively.

"You mean no SA. Or BO."

"No *lah*. I mean BA. *Buaya* Action!"

Buaya was Malay for "crocodile" but in Singlish it meant a woman chaser. Aunty Lee joined in the mild laughter but Vallerie did not find it funny.

"How can you laugh? Somebody killed that woman! Maybe the same somebody that killed my sister. You find that funny?"

"Maybe the same person that started the fire at the vet clinic," Aunty Lee suggested. She realized Vallerie was really frightened.

Vallerie shook her head. "Forget the stupid fire. I'm sure that was just an accident," she said firmly. "It's those damned animal activists. Can't any of you see? If only I had stayed in the hotel with poor Allison—"

"You might have been killed as well," Aunty Lee said quietly.

This silenced Vallerie. Salim took the opportunity to say, "So can we set a time for you to show me around your room at the hotel? Just not today. I'm on my way over to Holland Village now."

"I don't know how long they'll keep the room for me. I don't know whether they're going to make me pay for it. My sister was supposed to be paying for this trip. We're only here because she wanted to come. I was only supposed to be here to give her sisterly support. And all my things are still there. I don't know what I'm going to do! How long are you going to make me stay here like this?"

"We would like you to stay here in Singapore for a while, but there's no reason you have to stay in the hotel where it happened."

"I never want to stay in a hotel again!"

"You can stay with me as long as you want to," Aunty Lee said to Vallerie. "But you must get your things from the hotel. If you are scared it is safer to go to collect your things with a police officer."

"Somebody may be waiting there to kill me. Or somebody may follow me back from there and come and kill me here!"

"Miss, I'm sure nobody is trying to kill you—" Salim stopped, perhaps realizing he had no way of knowing if this was true.

"Allison was killed. Samantha Kang was killed. The animal people who were threatening Allison online threatened Samantha too. They're obviously the ones behind this." The problem with dealing with these natives was they were so slow, Vallerie thought. "You pretend to be so clean and safe in Singapore, but it's still the Far East. It's still dangerous."

"Maybe we should go to the hotel tomorrow?" Aunty Lee suggested into the silence that followed this.

"Tomorrow." Salim was nodding even as Aunty Lee was speaking, but she had not finished.

"They may not have been killed by the same person."

"Very likely she was."

It was usually Salim who warned against jumping to rash connections and Aunty Lee looked at him curiously. He clearly knew something more about both deaths. "Samantha Kang was killed the same way as Allison Love, wasn't she?"

"That is not for me to say, madame."

Aunty Lee knew how much Inspector Salim trusted her. If he would not tell her that meant he had been ordered not to, at least not in front of Vallerie. It was fortunate Aunty Lee was having dessert with one of the few people in Singapore Salim took orders from.

"Cable ties?"

Commissioner Raja's personal assistant, Lynn, had called to tell Aunty Lee the commissioner had been held up and she had no idea how late he would be. Would she like to make it another night? But Aunty Lee very much wanted to speak with him—and privately, away from the sister of a murder victim who was currently staying with her. So she was a little surprised, and very pleased, to see his familiar large figure in the doorway of Aunty Lee's Delights that evening only a little after eight, holding the door open to show he had parked less than legally and did not mean to leave his car there for long.

Commissioner Raja (now semiretired) had been spending more time with Aunty Lee since her ankle injury, so it was hardly surprising to see him. He had only dropped by as often as was proper, of course. Commissioner Raja was nothing if not proper. An officer of his seniority in the Singapore

Police Force had to be as carefully discreet as any member of parliament or megachurch leader. Singaporeans were much more interested in the personal failings than professional achievements of public figures, and several institutions had had their respectable reputations crippled by personal shenanigans. Vallerie stared at him with hostile suspicion. This did not surprise Aunty Lee, who had come to realize Vallerie regarded the familiar with resentment and the unfamiliar with suspicion.

"Raja!" Aunty Lee called out. "I am so glad you are here. I've got so many things to talk to you about. Did you come for dinner? We are closed today you know, but Nina can fix you something."

"Closed means closed," Vallerie muttered. "Can't people bloody understand that?"

"I know you're closed today. I just happened to be in the area," Commissioner Raja said blandly. "Since you're a semi-invalid I thought I would see if I could persuade you to leave things to Nina and let me take you out to dinner." He looked around the café, his eyes pausing on Vallerie, who was making for the washroom without being introduced. Aunty Lee nodded without waiting for his question.

"I've eaten dinner already. I eat at six P.M. Sometimes five thirty. Before the dinner crowd comes. Even when there is no dinner crowd."

"Ah yes, I thought so. That's why I brought dessert. I thought we could eat up at your house, where we can talk."

Aunty Lee seized her walking stick. "You drive."

Aunty Lee waved her stick at Nina, ignoring Vallerie's "I

have to go back to the house too. Are you leaving me alone with your maid?" whine. Nina would get Vallerie safely back to the house . . . after she had finished in the café.

People tended to have misconceptions of the police, Aunty Lee felt. All the police officers on the imported American and Korean crime dramas seemed to be clever or good-looking or both, and adept at hunting down criminals while cracking jokes and having love affairs.

Most police officers in Singapore were quiet and respectful young people who reminded Aunty Lee of the sons and daughters of friends. They were physically fit but drank too much coffee, ate too much fast food, and got too little sleep while trying to figure out the best way to handle difficult situations with no perfect solutions.

Then there were senior police officers like Raja Kumar, who had been a good friend of the late ML Lee and whose girth made Aunty Lee feel girlishly slim by comparison. He growled and let her lecture him on exercise and healthy eating as though he were stupid, but she knew Commissioner Raja Kumar was a very clever man, plus one who recognized talent and intelligence in others. As for love affairs, Commissioner Raja had been single since the death of his wife years ago. Recently Aunty Lee had wondered whether he had been getting more friendly with Anne Peters . . . and if not, whether he could be persuaded to. But that was something she would have to follow up on when she did not have a murder to solve.

Commissioner Raja had been concerned about Aunty Lee. Her physical injury did not worry him—it was nothing more than a sprained ankle, after all. But when he brought colleagues to Aunty Lee's Delights for a weekday lunch Aunty Lee had been uncharacteristically *bo chap* as Selina and Cherril battled over their seating arrangements. *Bo chap* was a Singlish term that might be translated as "don't care" or "can't be bothered," and he recognized it as something he had seen too often in newly retired officers when their change in status made them see themselves as old and useless. It was this attitude, rather than any physical disability, that ruined the richness of their well-earned third age. Some created new ways to make themselves indispensable, like volunteering for ex-offender rehabilitation or driving grandchildren around, but those who sank into the lethargy of pointlessness were often dead within years of retirement. Raja had feared Aunty Lee was headed in that direction. Plus the seasoned investigator had sensed his old friend was hiding something from him.

But this evening he saw at once Aunty Lee had perked up. Her eyes were as bright as they had been before her fall, and he had not seen her so animated and full of life since last analyzing a new dish or old murder.

"Shall I get dessert forks from the kitchen?"

"No, don't go in the kitchen! I mean, why don't we use back the same plates and forks—we are supposed to be having an indoor picnic, right?"

Commissioner Raja was glad he had not forgotten his desserts. And he could tell that even if Aunty Lee was not hiding anything from him, she was definitely hiding something.

Knowing Rosie Lee well, he had brought a copy of the menu. She liked to read about any innovations she was sampling so she could have Nina look up ingredients and recipes later. The mid-autumn Moon Cake Festival was coming. Though celebrated by Chinese people worldwide, in Singapore this festival was celebrated by anyone with children and anyone who made, bought, or ate moon cakes. Traditional moon cakes were heavy palm-sized baked pastries containing lotus seed paste and often a salted egg yolk. But Commissioner Raja (thanks to an office party) had discovered snow skin moon cakes, ice-cream moon cakes, and mini jelly moon cakes, small and light enough to be swallowed in two mouthfuls.

He had picked up a selection from that last category: pandan jelly moon cakes; chrysanthemum honey and goji berry moon cakes; and osmanthus, chrysanthemum, and plum *konnyaku* jelly moon cakes. Nothing too heavy, as he proudly said. Indeed, these might even be considered healthy offerings.

Aunty Lee's little espresso spoons were soon abandoned as she adopted Raja Kumar's more efficient finger-pick method. She was fond of jellies as well as of moon cakes and almost forgot the murders in her delight at their sweet and slightly tart taste, their firm yet smoothly elastic texture. "To work as moon cakes, the jelly has to be both firm and elastic. I wonder whether Cherril has tried these." Food purists would scream of course—but that only heightened Aunty Lee's pleasure in the little treats.

"I can make shark fin jelly instead of shark fin soup for New Year's. One big bowl shape and you can see all the ingredients, thick in the jelly. Much better for our climate here, right? And serve it with warm vinegar. Of course cannot use real shark fins nowadays. I can use agar-agar or *konnyaku . . .*"

"Shark fin is banned in Singapore now? I didn't know."

"Banned by Mathilda. For me that is same as banned by Singapore. And nowadays vegetarians and animal lovers won't come to your restaurant if you sell shark fin, you know. But first tell me what happened to the vet girl. I don't even know how she died. Usually murder is not so hush-hush, right? Government ministers having affairs or church leaders stealing money—that I can understand must be hush-hush. But this is just murder, right? Why cannot tell people how she died?"

"You haven't found out yet? Not even Inspector Salim would tell you anything?" Commissioner Raja teased with a straight face.

"I've got this thing stuck on my leg, how can I find out anything?" Aunty Lee thumped her cane on the floor with exaggerated frustration and then (more gently) on her ankle-stabilizing cast. She had phoned the police post several times but had been politely told they knew nothing. As far as Aunty Lee was concerned, nothing worked as well as pinning down someone in person and making them tell you all they knew. If only she could get about on her own, she was certain she could have gotten it out of a member of Salim's staff by now.

"So how long do you have to keep the cast on your foot?" Raja segued away from the murder. "How long until you're back to walking normally?"

"Actually this is just to keep the ankle stable. I can walk already. You know they wanted to keep me in hospital longer for observation? They said at my age must be careful. I told them I cannot sleep in hospital; I can sleep better, recover faster at home. I already took their MRI, nothing wrong they said. Very expensive you know, these tests, but didn't find anything."

Raja Kumar nodded without admitting he had already seen her medical reports. "Best thing is if it was a waste of money, because you don't want them to find anything. They probably just wanted to make sure there is no risk of you falling again."

Aunty Lee popped a whole jelly cake into her mouth and said around it, "So how was the vet killed? You think the same person who killed the puppy killer killed her, right? Her sister is staying with me so she is my responsibility and you should let me know. Her sister thinks those Animal Re-Homers people killed them both."

He nodded. This was not news to him.

"Must try putting sweet fungus in the goji berry jelly cake," Aunty Lee murmured. But she was only temporarily diverted. "Josephine said Allison Love was the kind of person that would poison herself to show you how bad your food is." Aunty Lee looked at her friend hopefully. "Was Allison poisoned? I thought she was strangled. They wouldn't let us see her neck. They pulled down the cloth from the top to her chin, and then when I asked to see more they pulled it up from the bottom to show her legs. Did she hang herself? Her head looked like somebody hit her very hard in the face. I thought her sister was going to faint or vomit."

"Did Josephine really say that? Josephine DelaVega?"

"She wasn't talking to me but I heard. Could that Allison woman have set this up? Maybe she found out she was dying of incurable cancer or something, so she came back and killed herself in such a way that the Animal ReHomers would be blamed. Her lawsuit against them was probably just her excuse to come back to Singapore. Nobody here would take it seriously, right?" The plump old lady paused, looking at Commissioner Raja with all the eager anticipation of a puppy that has just laid a precious dead frog on its master's foot. "Could Allison Love have killed herself? And then gotten somebody to come and hit her in the head after she was dead? Because that only happened after she died, right? That was not what killed her."

"What makes you think so?" Commissioner Raja asked impassively. Even after so many years he could not tell whether Aunty Lee was stating a fact or fishing for one.

"The meat on her face—I mean the flesh. The way it looked. There's a difference in how the meat looks if you hit a pig to stun it before killing and if you hit it after killing for tenderizing."

Aunty Lee pushed the little tray of unfinished jellies away from her. She fully acknowledged the need to kill in order to eat, but she suddenly no longer felt like eating. "If your hospital pathologists did not tell you that, then you go and tell them I said they don't know their stuff!"

"She didn't kill herself, Rosie. I'm only telling you this because I don't want you going and getting involved in something that may turn out to be dangerous—no, listen to me. This is not some poisoning case that you can solve by finding out who has been using bad meat."

Aunty Lee's lips pursed at this but she continued, refusing to be distracted. "I want to know how she died because I don't want to get blamed for poisoning people again. The last time you people blamed my special *buah keluak* dish and shut me down when it was nothing to do with me." It could not hurt to remind Commissioner Raja that Aunty Lee had not only been wrongly blamed but had also helped apprehend the real killer.

"And you know I won't tell anybody. Except Nina. But telling Nina is like outsourcing my brain. With other people I just tell them enough small gossip to keep their brains occupied so that they don't notice I'm not telling them the big thing."

Her convolutions would likely have knotted up Raja's brain if he had tried to unravel them. So he didn't.

"Allison Love was hit in the face with something like a fire extinguisher. Very likely the fire extinguisher from the hallway outside her hotel room. And yes, the forensic report suggests it happened after she died."

" 'Very likely'?" Aunty Lee took all kinds of liberties with the English language, but she knew it well enough to know Raja Kumar did not.

"We have to wait for confirmation of the samples sent to the lab."

"Just in case it was used to bash somebody else in the same hotel who you haven't found yet. *Hiyah*." Aunty Lee accepted the need for professional caution but could not help a sigh of exasperation. "So how was she killed?"

"There was also a cable tie pulled tight around her neck to suffocate her. It was a loop of two cable ties, actually. There would have been no way to get it off without cutting once it was pulled tight. That would have been enough to kill her, but it looks like the killer panicked because he thought she was not dying fast enough and went out to the hallway to get the fire extinguisher. She was already dead when he came back with it, but he hit her with it just to make sure."

It was not a pretty picture. Aunty Lee winced slightly. "Not a very experienced killer." She had seen enough animals killed to prefer a calm, experienced killer to a sympathetic, clumsily shrieking one. But she had no sympathy at all for people who ate meat without acknowledging it came from dead animals. That honesty was one of the things about her that made Commissioner Raja trust her.

"The blows suggest great rage or great panic. I would say some kind of emotion that goes beyond sanity."

Aunty Lee shivered slightly. It was always easier to deal with the greedy than the crazy, because you could follow their reasoning even if you didn't share their values.

"Vallerie's really upset, but I still feel she is hiding something. I can tell that she is really frightened. But I don't see why any animal activists would attack Dr. Kang after she apologized publicly for euthanizing the dog. You remember she also donated two months of her salary to the Animal Re-Homers. And just days ago she was one of the heroes who saved all the animals during that clinic fire. Couldn't her death be just a coincidence or an accident or even a suicide?"

"We are quite certain that Allison's killer also killed the vet because they were both strangled by cable ties. That incidentally establishes that Mike Fitzgerald is unlikely to be Allison's killer since we had already located and were keeping an eye on him when the vet was murdered."

"And unlikely to be Vallerie also. She cannot even tie up her own hair, how to strangle somebody with cable ties? Was the vet also whacked on the head?"

"No. The only thing that links them is the cable ties."

Cable ties? Aunty Lee thought about the sturdy nylon tie wraps that locked irreversibly once their pointed tips were pulled through the ratchet case teeth. Once through, they could be pulled tighter but not released. Aunty Lee used cable ties for everything from hanging up waxed ducks and smoked sausages to holding up Christmas and New Year decorations and fastening flower arrangements to invisible supports. Cable ties were indispensable, but she would never look at them the same way again.

It was difficult to think of cable ties as a murder weapon. Cable ties had come into the news in Singapore when it was revealed that they were used to secure rail claws on the island's Mass Rapid Transit lines after some major line disruptions. They had subsequently fallen into disfavor with the subsequent report that rail claws on the MRT's rail network continued to dislodge despite the cable ties. But that would be nothing compared to a revelation that cable ties had been used in the murder of a British tourist and local veterinary surgeon Samantha Kang.

"Are you officially ruling out suicide in the vet's case? Because if you don't have anything to cut them with, strangling yourself with cable ties sounds like a good way of committing suicide."

"She didn't."

Aunty Lee accepted that. "I wish there was some way to find out about Allison's state of health in England, state of her mental health also."

"I'm sure Salim already has someone looking into that," Commissioner Raja said. "How is the sister doing, by the way?"

"Holding up very well, all things considered."

"Rosie, just between us, your having the woman's sister staying with you makes things a lot easier for us. Feed her, look after her, listen to her. And I want you to let me or Salim know everything the sister tells you, even if it doesn't sound important. And if anybody contacts her, I want you to let Salim know immediately. I'm not asking you to spy on your guest"—he held up a hand to forestall the percolating objection—"I am asking you to help us keep her safe. You will be my undercover operative, how about that?"

"Undercover operative." Aunty Lee turned the words over on her tongue. "It makes it sound like I am doing illegal operations. I can be your undercover cook. But why is Salim in charge of this case? It is not his district, what."

"I asked Inspector Salim Mawar to take it and he agreed," Commissioner Raja said. "Officially anyway. After all, Allison Love's only appointment in Singapore was in your café, and that is in his district."

"And unofficially?"

"Salim asked if he could look into it. He's got experience in this sort of thing and he's got more time to look into it than the guys in town—tourist season, you know what that's like."

Aunty Lee did know. As tourists flocked into Singapore with money to spend, many others came to relieve them of it via cheating, stealing, or sex acts. Processing their victims' complaints occupied a great deal of manpower, let alone following through on them.

"Vallerie feels responsible for what happened to her sister," Aunty Lee said. "She says that just by coming to Singapore with Allison she was responsible. If she had refused to come, if she had broken her leg or didn't want to leave home for some reason and Allison didn't want to make the trip without her, then Allison wouldn't have come and she wouldn't have gotten herself killed."

"Whoever wanted to kill her could have killed her somewhere else."

"And that would be sad for her. But she wouldn't have been killed here and it wouldn't have been our business."

Commissioner Raja studied Aunty Lee. "So you're saying this is our business? And if she had been killed anywhere else it wouldn't matter?"

Aunty Lee jumped in to answer. "Of course it matters, *what*. It's just not our business. Every day women are being killed in Gaza, in Ukraine, in airplanes getting shot down, and we say, '*Aiyoh*, so terrible,' and think about what are we going to eat for dinner tonight. Allison Love is Singapore's business because she died in Singapore. Bad for Singapore's reputation if people come here and get killed. Her sister is my business because she is staying in my house. And, of course, Josephine DelaVega is your business as well as my business because she is a Singapore girl who grew up here. This Vallerie is going around telling everybody that Josephine hired somebody to kill Allison so that she can marry Allison's husband."

"Josephine is Jojo and Constance DelaVega's youngest?" Raja had made a point of not seeing Josephine himself and not taking calls from the DelaVegas till he understood more about the case. They were old friends and he understood their reaching out to him. Parents always believed their children either innocent or justified. As an old friend he sympathized with them, but as a police officer he could offer no comfort.

"Yes. She's one of the people Allison came to Singapore to sue for breaking up her marriage." Aunty Lee shook her head. "Crazy woman. Husband already left you, you think that acting more crazy will make him come back?"

To her surprise the commissioner did not agree immediately. "That puppy killer business must have been a terrible experience for Allison and her whole family. There were tens of thousands of people signing on to the 'Justice for Lola' page online and crying for her blood. It's mob justice. Many people don't feel responsible for their behavior when they are part of a mob because they see everyone around them doing the same thing. And the Internet amplifies this because you don't see your target's reactions, so there are fewer social inhibitions. It can get really ugly."

It did sound frightening. Aunty Lee felt the first stirrings of real sympathy for the dead woman. "But nobody actually attacked her, right? All she had to do is not go online and read what people were saying about her *lor*!"

"Given she was an expat wife far away from family and friends, that wouldn't have been easy. The puppy killer story went viral. It was shared over a thousand times on Facebook even before the full story and facts were established. Because they feel anonymous, online people post things they may not say in person. Mob vigilantes post things that make other people even angrier. Tensions really boiled over and it got really ugly. Maybe they were taking it out on her because she was a rich white expat, I don't know. One of those sociologists will be able to explain it. And the online community was doxing her—'doxing' short for 'document tracing.' They found out where her husband was working and sent e-mails to the company asking for him to be fired and sent home. They posted photographs of the house she was living in and photographs of her with her children with comments on how she looked and what should be done to her. The vet and the clinic also got some hate mail, but Allison got it the worst. Probably because she insisted that she had not done anything wrong."

"If she said sorry like that vet did, maybe people wouldn't

have been so angry." Aunty Lee remembered how angry and upset Mathilda had been. "But she was behaving like Japan after the Occupation ended. Instead of saying, 'Sorry we invaded you and killed your fathers and brothers and raped your mothers and sisters,' they pretended it never happened and said, 'You shouldn't have dropped the bomb on us.'"

Raja Kumar did not follow the red herring Aunty Lee trailed across the conversation. The generation of Singaporeans who had lived through the Japanese Occupation was dying out. And with or without apologies being given, memories of atrocities would die out too. He held no personal grudge against Japan. The only problem he had with the whitewashing of history was knowing that lessons not learned were often repeated. Still, his responsibility was to deal with people's problems in the present—not those causing trouble five or fifty years ago . . . unless that was where present problems were rooted.

"I suspect expats coming here on huge incentive packages get unsettled by cultural differences from what they assumed was the god-given norm," he said. "Their natural biases are triggered and they react with defensiveness or disgust. It's not just cultural prejudice. I think Allison Fitzgerald was feeling insecure and trying to make herself feel better by belittling locals."

"But why did everybody focus on her? Her husband must have been involved too. He was living in the house; he must have known what was happening to the dog. Why didn't people get angry with him too?" It was not only because of what happened years ago that Aunty Lee wanted to get the answer to this. If Mike Fitzgerald was the sort of man who pushed blame on to his wife, Aunty Lee would make sure that any rumors that Josephine DelaVega was involved with the man would come to nothing.

"Allison was the one who signed the contract. She was the one who made the agreement. But I agree with you. The man had to have known what was happening. You could say that he's noble for standing by his wife no matter what she did. Or if you want to be really old-fashioned and patriarchal, you can say that he should have kept his wife in order and made her behave better. Other than that there really wasn't anything on him."

Aunty Lee did not fully agree. People who lived together influenced one another. It was part of the give and take of daily life and community. Either he had accepted his wife and her personality or he had failed to change her. And had he left her because of that? But she put that aside to gnaw on later. The problem with having too many questions bursting out at the same time was it got difficult to keep track of getting the more important ones answered.

"I'm surprised they didn't just leave."

"They did leave. And that should have been the end of the matter for us."

Not for the first time Aunty Lee wished the woman had not come back. "And the vet? The angry online people went after her too, right?"

"They did. But right away the vet said very publicly that she was wrong to have put the dog down, that she blamed herself. She cried on TV and gave two months' salary to the

ReHomers and the SPCA and was donating her time to sterilizing strays, so they left her alone after that."

"It seems unlikely she would be a target for them then," Aunty Lee said. "But Allison might have felt Samantha Kang betrayed her."

She studied Commissioner Raja, who was wearing his most impassive expression—and waiting.

"It could just be a coincidence. Or it could be somebody who wants you to think that the animal people killed Allison, not her ex-husband. Vallerie thinks Allison's ex-husband followed her to Singapore. Is that possible?"

"If he did I'm sure you'll know soon." In case Aunty Lee paid too much attention to pronouns he rushed on: "So overall sounds like the sister is holding up okay?"

"She's in shock, of course. But I think she's eating normally—no spicy stuff, she likes lots of sugar and crispy food. Not very healthy, but I get the feeling she's tougher than she looks. And I don't think she and her sister were all that close." Aunty Lee did not think it necessary to mention tabloid papers rather than Vallerie had been her source of information. "From what I gather, Vallerie Love moved to America years ago, just after her sister and her family came to Singapore, and she hasn't been back to England since. What's more, she didn't go back to England when her sister was getting her divorce. You would think she would have, if the sisters were that close, right? And that makes it more surprising that she accompanied Allison here. But she said it was the least she could do, and she had never been to Singapore before so why not? I suppose Allison's children went to stay with their father when their mother left England."

"The two children were already staying with their father. After the divorce the court gave custody to the father. In fact he took out a restraining order against Allison."

"Against her coming close to him or to her children?"

"Children. She was only allowed supervised visits, and she could not take them out of school without their father's permission."

"Poor woman." Aunty Lee had been as set against Allison the Puppy Killer as anyone else in Singapore, but she was definitely feeling sorry for her now.

"The court wouldn't have granted a restraining order without good reason," Commissioner Raja said. He looked thoughtfully at Aunty Lee. "Are you sure the sister doesn't know anybody in Singapore other than those three Allison came to Singapore to sue?"

"She doesn't even know them. Met them for the first time the day her sister died. Your sergeant Panchal gave her a list of contacts in the British Council and the American embassy but she refused to call them. She says they never helped her sister when Allison needed them. But it's not a problem. I want you to tell your people that it's all right for Vallerie to go on staying at my house. You know I have lots of room. Your people can reach her here whenever they want and she will be quite safe. You can put a guard outside if you want, but don't make him stand in the sun. And I want you to make sure we can get back into the hotel room to get her things. For somebody her size it's not so easy to just go out and buy clothes here. Of course I can go to Holland Village and pick up a few caftans for her, but just think about the underwear!"

"Hmm. Of course." Commissioner Raja grimaced involuntarily and made a weary shooing gesture. "Fine, fine. Just keep an eye on her. Don't let her fall into a drain or walk into a door and sue you for damages. And don't let her talk you into getting involved in investigating her sister's death. This time it is really nothing to do with you. We just have to sort it out with the hotel security."

"Didn't anybody from the hotel notice anything?"

"Hotels like this, guests are paying for them not to notice anything. But the girl on duty at reception did say that one call came through for room sixty-six after Vallerie left, and when she put it through it was answered," Raja Kumar said. "We would have asked them anyway, you know. We've been doing this job for a long time."

"That suggests whoever Allison let into her room knew she was staying at the hotel but not which room she was in," Aunty Lee said. "I know Brian made a call to the hotel from the café. Was that it?"

"Oh no. The hotel took his call. They already knew by then."

"How?"

"Someone else called it in. But they didn't leave their name. Some people don't like getting involved."

Singapore police could be so earnest and naive, Aunty Lee thought. It was one of their greatest strengths, but could also be a great flaw. Aunty Lee was about to point that out when a buzz made Commissioner Raja check his phone.

Aunty Lee knew better than to ask about the text that put a gleam in her friend's eyes, but she sighed and massaged the knee above her poor damaged ankle to make him feel sorry for her and started absentmindedly on another of the jelly moon cakes. They were really very good: not too sweet, not too large, and leaving a slight aftertaste of honeyed lemon curd.

"Anything important?"

"You might like to know Allison Love was not the only member of her family to come back to Singapore," Commissioner Raja said. "Apparently the ex-husband, Mike Fitzgerald, arrived a week ago."

He looked pleased and almost cheerful, Aunty Lee thought. But yes, if the police could show that Allison Love's ex-husband had followed her to Singapore, it would tie up things very nicely.

"Mike Fitzgerald is already in Singapore?"

"Looks like it. Can't say anything more right now."

"Can you say that he also killed that girl vet?"

"So, Rosie, what do you think of that place up in Kuala Lumpur that is advertising *nasi lemak* that is 'better than Aunty Lee's'?" Commissioner Raja rose to his feet, switching back into policeman mode. He knew food—especially food from a rival cook—was the only thing that could distract Rosie Lee from trying to dig out confidential information.

"Sounds like they are giving me free advertising. What are you going to do?"

"One day I'm going to take you up to KL to eat the *nasi lemak* there that is supposed to be better than yours. When all this is sorted out. We can drive there. Better still, fly up to Penang."

Aunty Lee smiled, pleased. She did not make the mistake of underestimating Commissioner Raja. He might look like a genial old man on the verge of retirement, and he did his best to bolster that impression. But though his social Singlish made his children and grandchildren wince, Raja spoke Standard English as well as Hokkien, Malay, Japanese, and Mandarin, and could make himself understood in French, German, Korean, and Tagalog. He loved languages and traveling. And he loved food and gossip almost as much as Aunty Lee did . . . something his comments underlined. But while Aunty Lee loved solving crimes because she really loved untangling glitches in people, Raja Kumar preferred setting up systems to run smoothly without interruptions.

"We'll talk about KL *nasi lemak* another time. Now you tell me what are you going to do with the dead woman's husband!" Aunty Lee hurried to get between her guest and the front door.

"How can I talk about death first and then talk about life? *Nasi lemak* comes first. Life comes before death. And this is one of the rare times I discovered a stall you don't know. We should run away up-country to eat and give the kids a scare!"

In losing their life partners each had also lost a primary dining companion they had comfortably taken for granted for years. Though theirs was no more than a culinary flirtation, they were aware their offspring had vague apprehensions that Raja Kumar and Rosie Lee might decide to marry. They would be good company for each other and it was unlikely there would be children, but who would control the fairly substantial inheritances they had been counting on?

"We worried enough about them when they were growing up and going out with boyfriends and girlfriends. Now let them see how it feels!" Commissioner Raja had once said to Aunty Lee after deflecting a series of probing questions from Selina.

Actually they were both happy with how things were. The commissioner could talk to Aunty Lee about how Sumathi, his late wife, had first discovered kokeshi dolls (she had left an impressive collection) on their thirtieth anniversary trip to Japan and how, on the same trip, he had first tasted kelp-fed sea urchin sashimi. And Aunty Lee could tell him about how exasperating ML had been, giving up smoking "for good" every two years and donating all his pipes to the Salvation Army, and then buying them back (in their unopened donation box).

And they both enjoyed talking about food, of course.

"So where is this famous new *nasi lemak* stall?"

"It's not a new stall. It's an old one. Nasi Lemak Tanglin. In the Tanglin Food Court along Jalan Cendrasari, opposite the Poliklinik."

"Old man, you don't know what you are talking about. What's so special about their *nasi lemak* there?"

"Quite a number of dishes are special—fried chicken, chicken *rendang*, beef liver, beef lung, *sambal sotong* . . . I think we need to go up-country soon."

"Here I also got chicken *rendang, sambal sotong* . . ." Aunty Lee made a mental note to tell Nina to source beef liver and beef lungs, but there was something else. "The seller's name is Zainal, right?" Aunty Lee remembered. "He was running the stall with his mother—what was her name, I can't remember. They used to have a stall along Jalan Tanglin. ML brought me once. We sat on stools by the roadside under a tree—"

"That's it! *Wah*, Rosie, you are as old as me if you can remember. You look so young I keep forgetting." Raja Kumar roared with laughter. "That's it exactly. Zainal is still there. Old like us now. His daughter is helping him. Getting ready to take over. I want to go back up and eat one more time before she takes over. These young people always try to improve here, cut cost there. They say it is the same but it is never the same."

Aunty Lee thought about Cherril's factory automation plans and sighed. There were different ways of taking over. She would have to think about it, but for the moment her attention was focused on Vallerie and her dead sister. It was almost a relief to have someone with more problems than yourself to think about.

12

Problems

After Commissioner Raja left, Aunty Lee felt something was not quite right with her insides. When food provoked such a feeling it usually meant an upset tummy and runny stools later. She hoped it was not something in the jelly moon cakes disagreeing with her. People often did not know what food allergies they had. They thought they had been born with ill health and went on eating dairy or nuts or mushrooms or whatever it was that made them sniff, scratch, or break out in spots and feel generally miserable. Aunty Lee was fortunate in not being allergic to anything other than falling off tables, but people were always engineering new foods and genetically modifying old ones, so she was always on guard.

The problem was, it could be difficult to tell which ingredient in a dish was making you sick. But that evening Aunty Lee suspected she knew what was wrong: nobody was asking her what secret information Commissioner Raja might have shared with her. Aunty Lee could have resisted any amount of pressure and questioning, but with nothing to resist she felt the nugget of news (Cable ties! How bizarre was that?) swelling and threatening to leak out of her like gas out of swollen bowels. She wondered why Nina had not yet returned with Vallerie, and when Aunty Lee heard the gate opening she hurried to the front room. Even Vallerie would do. Vallerie would want to know what the policeman had said about her sister's death, and Aunty Lee would be sympathetic, but nobly refrain from saying what she had learned. But it was Cherril who knocked tentatively at the unlocked door and pushed it open.

"Nina took Vallerie to buy some rash powder," Cherril explained. "There's something I've been wanting to talk to you about privately."

Aunty Lee winced, fearing Cherril wanted to talk about her expansion plans, or perhaps ask about the mountain of mangoes or cache of cooking oil samples still untouched in the Binjai Park kitchen. Aunty Lee knew Cherril had already started looking for a factory; in fact she had wanted to bring Aunty Lee around to tour possible options. Fortunately her twisted ankle had gotten her out of that without offending Cherril, but how long could she go on using that as an excuse? She winced at Cherril's projections of how, once they got automated production in process, they could start negotiations to distribute "Aunty Lee's Frozen Microwave Meals" to supermarkets and school canteens. And Cherril had also been looking into leasing "Aunty Lee's" franchises to *kopitiam* stalls and kiosks. "There's a limit to how many people we can serve here. And as long as we are making *achar* and *sambal* by hand, production is limited," Cherril had pointed out. "The only way for Aunty Lee's Delights to grow is to expand in other directions. And on that subject we should start looking out for larger premises." It all sounded very businesslike and professional and had impressed Aunty Lee's stepson, Mark, and even his far harder to impress wife. But Aunty Lee knew that what made her Peranakan pickles and fried fish paste so special was precisely that it was made by hand in limited quantities!

And Aunty Lee had never wanted to make a lot of money from cooking. Indeed, for Aunty Lee the business side of things was more an excuse to cook than anything else. To live in a land where there was enough clean water and food for everyone to eat in peace side by side was already a blessing. Aunty Lee was fond of Cherril. But why did she want to change everything?

Aunty Lee was a firm believer in change when it came to sink filters and underwear, but she saw no point in changing something that worked well and didn't smell. And her little café with its kitchen and shop worked well for her. It was within walking distance of her house, friends and neighbors could drop in to chat, and the police post nearby kept everyone safe. Best of all, she could watch people enjoying the food she had prepared. Wasn't that the whole point of cooking good food? Not for Cherril, apparently. Cherril, who was definitely also one of the blessed if only she let herself realize it, only talked about profit margins and brand visibility.

In her role of business partner, it seemed to Aunty Lee that Cherril was focusing on the business side of things and forgetting it was really all about food.

Aunty Lee tried to change the subject before Cherril could bring it up. "I'm thinking of making savory jellies. What do you think of a seafood *tom yam* jelly? Our seafood *tom yam* is already quite thick. We can boil it up with gelatin then set it in the fridge. Cold and spicy instead of hot and spicy."

Cherril said vaguely, "I'm not very hungry," which made Aunty Lee stop and look at her with more attention. Cherril was never hungry, which Aunty Lee considered almost unnatural for someone in the food business. But she usually paid attention to what Aunty Lee was saying.

Cherril was a woman who seemed to look good naturally. Aunty Lee now knew this was not true, having seen for herself how much effort Cherril put into maintaining a perfect complexion through a workday. This had impressed Aunty Lee though she had no desire to emulate her. It was the same respect Aunty Lee felt for people who dedicated time, energy, and money to hybridizing orchids or restoring vintage cars. It was how she felt about her *sambals* and spiced sauces. They were artists, or perhaps acolytes. But that day Cherril was not looking good. Her makeup was still impeccable but she looked drawn, tired, and intensely worried about something.

"Is it Mycroft?" Aunty Lee asked, careful not to say too much.

Before her son's wedding, Anne Peters had told Aunty Lee (swearing her to secrecy) that the girl he was going to marry was not only a former air stewardess but had had an abortion. The fervently Catholic Anne had been shocked. "I got a private investigator to check up on his fiancée, this Cherril Lim. He can't marry that girl and I can't tell him about the private investigator—what am I going to do?"

"Why do you have to do anything?" Aunty Lee had asked. "Your son the lawyer can tell you that abortion is legal in Singapore *what*. As long as you can *tahan* all the check-ups and counseling and mandatory waiting period if your baby still not yet twenty-four weeks and you still don't change your mind, you can get abortion. Did she get abortion in Singapore?"

"I don't know. All the report says is that she suddenly left the airline after a routine medical check-up. After that she went to the Female Focus clinic twice. Their records are confidential, but no sign of any baby, so it must have been an abortion, right?"

Aunty Lee had kept to herself thoughts of several other things "it" might have been, and did her best to calm her friend down. It was at least partly thanks to Aunty Lee that Anne's private investigator and his information had not been allowed to stop the wedding. Aunty Lee had never regretted that. Anne might well have lost a son as well as a daughter.

Remembering how well she had kept information to herself made Aunty Lee feel pleased with herself and eager to tackle new problems. Cherril was always a good source of problems—young women these days were so bad at saying what they wanted, despite their multitude of communication devices. Life would be so much simpler if people said what they thought. But then without that drama life would be so dull.

"Mycroft!" Cherril stared at Aunty Lee. "Why? What's wrong with Mycroft? Did Mother Peters say something to you?"

"No, no. Nothing," Aunty Lee said quickly. Too quickly, she instantly realized.

"He's unhappy, isn't he?" Cherril said. "I've been going through his financial accounts and everything—no, of course he doesn't know—and everything looks all right. He's not a secret gambler and he hasn't been signing over half his income to some mistress or some church, so I know it's not that."

Cherril knew only too well she was not getting any younger. And she did want children. She just did not know whether she wanted children enough to get herself checked out by a doctor who might find out all kinds of other things about her. Cherril could talk to Aunty Lee about almost anything. But she didn't think Aunty Lee (contentedly childless herself) could understand this. Or worse, if Aunty Lee did understand and had felt the same way, what right did Cherril have to bring it up? Almost superstitiously Cherril was afraid of ending up childless like Aunty Lee. She dealt with the fear the best way she knew how: by not thinking about it. She wasn't sorry that Allison was dead. It would distract everybody for a while, and at least it hadn't happened to a nicer person.

"Mycroft deals with facts," Aunty Lee said. "And one of the facts is that he loves you. That is a very big fact, bigger than all the other facts in his head."

"Facts don't come in different sizes," Cherril said.

"Of course they do. Just like people. I am a bigger size than you, that is a fact, right? So my facts are bigger than your facts. What did you want to talk to me about?"

"Aunty Lee, I know you've helped people solve some . . . problems."

That was true, Aunty Lee thought. However unfairly people might describe her as a bossy busybody, she had certainly managed to solve a couple of murders while satisfying her own curiosity.

"Please, will you help Josephine?" Cherril asked.

The sudden change of subject took Aunty Lee aback.

"Only Josephine?" As far as Aunty Lee could tell, Cherril and Brian were also suspects, though Aunty Lee did not for a moment think Cherril had killed Allison Love.

"I didn't kill that woman," Cherril said carefully. "That's one thing I'm sure of right now. And I know that Brian couldn't have done it. I'm sure it was that woman's husband. I hope they prove it is, then it would just be their domestic problem and it just happened to blow up in Singapore but have nothing to do with us."

"You sound like you are worried that Josephine had something to do with it."

"I'm worried that people will think she did. I want you to somehow prove that she didn't."

"But you were with Josephine the whole time the woman was getting killed," Aunty Lee pointed out. "I heard you tell the police that she and Brian were here in the café with you."

The problem with this old woman, Cherril thought, was

that it was impossible to tell whether she was really missing the point or just pretending to. Or could she really have forgotten how long Cherril had waited, alone, for the other two at Aunty Lee's Delights that day?

"They weren't." Cherril was impatient with Aunty Lee's stupidity. "But I said they were. Look—I'm just trying to help Josie."

For a moment Aunty Lee felt cross with Josephine. She felt certain the other woman was not half as concerned about Cherril as Cherril was about her. Unless—

"Did Josephine ask you to help her? Did she tell you to help her?"

Cherril's startled, slightly guilty look told Aunty Lee she was right. She continued, with the air of hazarding a guess: "Josephine knows about you and Brian Wong." This was another nugget of information from Anne Peters's private investigator.

When Cherril did not deny this, Aunty Lee went on. "And she knows Mycroft doesn't know." She did not try to hide her disapproval, but by now Cherril knew her boss well enough to tell whom her disapproval was directed at. "Mycroft is not going to be angry with you for anything that you did before you were married, you know. Nothing that you did last time can make trouble between the two of you as much as you not discussing it with him now. You two are married now. You should be able to tell him anything and not be scared of what other people threaten to tell him about you!"

"It's not what you're thinking. She's not blackmailing me.

It's more like—well, friends helping each other out, you know."

Aunty Lee would have pursued this further, but just then—

"What's the big discussion?" Selina came in with Vallerie, followed by Mark. "Aunty Lee, I have to talk to you," Selina said as Vallerie headed for the stairs without greeting her hostess.

American manners, Aunty Lee thought, then quickly quashed the criticism, remembering the many lovely Americans she knew. It was too easy to spread a bad smell over a whole nation after encountering one bad egg. Better just to call them "Vallerie Manners."

"Aunty Lee and I were talking about a business expansion plan," Cherril said quickly.

"More plans? You should listen to her, Aunty Lee," Mark said. "This girl's on fire!"

Aunty Lee was prepared to listen to anything. But a quick glance at Selina's dark face reminded her that there was always more than one story to listen to. Cherril quickly said good night and disappeared.

Selina lowered her voice. "You should put her on leave so that if this blows up, people won't associate her with your shop."

"I'm sure Cherril didn't have anything to do with it," Mark said. Mark had always had a soft spot for Cherril, which didn't improve Selina's opinion of her.

"You don't know that. Even the police don't know anything yet. How can you know that?" Selina put a hand on Aunty

Lee's arm. This was a novelty for Aunty Lee. She was more used to Selina warning people against her than warning her against people. "I'm not saying Cherril had anything to do with that woman's death. But she's one of those animal activists so she's definitely involved. You don't want your business to be associated with that kind of thing. You should just put her on suspension or something during the investigation. Like secondary school teachers accused of supporting sex education or married government ministers suspected of having affairs. You don't need to have proof of anything. Just say that food preparation is a sensitive area and having her around will make your customers uncomfortable. Then if there's nothing wrong she can come back after it blows over. And you know she's a friend of Josephine's, which makes it worse."

"There is no need to see Josephine as a pubic enemy, you know," Aunty Lee said to Selina.

"Public enemy you mean."

"No, I mean pubic," Aunty Lee said firmly.

Selina frowned, then laughed.

"There's no point hating her. She's a poor thing," Aunty Lee said. "And after all you are married to Marko."

"So I'm supposed to think I'm so lucky and be grateful?"

"The same way Mark is so lucky to have you. And so grateful."

For once Selina did not have a sharp comeback.

"You should feel sorry for her," Aunty Lee said. "I feel sorry for girls who were pretty when they were young. People keep telling them they are pretty, and when they grow up they never try to be anything more."

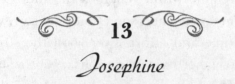

13

Josephine

Despite Selina's dire warnings, none of the customers at Aunty Lee's Delights seemed put off by the fact that Cherril had been questioned by the police. Indeed this stirred up much excitement, along with rumors of Singapore's ex–beauty queen Josephine's relationship with Mike Fitzgerald. Everyone seemed certain that Mike had killed his ex-wife and showered Vallerie, the bereaved sister, with sympathy, buying her drinks and even meals.

Even Selina contributed, given Selina and Josephine had attended the same girls' school at Emerald Hill.

"She was one of the havoc girls in school. You know, with too-long hair and too-short skirts, always looking at boys instead of books."

"That's Josephine DelaVega!" Aunty Lee said.

"Exactly."

"No, I mean that's her—Josephine—by the door. She just came in."

As far as Josephine DelaVega was concerned, maintaining her beauty required time, energy, and money. If you put in more money, you could sometimes get away with skimping on the time and effort. Even with the stress she was under that day, her hair extensions, eyebrow tattoos, and smudge-proof eye shadow made her look fragile and even more beautiful.

"Josephine, come! Come over here!" Aunty Lee waved her over to where she and Vallerie were sitting by the serving counter where Selina stood. "You already met poor Vallerie, right? And this one is my stepson's silly wife."

"Aunty Lee, I already told you Josephine and I know each other. I've probably known her longer than anyone else here! Are you looking for Cherril? She's not here," Selina said. She was torn between her desire to ignore her old schoolmate and to show her how well-informed she was. "She had to go and check on one of our suppliers. We're very particular about the quality of the ingredients we use here. Even when we're not full we're very busy. Can I help you?"

"Hi . . . What do you do here?" Josephine seemed puzzled by Selina's spiel, as though she was having trouble remembering her.

"I'm married to Mark, Aunty Lee's stepson," Selina said. She looked tense and insecure standing next to the vibrant, vague Josephine. "Mark and I are running the café while Aunty Rosie is incapacitated. After all, the show must go on, right? We can't have all the customers leaving and going to Violet Oon's kitchen instead because she closed shop without warning, ha ha!"

Josephine ignored Selina. "I heard you were staying with Aunty Lee," she said to Vallerie.

Aunty Lee patted the seat next to her. "Sit down."

"They are saying you are Mike Fitzgerald's girlfriend," Vallerie spoke up. "The newspapers said that according to records from the Immigration Department, Mike Fitzgerald is in Singapore now. And not only that, Mike Fitzgerald arrived in Singapore over two weeks ago. That means he was already in Singapore when Allison died. They just found him hiding in a hotel. They haven't arrested him yet but it's only a matter of time." Aunty Lee saw a malicious look flash across Vallerie's face. "Were you hiding him?"

"Don't be absurd!" Josephine said automatically. "I didn't even know he was in Singapore. He lied to me too!" Perhaps coming here to try to win over Allison's fat sister hadn't been such a good idea after all.

The police officers who had interrupted her Skype conversation with Mike Fitzgerald had indeed been Singaporean. She had been questioned by the police again, but could only tell them she had thought Mike was on a business trip to India . . . or Cambodia, or Vietnam . . . somewhere in Asia other than Singapore. Because she had not said anything earlier about her relationship with Mike, Josephine could tell they had not believed her.

She was distracted by Aunty Lee's next words.

"You are expecting, right?" Aunty Lee asked.

"What?"

"Expecting. You got baby coming, right?" Aunty Lee happily sketched the outline of a bulge over her own generous midsection.

Since Josephine came into the café more than a week ago, Aunty Lee had been wondering about the barely suppressed excitement that hummed around the woman. It was energy that suggested she was anticipating something big, a positive promise she was excited about, but also a little afraid of—Aunty Lee saw this in a lot of customers looking at her menu or buffet for the first time, but Josephine had not even glanced at her food.

"Aunty Lee, you cannot anyhow say things like that—" Selina started to say, but—

"How did you know?" Josephine laid a hand on her still flat stomach. "Who told you?"

"I can see in your face. All pink and fat, no more lines. Your body is happy even if you are not yet happy."

"I am happy." Josephine realized with some surprise as she spoke that this was true. "I am happy. I'm twenty-eight years old. I know it's late but I always wanted to get married and have a baby. I just didn't think about it for years because I thought there was no hope. And now—now I'm really happy, no matter what happens." It was the first time she had laughed out loud since finding out she was pregnant. And suddenly the secret inside her did not seem like such a terrible thing. Aunty Lee was the first person in Singapore other than her doctor who knew about Josephine's pregnancy, and

Aunty Lee had not whipped out a scarlet *A*. Indeed Aunty Lee looked happy too.

"You should be happy," Aunty Lee said. "If you are happy now, then the baby after birth will also be happy. Won't cry so much. And you must let me do catering for your baby shower—I give you discount!"

Vallerie got up and left, pushing roughly past Josephine as she went and slamming the café door behind her.

"It's okay," Aunty Lee said. "She has the house key. How are you feeling?"

"I feel sick," Selina said from behind the counter.

Aunty Lee didn't look round. "Nowadays everybody also can have babies. You should read those *Family Is Love* pamphlets."

Selina ignored Aunty Lee. "I mean I'm going to throw up—" She stumbled toward the toilet. "It must be the *laksa* I had in Holland Village. I don't normally take it with cockles, but today I was suddenly craving them and I even asked for extra—" The toilet door slammed behind her.

"This is a waste of time." Josephine stood up abruptly. "This is stupid. I'm not wasting any more time." It seemed to Aunty Lee that her change of mood had been triggered by Selina's mention of *laksa* or Holland Village or cockles—but why would that be?

Aunty Lee put a hand on Josephine's upper arm. "You are worrying too much. When you are old, like me, you will wish you didn't take things so seriously and enjoyed your life more."

"But things are serious." Josephine's careful social facade faltered but she sat.

"How serious? The man don't want you? Don't want baby? You tell me who I go *hantam* him!"

Hantam was Malay-Singlish for "beat" or "hit," and Aunty Lee's threat carried all the ferocity of a plump chicken clucking angrily at a stationary pile driver. Josephine laughed, letting some of her tension go. Despite the garrulous surface chatter, she saw Aunty Lee was studying her with kind, nonjudgmental curiosity. Even through the throb of her ever-present headache and twinge of nausea, she could tell there was nothing malicious there. Aunty Lee wanted to know more in the same way a new lover would. To her, feeding people well was a calling rather than a career, and to do that she had to understand the people she was feeding.

"That's not a problem at all. We're getting married. It's just that he's not from around here and it's complicated. You know what parents are like."

"Parents always worry," Aunty Lee agreed. "But they only want what is best for you."

Josephine shook her head but with a small, genuine smile this time. It was nice of the old woman even if she didn't know anything. "It's complicated."

Aunty Lee nodded. Once she got hold of the man's name she would have Nina look him up online. "It's complicated" rang all kinds of alarm bells in Aunty Lee's head. Was it Mike Fitzgerald, the dead woman's ex-husband? That would definitely be complicated!

"You young people think getting married is not important. But if you got two names on the birth certificate, you got double chance to get into a good school. Is your sweet man from a good school?"

"He's not from around here," Josephine said again. There was a small smile on her face and a faraway look in her eyes. "Maybe we won't be needing a Singapore school . . ."

Aunty Lee continued her cross-examination. "Not in Singapore or not from Singapore?"

"Both . . . I mean, not from Singapore."

If the man's only drawback was his geographical location, then he might do very well, Aunty Lee thought.

"That's why you so sad, is it? Don't worry *lah*! Nowadays all you young people nonstop fly here, fly there, frequent flyer everywhere. What's the problem? And you tell your parents, once you teach him to eat Singapore food then he will be Singaporean *lor*. Case closed. So you are getting married and getting baby, you should look more happy!" Aunty Lee said. "What's his name? When can you bring him here to eat in my café?"

"Like I said, it's complicated. Even my parents don't know yet. So please don't say anything—"

"Don't worry," Aunty Lee said with deliberate vagueness. Aunty Lee was genuinely fond of Josephine's mother, and it was no more than her responsibility to find out what was going on for Connie's sake, even if she never told Connie what she learned.

"I'm going to drive Vallerie to Holland Village to get some things," Selina said. Aunty Lee had forgotten about Selina till now. "She heard there's a shop there where they have decent plus-sized clothes. And because she doesn't feel comfortable here with some people around."

Vallerie was already standing by the front door with her back to them.

"Good idea," Aunty Lee said, disappointing Selina, who expected awkwardness, apologies, and invitations to stay. "Good-bye."

Once they were gone, Aunty Lee returned to the subject. "Don't think you must marry that man just because you are having a baby."

"What?"

"That man—that dead Allison's husband. He is your boy-friend, right?"

Aunty Lee talked fast to explain before Josephine had time to feel offended. "I am not against that Mike Fitzgerald because he is a) divorced, b) foreign, or c) much older than you. Of course those are things to keep in mind. But you should not get married *for* the baby. It's not good for the baby."

"My parents will freak out because he's a divorcé. They've got this whole church hang-up thing."

"A man who gets divorced once finds it easier the next time," Aunty Lee warned. "Same like killing chickens. Better for a baby to have no father than to have a murderer for a father."

"You have no right to say such things. Even the police aren't calling him a murderer!"

But Josephine did not walk away, and Aunty Lee was encouraged to ask, "This Mike Fitzgerald was not your boy-friend at the time the dog was killed?"

"Of course not! After Allison accused us of harassment and libel and trespassing, the police set up a mediation meeting to try to calm everyone down. It didn't work, of course. It lasted twelve hours and that was the first time Mike and I met. I was all fired up to make sure Lola wasn't just forgotten, and of course Mike was there to back up Allison. I remember being so mad at him for saying over and over again that it was just a dog and unwanted dogs were being put down every day, why didn't we just go and pick up another one instead of wasting time and money on this one." Josephine paused and looked at Aunty Lee with tears shining in her eyes, as though to give cameras time to focus (they always had on previous occasions when she delivered this speech). "He just didn't get the point."

"What was the point? Why was that dog so special?" Aunty Lee was not sure she got the point either.

"Every dog is special, given the chance," Josephine said, returning to her script. "But that was not the point. The point was that that wife of his signed a legal agreement without reading it, and then lied to us, and still thought she hadn't done anything wrong because she was above the law here.

"Allison knew very well we needed a couple of days to find someone else to foster Lola. Cherril told her so. She asked if Allison would help pay for boarding costs, but that was only because Allison wanted someone to go and collect Lola immediately. We were all volunteers because we loved animals, and I thought Allison and her family did too. I remember feeling so happy that an expat family had adopted Lola, because they could afford a house with a little garden in front and I thought she would enjoy that. Instead she ended up dead.

"Allison refused to back down and everything just dragged on and on. Mycroft Peters was helping us pro bono and I thought that meant we would have no problem. Mike tried to get us all to say it was a misunderstanding and shake hands and move on, but his wife called him a traitor and swore at him. I remember feeling sorry for him. But by nine P.M. I was too tired to think or to care about anything other than I didn't want Lola just swept away and forgotten."

"Cherril got Mycroft to help?" Aunty Lee asked as Cherril came to join them after watching Selina drive away with Vallerie.

Cherril looked awkward but sat down with them as Josephine answered, "No—in fact I think that's probably when Mycroft and Cherril first met. Is that why we didn't win the case? Because Mycroft got so caught up in you he wasn't paying attention?"

"Don't be nuts."

"But once you decided to go after Mycroft you abandoned the animals, didn't you?"

"What?"

"I'm just kidding. That lying bitch swore she thought the puppy was going to spend the rest of its life in a cage and she was doing it a favor by putting it down. She wouldn't shift from that. It was all one huge waste of time."

"I think Allison Fitzgerald convinced herself that's what I said." Cherril shook her head. "It was like she had a filter around her: only certain things got through."

Aunty Lee smiled at this. "We all see things through filters. But like air-con filters and fish tank filters, we must regularly clean out the rubbish from our filters otherwise everything gets blocked. But you are saying that it was during that long meeting that you and Mike Fitzgerald sat down in the same room for the first time?"

"I suppose—yes."

"Then it was not a waste of time. You got so tired that your filters came off, both of you. But if your Mike is innocent, then why did he have to sneak back into Singapore without telling you? You didn't know he was already in Singapore until the police found him, right? If Mike Fitzgerald did not come to Singapore to see you, then why did he come?"

Josephine looked pointedly at Cherril. "You should ask her."

"Cherril?" Aunty Lee said in disbelief.

Cherril took a deep breath. "Mike Fitzgerald contacted me and said he was looking for business opportunities here, because of Josie. He wanted it to be a surprise for her. It was too good a chance to pass up, because to go big scale and international we're going to need an international guy, someone with international business experience. And he was willing to come out without expat pay so that he could be in Singapore with Josie."

"Why did you do that without even discussing with me? And that means you knew that Josephine and Mike were a couple and you never told me!" Aunty Lee saw the younger women exchange glances.

"I guessed there was something but I didn't know for sure.

The important thing is Mike Fitzgerald knows about running big businesses and he has contacts in America."

Aunty Lee looked doubtful. She shook her head and waved her hands. "So confusing, all of your men. Got one 'Mark,' now got one 'Mike.'"

"It's easy to tell them apart," Josephine said smoothly. "With Mark, what you see is what you get. There's nothing more to him. But Mike is really Michael. There's more depth to him."

Cherril giggled. "Lucky *someone's* not here. That would make her so mad!"

"You must tell that Silly-Nah when she comes back!" Aunty Lee said.

"I want you to meet Mike," Josephine spoke up. "Right now the police are talking to him. Cherril, you have to go and tell the police why Mike came here without telling me. And, Aunty Lee, you're friendly with the police commissioner, right? You have to tell him that Mike didn't do anything to his ex-wife."

"I'm sure that if he didn't do it the police will find out soon enough," Aunty Lee said. "Besides, it's a bit funny, isn't it? The way he came to Singapore so sneakily without even telling his girlfriend? What kind of man does something like that?" Aunty Lee wondered what Josephine saw in that foreign man, why she couldn't have ended up with someone like Brian Wong, for example. She sighed. Josephine DelaVega and Brian Wong were both so energetic and passionate about changing the world for the better. And they were both so tall and good-looking and rich and would have such pretty babies that they could afford to dress up. Plus they might have asked her to cater their wedding buffet.

Instead Josephine was throwing herself away on some divorcé with two children who might or might not have killed his mad wife.

"I know you don't like Mike. But you've got to help prove that he didn't do it because he didn't. It's just something else that ex-wife of his is trying to set him up for."

"His ex-wife is dead."

"She may be dead but this is all still her fault."

Aunty Lee felt sorry for Allison—even sorrier than she had on hearing of her death.

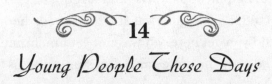

14
Young People These Days

"Josephine really didn't know that Mike Fitzgerald was here because he came into Singapore early to meet Cherril. No, nothing like that, Raja. You and Brian Wong are both so biased against *ang moh* men. Mike went and got in touch with all three of them after he and Allison got divorced. He said he wanted to apologize for his part in what had happened to the dog in Singapore. That led to Josephine falling in love with him and Cherril asking him to help expand the business. He came to Singapore early to discuss working with Cherril on business expansion plans."

Aunty Lee knew from experience how difficult it was to get into Commissioner Raja's office in the police headquarters, even if you knew he would want to see you. So instead of trying to get through the various levels of administration, she had gone to the staff canteen in the basement and phoned him from there. Since her fall, Commissioner Raja had dropped in on her often with gifts of food and genuine concern, so it seemed only right, now that she was more ambulatory, that she should drop in on him. Admittedly she came bearing chicken curry, pineapple tarts, and a request . . . but as she had expected, Raja Kumar was still glad to see her.

"How did you get here?" It was not yet lunchtime for most people, and only the coffee and dim sum stall was busy with takeaway business.

"Nina dropped me off. She's going to pick up some more chickens and she will come back and get me in an hour."

"With a car full of live chickens?"

"With the freezer in the car boot full of dead chickens. They kill them with electric shock, very fast. And then they have a machine that can clean and remove feathers very fast." In the old days killing chickens had been a far more laboriously messy business. Aunty Lee still felt a twinge of nostalgia for her younger self, the girl who had decided that the best thing for both chickens and herself was to learn to kill them as quickly and painlessly as possible. There were "high-class" girls who preferred to shriek and considered themselves superior to tasks only suited for servants, but Aunty Lee believed that what could not be avoided should be tackled as quickly as possible. So—

"I want to talk to you about Mike Fitzgerald. How is the curry?"

"It's good, but not as good as Sumathi used to make."

Commissioner Raja had already dipped a convenient teaspoon into the curry gravy. He always remembered to pay tribute to how well his late wife cooked. Aunty Lee remembered Sumi too, and her advice to the much younger Rosie Lee on the secret of her chicken curry: "If it looks funny, dump in a tin of Amoy chicken curry to make the color right." It had worked too, though Aunty Lee had not had to resort to tinned curry for some time now. But Aunty Lee knew that the reason Raja Kumar fondly remembered Sumathi's curry as the best in the world was a testimony to the power of love and memory rather than the Amoy brand.

"I must get some French bread. It soaks up gravy better than rice. Sorry, what did you say?"

"Mike Fitzgerald." Aunty Lee repeated what Josephine and Cherril had told her the previous day.

"So Cherril is talking to strangers about expanding Aunty Lee's Delights without telling you first?"

"She tried to talk to me. I told her it was no use even thinking about overseas franchises for the business unless we had someone with overseas experience. I thought that was the end of the matter. Cherril thought I was telling her to go ahead and recruit somebody."

"Young people," Commissioner Raja snorted. "Young people these days think they know everything and try to tell their grandfathers what to do! You know what they call young people these days? The YOLO generation—the You Only Live Once generation. And because they only live once they cannot be bothered to work on things that will take longer or benefit other people. But at the same time they feel entitled to take, take, take everything that other people have worked to build up!"

Aunty Lee was familiar with Raja's rants over the quality of new recruits and young officers. And he had other reasons to be frustrated by young would-be tyrants. His son-in-law was strongly hinting that Raja Kumar think about signing a pre-nuptial agreement if he wanted to marry again, while tiptoe-ing around the question of how much Rosie Lee was worth. Or even better, dividing his assets among his offspring now, before he inconveniently descended into death or dementia. When he was in a good mood he laughed about it, but at the end of the day when his energy was low and he most missed his wife, it got him down and left him drained the next morning.

"I never thought they would grow up so mercenary."

"They are trying to protect you, you know. They are prob-ably afraid I'm going to take all your money and spend it at the casino and leave you with nothing to pay your medical bills in your old age."

"So? That's still my business, not theirs. And the café is your business. Cherril should have talked to you first!"

"When Mike offered to come out and look over the facto-ries Cherril had short-listed, she thought it would be a good idea. She says he was willing to come on board as a partner investor."

Commissioner Raja looked skeptical. "There are people selling plots for time-share holidays on Mars if he's looking for something else to invest in."

"I doubt he would be interested unless Josephine DelaVega is going to be living on Mars. The point is, he was going over factory costs with Cherril when the vet was killed. He couldn't have done it. And if you are sure that the vet was killed by the same person who killed his wife, that means he did not kill his wife either."

"Because Mike Fitzgerald was with Cherril the morning it happened." Raja Kumar had reached for a notebook and was making notes. The investigator in him had surfaced and Aunty Lee knew he would confirm all the details.

"That's what she says. I would be very happy if he killed his wife. I mean, better him than Josephine or Cherril or Brian. But if you say whoever killed his wife also killed the vet, then he didn't do it."

"Unless they were in it together." But it was clear he didn't believe it. "And the girlfriend really didn't know he was already in the country?"

"It was supposed to be a big surprise for Josephine. They didn't want to get her hopes up in case they didn't manage to talk me round."

"At least Cherril was going to ask you before signing him on!"

It was hardly necessary to comment on the failings of the younger generation again.

"Can you really believe that if Cherril knew her good friend's boyfriend was in Singapore she didn't say anything to her friend? Girls like that talk. Cherril would have told her."

"They both swear she didn't know. Mike says he didn't want to raise false hopes in case it didn't work out. But I think it's more likely he's just secretive by nature and being married to Allison made him more so. He made each of them promise not to tell anybody that he had got in touch with them.

Remember, the three of them also went through quite a difficult time during the dog business. They didn't want to dig things up again."

"But Josephine goes and falls in love with him." This seemed to be the major point Commissioner Raja held against Mike Fitzgerald, even outranking the possibility that the man had killed his ex-wife. "And they really didn't tell anybody, didn't even discuss it among themselves?"

"They were not as close as they used to be." That was another unpleasant aftermath of the puppy killer case, Aunty Lee thought. It would always be something the friends reminded each other of.

"What about Brian Wong? He was also involved in that puppy killer business."

"He's a big-time entrepreneur now. Sitting on government boards and committees and handing out grants, he's practically a national resource."

"That means the big bosses won't be very happy to find out they've got an infamous activist handing out their big-time grants. You know what Singapore is like about such things. He's the one that had the most to lose from Allison's suit. Even if she didn't win his entire activist past would have come out. He would be the one hiding his head and running out of the country!"

"Of course Brian Wong didn't kill Allison," Aunty Lee said firmly. "I know Brian Wong. Brian can't even kill cockroaches. Oh, I wish you could just prove Mike Fitzgerald was the murderer."

"Because he's a white man or because he's a divorcé and unemployed?"

"Because he is not from here and I don't know his parents," Aunty Lee said honestly. "And because he's got such good motives here—if that vet had not put down that dog for his wife, if his wife had not made such a fuss about everything, he would still have his cushy lifestyle and expat benefits, and Josephine would be in love with Brian Wong by now. But he didn't kill them."

"So what do you want me to do about it? Go and spring him out of prison? If I do that they'll fire me and take away my pension!"

"He hasn't been arrested," Aunty Lee pointed out. "He's just 'assisting inquiries.' Let me assist him to assist you."

"Here's Nina. That means there's a car full of dead chickens in the car park . . ."

Aunty Lee chatted triumphantly as Nina made sure her boss was safely settled with her stick by her feet and her seat belt locked in.

"I could see what Raja was thinking, but I know Cherril would never go after somebody else's boyfriend."

"Madame, I thought you said Madame Cherril didn't know that man is Miss Josephine's boyfriend?" Nina started the engine and looked over her shoulder, preparatory to reversing. It would not do to run over someone in the basement of the police headquarters.

"Anyway, Cherril is happily married, so that's not an issue."

"It's hard enough to be happily married when you come from the same background. But when your backgrounds are so different, there will be so many more problems."

Aunty Lee's happy flow of murderous thoughts ran into a sudden stop. Was she imagining things? Nina's voice did not sound any different, but it was unlike Nina to express such decided opinions. Aunty Lee stole a look at Nina, but her helper's eyes were fixed on the electronic payment reader, as though daring it to overcharge their car. Josephine was not the only woman involved with a man from a very different background, Aunty Lee remembered. There was also Cherril, whose upbringing had been so different from Mycroft's though in the same country, and Nina herself, come from a country and culture completely alien to the young police officer who . . .

"It can be good that two people are from different backgrounds." Aunty Lee put on her sunglasses as the car emerged from the dim car park into the brilliant Singapore sun. "Because then you know you must make adjustments. You remember that you are two different people. Otherwise you assume the other person is exactly like you, the smallest difference also very easy to get angry."

Nina shrugged and signaled a lane change. "Too different is not good. Different religion, different food, different families, different countries—all not good."

"All people are different, Nina. It's just that most people don't realize it. As long as they agree on the important things you can work out everything else."

It seemed Aunty Lee had been successfully distracted

from her fall-induced listlessness. Unfortunately Nina liked this new direction even less.

"Madame, I must concentrate on driving. Cannot talk." Domestic helpers were not supposed to drive in Singapore, and it was only Aunty Lee's pleas of helplessness and the late ML's influence that had gotten permission for Nina's special license. Aunty Lee ought to understand she could not afford to jeopardize it.

Later, with Nina safely in the kitchen tending to the fresh chicken meat, Aunty Lee put in a quick call to Constance DelaVega, Josephine's mother. Aunty Lee was old-fashioned enough to prefer talking to people face-to-face, especially friends whom she had not seen for some time and about subjects as potentially sensitive as their daughters being involved with potential murderers. But fortunately Connie had heard about Aunty Lee's fall and was understanding. Even more fortunately, she was not offended when Aunty Lee brought up the subject, saying that she was only calling because Josephine had just spoken to her about Mike and she wanted to know how her friend Connie was taking it.

"Then she's said more to you than to me," Connie said. But at least she sounded resigned and hurt rather than angry and raging, Aunty Lee thought. And at least she had not put down the phone immediately. If anything, Connie sounded eager to talk. Aunty Lee suspected the family had been avoiding the subject of Josephine's *ang moh* boyfriend and she was longing to discuss it. Plus the relative anonymity of a telephone call might have made it easier—almost like the anonymity of Catholic confession boxes, where you trusted the unseen person but where you could discuss things you might prefer to avoid face-to-face. Aunty Lee told herself to remember some people were less rather than more comfortable face-to-face, whatever she herself might prefer.

"Josie's young," Aunty Lee said vaguely. "She's in love and she thinks you don't approve of the man she's in love with—how can she talk to you?"

"Of course I don't approve of that man. I don't even know him, how to approve or disapprove of him?"

"She thinks you won't approve of him."

"Maybe that is her own guilty conscience speaking, then!" Connie's voice rose slightly.

"Because he is a white foreigner?"

"No. Not really."

"Because he's divorced? Because he's much older than Josie? That is not necessarily a bad thing, you know. ML was much older than me. He said it gave him patience and I think that was a good thing for me!"

Although Aunty Lee did not mention it, she knew Joseph "Jojo" DelaVega was her friend's second husband. Connie had married at eighteen, to a handsome boy her own age. They had separated after less than two years and somehow their families had managed to get an annulment, back in the days when divorce was seldom spoken of in Singapore.

"I'm not against this Mike Fitzgerald being white, divorced, or much older than Josie." Constance DelaVega's voice came quietly over the line. "I am concerned about my daughter marrying a man who may have treated his first wife badly.

The newspapers quoted the sister—Vallerie Love, right?—saying how badly Mike always treated Allison, his first wife. Men like that get into a habit. They don't even consider it wrong. To them it is just the normal way men behave."

"Vallerie may have a habit of exaggerating," Aunty Lee pointed out. "Vallerie has also been saying their parents—her and Allison's parents—treated Allison so badly while they were growing up, but she was talking about things like not giving her opportunities and not encouraging her, so it's possible that after Allison's death, Vallerie feels so bad for her that she thinks everyone, including the husband, mistreated her sister."

"So you think that Mike's bad behavior may have been exaggerated?" There was wry doubt in her voice.

"Josephine is bringing Mike here to talk to me. Would you like to come and meet him at the same time?"

"They didn't arrest him? I thought they did. Where is he now?" Aunty Lee heard real fear in Connie's voice. "Is he staying with Josie? Do you know if that's where he is?"

"No, he's not," Aunty Lee said, having asked the same question herself. "He's got a room at the Grand Hyatt." The Grand Hyatt on Scotts Road was part of the Orchard Road prime district and in a far higher and far more expensive class than the Victoria Crest Hotel.

There was a silence over the line. Then, "Can you meet him and tell us what you think of him?"

Aunty Lee considered telling Connie she ought to see for herself—bringing Aunty Lee with her to keep the peace, of course—but just then Nina interrupted.

"Madame! Did you order a lot of mangoes online?"

"Mangoes? Oh, Nina, you won't believe the price they were going at. And they had Thai and Indian mangoes as well as Malaysian mangoes—"

"Madame, there is over twenty boxes—"

"Connie, I have to go. Do you like mangoes?"

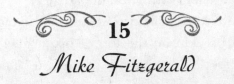

15

Mike Fitzgerald

To Aunty Lee's surprise, she liked Mike Fitzgerald.

After all she had heard, Aunty Lee had expected to meet a dangerously seductive killer. But Mike Fitzgerald turned out to be more like a middle-aged lawyer or businessman. He had the look of a successful man gone paunchy, the posture of a tired one, and he was not what Aunty Lee considered "handsome," with a bald head that made her think of a healthy brown egg.

"So you are the husband of the dead woman," Aunty Lee said when Josephine introduced them. She had called Aunty Lee about bringing Mike over before Aunty Lee had had a chance to think about her mother's request. "Do you like mangoes?"

"Of course! And I like you, the wonder woman who got the

police to let me out." Mike Fitzgerald brushed over the question. There was definitely some charm there, she thought.

"You have been in Singapore for some time."

"He got in last week to meet with Cherril. We told you that," Josephine said with some impatience.

"Not last week. At least two weeks, maybe more. Look at the color of his skin on the top of his head. He has been eating local food and going out in the sun." The signs were obvious to Aunty Lee.

"That's crazy. He's been traveling for work in—" Josephine automatically started to defend her lover. Then she stopped.

Mike ran a hand over his head, sweeping hair over the emerging egg of his thinning crown. Aunty Lee estimated he was coming to the end of his forties. Quite a bit older than Josephine. But then who was she to talk? ML had been quite half a generation older than she when they married. And his friends—including Raja Kumar, Aunty Lee remembered with a smile—had been concerned about the age difference though they had all been too well bred to say anything openly. The young Mrs. Rosie Lee had been aware of how her husband's fuddy-duddy old friends felt about her. And she had thought them all old and stuck in their ways.

Aunty Lee was older now than they had been then. And yes, she was doing to Josephine what she had resented them doing to her. And more. Unlike her late husband's friends who had been always punctiliously polite and merely radiated disapproval through their eyes and body language, Aunty Lee meant to ask questions and probe into the man's motives and any murderous intent. That was the real reason she had asked Josephine to bring Mike round to Aunty Lee's Delights. "You are a bit older than Josephine, aren't you?"

"Oh yes. Fortunately she's quite a bit older than my two kids, so that's one minefield avoided," Mike said languidly.

An old egg that wouldn't crack as easily as a fresh one, Aunty Lee thought. And hard-boiled old eggs were always difficult to get out of their shells. Aunty Lee was momentarily distracted by how much she missed having her own chickens. Perhaps she would speak to Nina about that. It would be nice having chickens in the back garden again even if they didn't produce many eggs and what eggs did come out of them couldn't be officially certified "free range" or even "organic" though they would be. Chickens would be one more diversion in her old age, which suddenly seemed round the corner.

"That's why you wouldn't let me phone you," Josephine said to Mike. "That's why you always had to be the one that contacted me on Skype. Did everybody know you were in Singapore except me?"

"You believe some old woman who looks at my skin and tells you where I've been?" Mike asked genially. Clearly Josephine did. "Josie, I told you it's complicated."

Mike threw Aunty Lee a half-humorous, half-pleading look. The message was clear: *Go away and give us some privacy—time for a heavy couple conversation.* But Aunty Lee chose to ignore this. There was no telling what nonsense the man would feed Josephine if Aunty Lee and her lie detector weren't there to keep an eye on things.

Aunty Lee wondered whether Josephine had told Mike

about the baby yet. Somehow she didn't think so. The girl was still young enough to think that she could handle everything herself if only she made more of an effort. It was the result of the competitiveness in schools that told children it was more important to "try harder to come out on top!" than work together and help each other. But that was not relevant right then. It was also not really relevant that Aunty Lee did not believe in couples telling each other everything. You could end up doing nothing but talking and analyzing each other. And anyway, being told things was never as interesting as finding them out for yourself. Much as Aunty Lee loved reading recipes, she did not enjoy being regaled with recipe details every time she sat down to a meal.

However, some things like "I killed my ex-wife" and "I am having your baby" definitely needed to be said if you wanted a marriage to work.

"Why did you come to Singapore earlier than you told Josephine you would? She is supposed to be the woman you say you are in love with and want to marry," Aunty Lee asked.

"Because I wasn't sure the job with your company—the franchising and everything—would work out. Since I was going to be in the region, I thought, Why not get in early and talk to some other people? I met with someone from an Indonesian company and another guy from Thailand. I didn't want Cherril to know in case it put her off me for this business. I knew if I said anything to Josephine she would have told her. That's what women do, isn't it? They talk about things. They just can't stop talking."

It took a great effort, but Aunty Lee said nothing in response to that. She would not validate his absurd statement by opening her mouth to reject it. But Mike's opinion of women did not bother Aunty Lee as much as his assumption that Josephine would go along with any plans he made for them without consulting her.

"Did you know about your ex-wife's lawsuit? Why didn't you warn Josephine and the others?"

"Allison had trouble letting things go sometimes."

Aunty Lee found Mike's choice of words curious. Someone else had used that phrase recently—it had been Brian, speaking of Josephine. When the Animal ReHomers merged with the local SPCA after the puppy killer incident, most of the volunteers had been glad to move on, but Josephine had not wanted to.

"I thought it was just one of her threats. She throws them out and makes a huge fuss, but then if you don't react she doesn't usually follow through. Even the children knew what she was like. If they give me any trouble I tell them I'm shoving them off to live with their mother, is that what they want? And that's usually enough to shut them up. With Gemma, anyway." He paused. "Nick missed her more. Anyway, I never believed she would come back to Singapore. When we left she said she wished the whole island would disappear under a nuclear bomb. No offense."

"Her sister said you took out a restraining order against your wife—why?" Aunty Lee saw Josephine start to interrupt her, then turn to watch Mike, waiting for his answer.

"I was worried for their safety. When she first moved out she used to come over to spend time with them while I was at work. One day I got a call from a neighbor saying that Allison had been shouting and the children crying for almost an hour. It wasn't a complaint. Mrs. Ameeta may be a nosy old fart, but she's a good-hearted old bag. When I'm not around she calls the kids over and gives them their tea. Anyway, when I got home Allison had wrecked the whole place: windows, TV, right down to carving up the backs of the cabinets with a kitchen knife. She was looking for bugging devices, she said. I wanted to call the mental health people but Nick begged me not to put his mum in the madhouse.

"Anyway, she's dead now. I want the children to remember her good side. She tried to be a good mother. I'm sorry you don't like me, but I really don't—"

"Stop." Aunty Lee said quickly. "I didn't say I don't like you. All right, when I heard about you I didn't like you, that's true. But that's past tense. Meeting you is like eating tangerines. You know what tangerines are, right?"

"Sure, but—"

"If you eat tangerines after you eat ice cream, then you will say they are so sour, they make your teeth sensitive, all kinds of bad things. But if you eat the tangerine first, then you will think, Oh, quite sweet, quite fresh, and quite delicious. After meeting your wife's sister, who had all kinds of good things to say about your late wife, even if you turned up here as Saint Francis we would have looked at you and said, 'What a terrible man, so bad to his wife and to animals.' But after a while the ice cream wears off. You know what I mean?"

"I think I do."

Strangely enough she thought he really did.

"We should all brush our teeth more often. Before we eat, in fact. Like you wash hands before eating, should wash mouths also, right? I don't know why people only brush their teeth after they eat. Like they cannot wait to get the taste of food out of their mouths. But anyway, I don't think you are so bad. Josephine is a nice girl. She has a good heart but she is not stupid. If she likes you that means you are not all bad. Anyway, you are her risk to take."

"Thank you. I think."

Mike Fitzgerald knew he had been left with some kind of compliment. Or it might have been a threat. He was not sure. But at least he was part of the discussion now and that was a definite step forward.

"Inspector Salim will be joining us for dinner."

"Oh Christ, more questions?"

"Last time he had to ask you questions as a suspect. Now you will both be my guests. Are you hungry?"

"I'm always hungry." Mike took Aunty Lee's hand in his. "I know you are keeping an eye on Josephine and keeping her safe and I must thank you." He raised her hand and touched it to his lips. "I owe you."

She smiled and he knew he had given the right answer.

"Dinner won't be until seven thirty. Some other people who met you before will be joining us."

"Brian? I remember him. We've been in touch, actually. Will be good to see him again."

Aunty Lee caught the surprise on Josephine's face and the embarrassment on his after she nudged him hard on the ribs. If those two ended up together, it would be a good thing if they learned to talk to each other. She changed the subject: "Did Josephine tell you that Allison's sister is staying at my house?"

"Yes, she did. Actually I don't know Vallerie very well. I just know she's fat and moved to the U.S. before Allie and I got married. She didn't even come back for our wedding. Said she was down with food poisoning or something. I remember Allie said it was just like her to get sick at the worst time. I met her when she visited Allie here in Singapore, before all hell broke loose. I should thank you for taking her on too."

"I was hoping to meet her here today, actually. I guess she doesn't want to see me?"

"If she thinks you killed her sister, that's not surprising," Josephine said.

"I didn't. I don't know how many times I'm going to have to go on saying this, but I didn't kill my ex-wife."

"Vallerie must have been close to her sister," Aunty Lee said. "She seems very upset. I think she's having some kind of breakdown."

"I don't think so. They didn't really stay in touch. Allie used to get very upset with Vallerie for being such a mess. She was so organized herself."

"What kind of a mess?" Aunty Lee wondered. She had assumed Vallerie Love's mood swings were due to the shock of her sister's death, but had she always been that way?

"Her weight for one thing. And her refusing to come back to England for our wedding."

"So you really don't know her very well? They weren't close?"

"They must have been once. If you look at their baby pictures, you'll see how alike they were. If you compare the photos of Allison at five years old and Vallerie at the same age, it's difficult to tell which was which. And just to complicate things their mother used to dress Vallerie in Allison's old clothes. You know how fast children grow, and Vallerie was just over a year younger, so I suppose that was natural. But then of course Vallerie started getting fatter and fatter, until they had to buy new things for her because she couldn't fit into Allison's old clothes. And Allison refused to wear fat-girl clothes, so from then on it was two sets of everything for them. Not so different from having a boy and a girl, I suppose."

Aunty Lee wondered whether the young Vallerie Love had deliberately used her size to get out from under her sister's shadow. She had heard of women who deliberately starved themselves skinny because their bodies were the only things they had any control over (some of them seemed to think they looked good as skeletons, but did anyone believe that?). Had Vallerie Love done the reverse, asserting control by growing larger than her sister? It did not feel likely, but Aunty Lee would have to think about it. In her experience, unless there was already something wrong with your body, giving yourself free rein to eat as much of everything available usually resulted in more discrimination and less indulgence. Animals overeat because they are conditioned to eating to excess after a kill and then fasting till the next successful hunt. Humans overeat because they remember scarcity in their past and fear it in their future. But if these fears were laid to rest, the human body was very good at detecting and selecting what it needed and in the quantities needed.

But Mike Fitzgerald did not look like he needed a lecture on Aunty Lee's pet topics of eating and appetites. Old photos taken at the height of the puppy-killing furor had showed a slightly overweight, slump-shouldered man. But now, despite his thinning hair, he looked better than he had five years ago.

Aunty Lee wanted to believe Mike Fitzgerald. She had nothing staked on him, but Josephine did and Aunty Lee was fond of Josephine, even if the girl had made some doubtful choices along the way. Still, she had survived and that was the main thing. Aunty Lee was not in favor of staying with safe choices. It would be like eating nothing but rice and steamed egg and spinach soup day after day after day. And given how many other things there were in Singapore to eat, that was an almost criminal waste.

"You could meet up with Vallerie," Aunty Lee suggested. "Show her that you are not a monster after all. If all she knows about you came from her sister, I'm not surprised she doesn't trust you."

"What's the point? Now that Allison's dead it doesn't matter what her sister thinks of him!" Josephine snapped. "Once this is taken care of, Mike and I can get married and everything will be all right."

"Right. We'll get a license or whatever once this is sorted out."

Josephine was glad Mike raised no objection to the mention of their marriage and said nothing about his lack of enthusiasm.

"No," said Aunty Lee. "If you are going to marry Josephine you should do it properly. You may have been married before, but this will be Josephine's first time. This is something that she is going to remember all her life. And if you are going to marry her, all her friends and family in Singapore are going to want to take a good look at you. That is what the wedding is really for. I think you better marry her here so we don't all have to fly over to England and find hotels."

Mike Fitzgerald looked uncomfortable, verging on overwhelmed. "It's no big deal—"

"Josephine should have warned you about Singaporeans," Aunty Lee said. "You can't just marry one. You end up marrying us all!"

16
Usual Suspects

"So, all the usual suspects are here!" Brian Wong said jovially as he joined their table that evening. As usual he was the last to arrive, and he slipped in beside Cherril. "Mycroft not coming? I'll sit here then." He nodded to Mike. "Good to see you again."

"We started first," Aunty Lee said, stating the obvious.

"Of course! I would have been upset if you'd waited!"

Dinner in the café was served family style that night, with everyone helping themselves from serving dishes placed at the center of their table. Nina and Lisa, one of the part-time helpers, served them and the two other tables of paying guests. Out of consideration for Mike, Aunty Lee had ordered relatively bland dishes—a chicken stewed in soy sauce and ginger, a steamed pomfret, steamed shiitake mushrooms and baby *kai-lans*, and battered fried prawns.

But from the relish with which Mike dunked his crispy-coated prawns in her sweet-and-sour chili sauce, Aunty Lee thought she could have gone with a more adventurous menu. Her mind had been dwelling on whether to try him on black pepper crab or chili crab when Brian arrived. After all, how a man ate his crab (and whether he had the tenacity to dig the sweetest meat out of the claw tips) showed so much about his character.

Inspector Salim nodded to Brian before continuing his conversation with Mike. "Your wife's sister, Vallerie, has been staying at Mrs. Lee's place. You haven't seen her yet?"

"No. I was hoping Vallerie would be here tonight actually. I haven't seen her since Allison and I split up."

"Have you any idea why she might want to avoid you?"

"Is she? Good for her. But seriously, we didn't have a problem before all this happened. Vall came to stay with us when I was posted here. Didn't stay very long, but it wasn't me she had trouble with." Mike shook his head. "But some sisters are like that. Someone gave us some moon cakes, the ones with lotus seed paste inside. Allison liked them, but she would only allow herself one tiny sliver at a time. Then Vall came and picked up a whole cake and took a bite out of it. Allison completely lost it. She screamed at her, called her fat and disgusting, told her she was ashamed to be seen with her. Vall left the day after that. I didn't blame her."

"Over a moon cake." Aunty Lee had to check: "Was it that good?"

"I've had better."

"She sounds like she had real problems," Brian said. "Psychological, I mean." Aunty Lee looked at him curiously, waiting for more. But it appeared that Brian was using "psychological" to mean crazy beyond explanation.

"My late wife always had trouble letting things go. Like she picked on Vall for being fat because when they were children Vall was the fat sister. By the time I met her, she wasn't so big, but to Allison she was always the fat sister, and I got the impression Allison resented her losing weight because she was supposed to be the 'fat sister.' "

"She's fat again now," Josephine said. "Maybe the stress brought it back."

"Same thing with Allison. I believe it was the stress of what happened in Singapore that pushed her over the edge. She saw it as an attack. All of you, all of Singapore, had attacked her and nobody was on her side. I brought her to doctors who suggested Allison might be bipolar, but there was no sign of that before the dog incident."

"And yet now you are marrying Josephine, who helped push your wife over that edge?" Aunty Lee said, handing him a platter of fried chicken with pineapple and sweet chili sauce.

"It wasn't Josephine's fault." Mike took the chicken automatically and gestured with it. "Josephine is very special, but we're not talking about getting married any time soon. Someday, sure, but right now I just want to try to be a good father and make up to my kids for what they had to go through."

"Hey, careful!" Salim steadied the plate Josephine was taking from Mike just in time to avoid his being showered with crispy chicken bits.

Mike didn't notice. "Another factor was how difficult Allison found readapting to life back in England. And the children made it worse. They weren't used to living without a maid and a driver, without two cars and the best of everything. There was a lot less money, of course. Allison wanted me to get another expat posting, anywhere other than Singapore. When that didn't happen she said the Animal ReHomers had got me internationally blacklisted. She was ranting against Singapore to everybody—friends, neighbors, strangers at the bus stop."

"What did she say was wrong with how people do things here?" Aunty Lee was curious. Criticism often revealed more about the complainer than what was complained about.

"Everything." Mike sounded suddenly weary.

"Hey, enough talk about Allison," Josephine said firmly. "We're all sorry she's dead, but talking about her is not going to bring her back. Hold out your plate, I peeled these prawns for you."

Aunty Lee remembered the "today peel your prawns, tomorrow peel your wallet" warning against overly solicitous women. Surely that did not apply to Josephine (especially as Mike did not appear to have a wallet worth peeling). But it was clear Josephine had the situation—and the man— well in hand. It didn't matter that Mike was not intending to get married again soon. It really wasn't up to him. But something about how carelessly Brian had greeted Mike puzzled her. She turned to him. "You already met Mike this trip?"

"What makes you think so?" They all saw Brian's quick, guilty glance at Josephine. The man was either a bad actor or a very good one.

"Have you?" Salim questioned. He might not be as good as Aunty Lee at sniffing out things, but like the best rat-catching dogs, once set on a scent he followed through.

"Mike arranged to meet to talk about sponsoring a child's school fees in Batam," Brian explained. "It's one of the projects I'm currently working on. Batam is so near Singapore, but some people there can't even afford basic education for their children."

"Why didn't you tell me?" It was unclear whether Josephine's question was directed at Brian or Mike, but both men looked guilty.

"It was just a briefing on the project," Brian said.

"I don't have any money to sponsor a kid with right now anyway," Mike said.

"Do you mind very much?" Aunty Lee asked Brian quietly when he came round to thank her and say good-bye. "About Josephine and that man? I used to think that you and Josephine would end up together."

Brian smiled. Aunty Lee was glad he did not pretend not to know what she was talking about. "People change, you know. I was in love with Josephine once upon a time, but now I think I'm almost scared of her. I don't think I could keep up. Good luck to Mike!"

And good luck to Brian too, Aunty Lee thought. He was

putting a brave face on things, but she doubted he was as over Josephine as he wanted her to think.

"Do you think Mike Fitzgerald is a murderer?" Salim asked after the other guests had left.

"I don't think he would be a successful murderer," Aunty Lee said thoughtfully. Mike Fitzgerald was the kind of man single women considered ideal husband material (educated, solvent, social), but who would probably bore his wife to death once married. Even if he had not killed his wife, Aunty Lee thought being married to him had definitely contributed to her breakdown.

Back at 88 Binjai Park, Aunty Lee walked slowly into the house while Nina parked the car and went to lock the gate. She was tired and wanted to think over the evening's conversation. But first she had to make sure her guest was all right. Vallerie had flatly and loudly refused to meet Mike Fitzgerald over dinner, repeating herself several times though it had been floated as a suggestion only once. Aunty Lee could tell there was real fear beneath Vallerie's almost theatrical anger, but found it difficult to believe it had been inspired by the man they had just met.

"Don't get involved with her, she can't be trusted," Selina warned Aunty Lee that afternoon. Unexpectedly, she was referring to Josephine DelaVega rather than Vallerie. Selina's distrust of Josephine appeared to have begun years ago in their schooldays. "She's one of those that puts on an *ang moh* accent when talking to *ang moh* men." Aunty Lee had observed that for herself that night. "You can't trust people who fake accents," Selina had said.

Selina had offered to take Vallerie out to dinner that night. The two were getting along well, perhaps due to their shared dislike of Josephine. Selina had supported Vallerie's refusal to meet Mike over dinner, agreeing it was dangerous, even though Salim's sitting down to eat with them should have precluded Mike murdering anybody at least during the meal. Selina and Mark had taken Vallerie out to dinner at a steak house, something Aunty Lee appreciated very much.

And why wouldn't Vallerie want to avoid the man? Given her sister's divorce and death, she would naturally be biased against the ex-husband she saw as the cause. The vehemence of her feelings was surprising given the sisters had not been close, according to Vallerie. Guilt, Aunty Lee decided. Guilt for having moved across the ocean to America instead of being there for Allison when her sister needed her. And guilt always led to anger.

Aunty Lee was quite pleased with her psychological deductions. During her early convalescence, Nina had tried to read her to sleep out of random tomes in the late ML Lee's library, and some passages on sibling rivalry had led to Aunty Lee feeling quite an expert on the subject. She was almost certain now that Mark's irresponsible approach to life was due to jealousy of his high-achieving sister, the overindulgence of his late father, or his fear of usurpation in his father's eyes by Aunty Lee and any children she might produce. These theories had been comforting rather than useful after Mark proclaimed his latest venture: photography. More accurately, photographic history—documenting and digitizing history as it happened. He would be appreciated and celebrated in five hundred years' time after all other documentation of our time had been lost, Mark said. He certainly seemed inspired and committed. Aunty Lee would probably have been more impressed if she had not already seen him express the same degree of inspiration and commitment for his wine business that was to revolutionize the Singaporean palate and, before that, his travel business that was to turn holiday seeking into voyages of shared self-discovery.

Mark had, of course, been put out by her refusal to hand over what he considered his money, but he had gotten over it in a day or two. Selina had been offended into boycotting Aunty Lee's Delights and (when that was not remarked on) sending friends to tell Aunty Lee how upset Mark was. But since those friends met Mark at the café (he still turned up for a free lunch or dinner several times a week), the effect was lost. Selina had only started coming around after Aunty Lee's fall and ankle injury, so that had at least brought about some family reconciliation.

Aunty Lee's real reason for refusing Mark another advance on his inheritance was that she wanted Mark and Mathilda to have something when she died. Because Aunty Lee had financed so many of his schemes, Mark had already gone through his share of the estate. Were it not for what Aunty Lee had brought to the marriage, there would have been little left for him. His late father would likely have been far stricter. And it was not fair to Mathilda. Aunty Lee was very fond of Mathilda. She was also much closer to her, perhaps because Mathilda lived so far away. Distance definitely made relatives grow fonder.

And that might explain why Vallerie had come to feel closer to Allison after moving away from her family and England. No matter how she had felt growing up as the overlooked sibling of a popular elder sister, it must have been easier for her to take her sister's side when she was no longer living in the same house or the same country . . . indeed, even more so when that sister was no longer living.

Perhaps it was because Aunty Lee sympathized with that, or perhaps she was feeling uncharacteristically low and lonely. Rather than restoring her, her enforced "rest" drained her of energy, leaving her miserably sluggish in mood and circulation.

Though Mark and Selina had bought Vallerie a good dinner (Selina had texted Aunty Lee, *V was starving! Must show you receipt!* when she dropped her back at the house), there were empty packets of crisps and a tub of ice cream on the coffee table in front of the living room television. Vallerie was not there, but Aunty Lee heard her upstairs. She sounded like she was in ML's study, talking in tones that suggested she was giving detailed instructions to a recalcitrant child.

"Calling home?" she called out pleasantly.

"It's the television," Vallerie lied immediately and badly. Aunty Lee looked at the muted downstairs television, no doubt where Vallerie had started the phone call. But she didn't say anything about that when Vallerie came downstairs and sat heavily on the sofa, not looking at Aunty Lee.

"I know how you feel."

"No, you don't."

"You're unhappy and angry and looking for somebody to blame. I know the feeling. After my late husband died I was angry with the doctors for not keeping him alive, angry with myself for not being dead, even angry with his ancestors for not giving him better genes! Sometimes I can understand why people commit suicide or take to drinking. You just want to stop the voices inside your head that are blaming, blaming, blaming nonstop."

Vallerie looked surprised but did not contradict Aunty Lee. Aunty Lee saw that whatever Vallerie was hiding, it was not grief at her sister's loss—and that she was happy to have Aunty Lee believe it was.

"Mike Fitzgerald sends you his regards. He said he was hoping to meet up with you."

Aunty Lee saw at once it was not just shock, grief, or post-traumatic stress syndrome that was troubling Vallerie. Vallerie was afraid of Mike; even hearing the man's name made her wince.

"There's no reason why he would attack you," Aunty Lee said, "even if he attacked your sister—which we don't know he did. Wouldn't he just want you to leave him alone to get on with his new life?" From everything Aunty Lee had heard of the late Allison Love, it seemed much more likely that she would have been the one unable to let go.

Vallerie shook her head. "You don't know what people like Mike are like. He can't stand leaving loose ends. He always has to have everything cleaned up and laid out, and he'll keep on at it until he can say 'case closed.' That's the only way to explain why the vet clinic got burned down and that vet got killed as well as poor Allison—either by Mike or those crazy activists. Or both. Just go back and read some of the things they were posting online. People who write stuff like that are capable of anything. They won't stop till they get what they want. If they are behind it, they're doing it for spite and revenge. But if Mike is behind it, then it's because he wants to marry that Josephine. Maybe she got him to do it to show that he's made a break with his past before she would marry him or something. Or maybe it's the other one, that Brian. He's all dressed up posh now, but you should have seen how he looked five years ago. It's all just an act—don't be taken in by him. I've seen him sneaking around. He's sly and can't be trusted."

The fear in Vallerie was definitely genuine. It was that fear bubbling up into panic that was making her eat savory prawn crackers by the handful now. But even if her fear was real it might not be directed at the right object.

"Brian would have no motive." Aunty Lee gestured and Nina, who had come in through the kitchen, put a large, warm bowl of milky sweetened bean curd and a dish of mango chunks on the table between them. The smooth, silky curds would soothe the damage done to Vallerie's stomach by all the salty foods, and fragrant, sweet mango was supposed to be good for the temper as well as the complexion.

"Brian loves that bitch Josephine. Just watch how he stares at her when he's around. He's almost drooling. You can see he would do anything for her, even knowing he can't have her.

Some men are like that, but not Mike. Mike is the kind of man who would find a way to destroy a woman if he couldn't have her. Do you know he wouldn't even give Allison her money after the divorce? And it was her money—that was the court decision. But he paid his fancy, expensive lawyers to come up with how she could only draw living expenses from what was supposedly her money but couldn't use any of it without his permission. How was it her money then, tell me that?"

Aunty Lee tried to paint the best scenario. "At least there will be someone to look after your sister's children if they get married. They must be how old now—nine and eleven years old? If Mike gets married again at least it will provide a stable home life for them. And there may be other children."

"No," Vallerie said.

The way she looked at her frightened Aunty Lee, even though there was no way Vallerie could know about Josephine's baby. As Vallerie drummed her fingers on the table as if deciding how best to put what she had to say, Aunty Lee tried to figure out what was bothering her. Was it something Vallerie had said?

"Allison would rather have seen her children dead than living under the same roof as Mike's new slut!"

Aunty Lee started picking up empty packets on the table and on the floor around it. She had always found cleaning up the best thing to do when trying to think. That way, even if you didn't find an answer you at least got a clean house.

"What are you doing?"

"Just tidying up. We can reuse one of those bags—"

"Oh, just leave it," Vallerie said carelessly. "The servant can clear it in the morning. That's what you pay her for, isn't it? I'll see you tomorrow."

Aunty Lee waited till Vallerie had gone up the stairs before resuming her tidying. Nina came in and repeated, in essence, what Vallerie had said, and the two women finished clearing the space together, knotting the debris into plastic bags that would not tempt ants or cockroaches. Then as Nina sprayed a soapy wash and ran a damp cloth over the surfaces, Aunty Lee commented, "Vallerie seems used to having servants pick up after her."

"No, madame."

"No?"

Satisfied with the surface of the low teakwood coffee table, Nina rested her weight back onto her heels before gracefully rising from her squat. Watching her, Aunty Lee missed the knees of her youth and her youthful self who had taken them for granted.

"People like you, madame, you are used to having servants in the house. For you servants are like family members, lower than daughter-in-law but higher than gardener. For people like Madame Vallerie, they one day want to be your good friend, ask you about your family, your boyfriend, cry to you about their problems . . . then the next day treat you like dog shit. Move one chair also cannot. Got to shout for you to put down the mop, wash your hands, change your shoes, come upstairs to move chair a bit closer to the door for her. And then scold you for not coming faster."

Aunty Lee took this in with interest. But one point rankled slightly. "I also ask you about your family, what."

"You are different," Nina said. But she refused to elaborate, changing the subject instead. "I put bowls of water under the legs of the table the mangoes are on so that ants cannot go up. But very ripe already. Must eat soon or will be wasted. I gave one box each to the neighbors and one box to Madame Cherril to bring home. Tomorrow I send one box to the police station."

Aunty Lee knew the mangoes were ripe. The kitchen and most of the dining room were fragrant with the delicate odor of sweet fruit. The importer had brought them too ripe, which was probably why she had gotten them at so great a discount. Today people who only knew markets and supermarkets wanted firm, smooth green-plucked fruit. But these mangoes had the spongy feel beneath the skin that wrinkled slightly under your touch that told you they were at the peak of ripe perfection. It was the pause before rot set in. It was the same with people, Aunty Lee suspected.

Aunty Lee remembered how she had taken an excess of tree-ripened mangoes for granted. In the old days every house had two or three mango trees in the garden. Left to ripen on the tree, you heard them falling in the night, and in the morning children and servant girls ran out to collect them in competition with the monkeys and the squirrels and the chickens already feasting. (Of course that was only at the beginning of the season. As the season wore on the animals got a larger and larger share of the fruit.) It was just one of the things she had thought was part of life and would last forever.

She knew Nina had brought mangoes in as a distraction—and it had worked. But Aunty Lee already knew—more or less—about Nina's family. And she had all kinds of plans and possibilities for Nina's future, which her helper would likely have pooh-poohed. But now what she was interested in was Vallerie Love's family. As far as Aunty Lee knew, Vallerie had no children of her own. Had she been talking to her dead sister's children? That was entirely possible of course, and Aunty Lee would not have thought anything of it if it had been done openly. But why would she deny it? That was something Aunty Lee meant to look into. That and recipes for mangoes.

17
Hotel

Of course Aunty Lee accompanied Vallerie to the hotel to collect her things. She had assumed they would bring Nina with them (Nina was a champion at packing big things into small spaces), but Vallerie said she didn't trust a servant touching her things. Aunty Lee almost asked Vallerie how she dared to put into her mouth food prepared by hands she didn't trust to put clothes into her bag, but reminded herself that Vallerie was a) shocked, b) bereaved, and c) a foreigner, and asked Nina to call them a taxi.

The Victoria Crest turned out to be a small business hotel that advertised hourly rates and backpacker rates.

Aunty Lee's morning phone call to the hotel had been taken by a girl whose accent suggested a recent arrival from mainland China. All Aunty Lee's queries had been met with

"Yes, you talk Chinese?" Aunty Lee had been forced to ask Nina for help, given Nina had picked up more Mandarin during her stay in Singapore than Aunty Lee had in all her life here. Nina got directions from the girl, who added, unprompted, that she had been promised a job in a five-star hotel in Singapore where rich single businessmen stayed on business trips, but once on the island found herself behind the counter in a budget hotel (that is, one or two stars) and was open to any job offers in any line. Innovation and enterprise were alive and well, Aunty Lee thought, but not all innovation was good for its parent enterprise.

Aunty Lee was prepared for a struggle to communicate. But at the hotel reception they were greeted by a young local (and English-speaking) woman.

"Hello, how may I help you?"

Vallerie said, "Give me my key," without preamble, but Aunty Lee stepped in with her usual friendly, curious smile.

"Are you the receptionist? I think I spoke to someone else on the phone. What's your name?"

"My name is Melvinia, but everybody calls me Mel. Right now I'm the front desk receptionist and the room service order taker—even though officially we don't have room service. Sometimes we help out in emergencies. After all, the 7-Eleven is just next door. And I answer the phone. Oh, and I calm guests down when they get too worked up." She spoke good English, with a comfortable Singlish accent. "Most of our staff quit when the police started coming in to question people, so I'm filling in until we get new people. How can I help you today?"

Aunty Lee plunged right in. "This is Vallerie Love. She and her sister were staying here when her sister was killed?"

"Yes, shocking, right?" Mel said with an exaggerated shudder that suggested more relish than disgust. She also looked at Vallerie with undisguised interest. "I remember seeing you around. So shocking, right?"

Murder had a way of breaking down social divides as well as the divide between life and death, Aunty Lee thought. Like hunger, death was no respecter of social class.

"Are you going to quit too?" Aunty Lee asked Mel.

"Of course not. Who would want to kill me? Anyway, I can't. It's a family business, so no escape, right? In fact I've been doing extra shifts since it happened. Half of the PRC staff quit right away. They said they were scared, but actually I think they are more scared that the police might come and check their papers. Then the last one quit less than an hour ago. She said the secret police called and cross-examined her on the phone. Even got a Mandarin translator to ask her questions! I told her it was probably just reporters trying to get a story, but you know what young girls are like—they want to believe the most frightening story."

"Did a lot of reporters come in to ask questions?" Aunty Lee asked innocently.

"Not really." The girl sounded disappointed. "The reporters just asked for a comment from the boss. And some other guests asked why there were police all around but nothing much. And now it's like everybody has already forgotten." She was still young enough to be intrigued by a murder, something Aunty Lee had never grown out of.

"Everybody's already forgotten Allison. They've all gone back to their stupid, boring lives and completely forgotten her!" Vallerie burst in.

Aunty Lee guessed Vallerie Love had a lot more to say, but this was not the time and she interrupted smoothly: "Her sister would like to get her things from their room."

"You look very familiar." The girl stared at Aunty Lee. "Are you the one they call the Sambal Queen? The Shiok Sambal lady?"

"Yes, that's me." Aunty Lee was pleased.

"And you solved some murders last time, right? I read about it in the Life! Section when they printed that review of your shop. Are you going to solve this murder?" The girl lowered her voice, her eyes darting around. "Are you recording this?"

"No." The girl looked disappointed and Aunty Lee hastened to add, "But I would like to find out what happened. Do you think you can help me?"

"Of course! That's what I'm here to do! And I'm sure the management would want me to help also. Last night I heard Jacky saying we had to extend the stay for Miss Vallerie Love, he is not sure for how long. But we can't move out her things because the police said she wants to pack them herself. And the room they had was on the dead woman's credit card, so he said he is not even sure we are going to be paid for it. Every time Jacky tries to phone and talk to her about it she gets upset and cries and says that the police want her to stay in the country and she cannot leave her sister's body and she has nowhere else to go . . . we can't just throw her things out, that would be so terrible. But she is not even staying here." She suddenly remembered that the woman she was talking about was standing in front of her.

"But you're here to get your things now, right? That's good. What would you like to do about the room charges?"

Vallerie let out a low warble that Aunty Lee had learned to recognize as the beginning of one of her wails.

"Who is Jacky?" Aunty Lee asked quickly.

"He's my cousin. He's also the hotel's assistant manager."

"He's a bloody poofter," said Vallerie.

Jacky, the assistant manager of the Victoria Crest Hotel, was not only beautiful, he was wearing lipstick.

"I've been trying so hard to get hold of you!" he said to Vallerie, who winced and turned away from him. "And of course you are our famous Aunty Lee. I'm a great fan of yours, Aunty Lee! Welcome to the Victoria Crest Hotel! I am Jacky Kong. Welcome to Victoria Crest. Isn't murder so terrible? I had surveillance cameras set up all over the hotel—computer surveillance is a little hobby of mine and my grandfather let's me practice here. I was hoping I got some footage of the murderer but the police said there was nothing useful."

"I wonder if we can get Vallerie's things from their room? I know it's a crime scene but . . ." Aunty Lee trailed off. "It's all cleaned up, isn't it? No blood or evidence left?" She hoped she was sounding like a squeamish old lady rather than a hopeful, inquisitive one.

"All my stuff better still be there!" Vallerie said.

"Actually we moved most of the things—the foodstuffs we mostly threw away—to the baggage storage area."

Vallerie took a deep breath, ready to protest.

"Did you clear that with the police?" Aunty Lee asked, more for Vallerie.

"Of course! The police said no problem. They were keeping everybody out until they went in there in their cover-up suits and took samples and photos and everything. We couldn't even use the corridor and the room beyond it because they wanted to test the walls and floor and everything, but I don't think they found anything because they haven't arrested anybody yet. But yes, after they finished they told us we could go ahead and clear the room."

"I can't believe you went into my room and looked through my stuff without even asking permission! I'm going to sue the shit out of all of you!"

"Why don't you see what they put in the storage?" Aunty Lee suggested quickly.

"Please take her to the baggage storage room, Mel," Jacky said. "Quick quick. Let's not keep customers waiting, sister. I'll keep an eye on the desk for you."

He settled himself behind the counter as a glum Melvinia led the grim-faced Vallerie away, Aunty Lee following. She was so caught up with taking everything in that she almost forgot she was still walking with a stick.

There were several suitcases along with a number of open bags. Aunty Lee looked into one and pulled out a pink plastic square divided into four square indentations and realized what it was: the thin plastic base liner of the sort used to stabilize moon cakes inside the more posh, expensive boxes on sale. But there was no moon cake box. "You like moon cakes?"

"Don't know what they are," Vallerie said. "Never saw that before."

"Maybe your sister bought them."

"No way in hell."

Aunty Lee asked Melvinia, "Maybe they were a welcome gift?"

"Where we can afford to give welcome gifts? I think they were delivered to the hotel for one of them—Allison Love. One of the girls would have brought it up; we don't allow delivery people in the rooms."

Vallerie was already shuffling inside the bags. She clearly wanted to make sure her "stuff" was intact. "Take your time," Aunty Lee urged as she slipped away.

Aunty Lee leaned conspiratorially across the reception counter. "I have never seen a place where somebody was actually killed. It's like reality TV in real life, right? Maybe you should come with me. Just in case I do spot anything. I'm very fussy about how people clean places. You could think of me as a quality control inspector. Her sister was murdered here in your hotel. If you don't check the room properly and miss something, your next guest in the room will phone the police and ask them to come again!"

Either this convinced Jacky to give in to his own curiosity or he was really concerned about what future guests might find (though Aunty Lee did not find this quite as likely). He pulled out a card stand that said RING FOR ASSISTANCE and put it on the front of the counter.

"There's nobody else here except me and Mel. But they can keep ringing until Mel comes back. At least that will give them something to do!" he said and pulled out a bunch of tagged keys from a drawer.

"You might be able to spot something our cleaners missed. Sometimes having an outside eye helps. At least it always seems to on TV, right?" Jacky led her to the elevator. "It's not as though we are so full up that we need the room. Half the rooms are empty right now. It's only during F1 or the Great Singapore Sale that hotels in this area are booked full."

"There might be a sudden flooding or other disaster in the area," Aunty Lee said encouragingly. "Then you would need all your rooms quickly and without warning. It's best to be prepared."

"That's true," Jacky said with resolute confidence. "There's so much construction going on here it's definitely possible underground pipes might get cracked or something." He slid a key case out of his man bag and searched through tagged keys. "I haven't been inside the room myself. I don't know if there's anything—you know."

The room where Allison Love had died was clean and drab and without any trace of blood or sinister atmosphere. It looked small for two people but was carefully, if blandly, styled with cream walls, beige curtains, and brown carpeting. Aunty Lee found the chemical odor of industrial-strength cleaner depressing.

Allison had clearly died in the bed closer to the door. The bedding and mattress had been removed, but there were dark stains seeped into the wooden slats of the bed frame and carpet beneath. It did not look like blood. Probably her bladder and bowel sphincters had relaxed in death. Aunty Lee sniffed and decided to leave analysis to the forensic technologists. Bodily fluids were fine, good, and necessary as long as they were inside the body, but once they emerged they were considered disgusting and repulsive. Aunty Lee shared this aversion, though it did not make sense to her. Perhaps it was survival instinct. Your insides were only on display outside of you if something terrible had happened. And that was probably why some people felt uncomfortable showing their feelings. For them feelings were also private things meant to be kept hidden, and for them to be displayed meant their lives had been torn apart.

"They must have decided to bring in a new mattress after all," said Jacky. He was clearly both relieved and disappointed. "We had a discussion about it. The old mattress was less than a year old and was still under a cleaning contract, but her bowels . . ."

Aunty Lee stood at the entrance and looked around the room. It was much easier to get a sense of someone from a home they had designed than from a hotel room they had only just checked into before getting murdered, but she was sure she could pick up something. This was a small, functional room with two single beds against one wall and a television on a cabinet containing a small fridge against the wall facing them. There was a built-in cupboard housing a safe at the entrance where Aunty Lee stood, and the window in front of her looked into the windows of the neighboring office block. Even without any other furniture there was barely room enough to walk around the beds. The door to the shower and toilet was at right angles to the room door. There was no sign of anything that might have belonged to the Love sisters.

"There's nowhere to sit and read," Aunty Lee said.

"Oh, people who come here don't do much reading," Jacky said. "Mostly day-rate people just come and dump their stuff here and then go to the casino or go shopping or whatever. Then they come back to dump their shopping and shower and go out to party. The hour-rate people only use the beds, if you get my meaning. The only reading they do is the 4D, TOTO, and racing results."

"Jacky, were you here the day Miss Love was killed? It must have been so awful for you."

"Oh yes, so shocking!" he said with relish. "It's the first time anything like that ever happened to me. There I was, sitting in the downstairs office, when right on top of me somebody was being killed. I can't believe it, I tell you!"

"Did anyone hear anything? Any of the people in the other rooms? Or underneath? You know people are always complaining about noise coming through their ceilings."

"There was nobody in the room underneath. Like I said, nowadays we are not full most of the time. And most of the time when you hear funny things around here you don't pay much attention, if you know what I mean. Plus they said very strictly they did not want to be disturbed. That's why I had to say no to the phone caller."

"What's that?"

"Somebody phoned for Miss Allison that day. It went to the switchboard because the caller didn't know what room she was in. But before going out Miss Vallerie had said Miss Allison had a bad headache and didn't want to be disturbed, so the girl put it through to me to take a message, and wow, I got such a shelling from the caller. All the bad words coming out."

"It was somebody local? Or was it a foreigner? Male or female voice?"

"Oh, a local woman for sure. Well, could be Malaysian also I guess. That's also partly why I didn't put it through to the room. I knew it wasn't Miss Vallerie or one of her friends calling for her."

"What time was this call, do you remember?"

"I don't know. About two songs into the *HOT 30 Countdown,* which starts at ten A.M. . . . so I guess sometime before eleven?" Jacky lowered his voice. "Of course I only found out later that Allison Love was Allison Fitzgerald the puppy killer."

"You heard about that? You must have been quite young." He did not look much more than eighteen, but Aunty Lee suspected Jacky was really in his mid- to late twenties—quite old enough to appreciate being called young.

"My whole family was following the puppy killer business. Allison Fitzgerald's son used to attend the playgroup that my aunt's sister-in-law was running. My aunt used to help out there, and when the news came out Aunty Joanne said she wasn't surprised, because that *ang moh* was the type that could be one minute happy happy, smiling smiling, the next minute got bad temper, shouting, swearing, threatening to sue like a big shot. One time, because they gave all the children some pineapple tarts to bring home before the Chinese New Year break, Mrs. Fitzgerald accused them of trying to poison her!"

"Poor woman," Aunty Lee said politely. "Sounds like she had quite a temper."

"It was not just a bad temper. Later Aunty Joanne told us that Allison Fitzgerald got diagnosed with bipolar. She followed the story online, even after they ran away from Singapore. You know what some women are like. Everything also want to know."

"Bipolar?" said Aunty Lee, another of the women who liked to know everything.

"That means one day depressed enough to kill yourself, next day so angry you want to kill everybody else," Jacky explained. "I know because we have a kitchen staff with it here. Very frightening when there's knives or hot soup around. But on medication she's okay. We keep an extra set of meds here in case she forgets to take in the morning."

"Medication for things like that no use," Aunty Lee said firmly. "Makes everybody addicted so that they have to go on taking the medication, that's all. She should just eat better, exercise out all the bad energy!" This was Aunty Lee's standard response to all ills, and if it worked for her, there was no point in arguing.

"And of course I donated to the puppy killer fund. Everybody did, right? Foreigners should not come here and kill our dogs anyhow. But Allison Fitzgerald was very quiet when she was staying here. Miss Vallerie was the difficult sister, not Miss Allison. Miss Allison stayed inside their room most of the time, in fact. Didn't even want to let the cleaners in. I think she wasn't feeling well."

"I wonder why Vallerie didn't mention that."

"And Miss Vallerie was always complaining." Jacky lowered his voice on mentioning complaints. "She already complained five times in the week they were here before her sister was killed."

"They were here a week?" Aunty Lee was surprised.

"Oh yes. And changed rooms twice. The first one was too small and the second one was too expensive—she wanted to pay the rate for the first size of room while staying in the second. Oh, she made such a fuss!"

"Allison? The sister that got killed?"

"Oh no. The one downstairs. Your friend—the pink fat lady."

Aunty Lee warmed to Jacky as he pointed out the cleaning equipment storeroom, lifts, and other exits in response to her queries.

"Latest upgrade—we installed lift indicator lights so you can see how long you have to wait." Both lifts were on the ground floor.

Aunty Lee was impressed. "What about the staircases?" she asked.

Jacky explained that the fire exits were locked (contravening fire regulations but conveniently in this case), but the service stairwell leading down to the car park could be accessed from all floors.

"When the staircase to the outside is open, too many guests walk out without paying. But if they go down the stairs to the lobby or car park, there's security there so it's all right."

"Was there a lot of stuff besides the luggage downstairs?"

"There was quite a lot of food that we had to throw away. Shall we go back down and join your friend?"

Aunty Lee asked about the cleaners who had packed up the room after the police left. "We should thank them. They did such a great job."

Jacky said he was sure he could find them.

"And the cleaners who took care of Allison and Vallerie's room while they were staying here. Can I talk to them?"

Aunty Lee had been slightly apprehensive for Melvinia. However, not only had the slight receptionist survived, but Vallerie seemed resigned to the condition of her belongings. Mel was tougher than she looked, Aunty Lee decided.

"Your toilets are so small—they remind me of toilets on board a plane," Vallerie was saying as Aunty Lee and Jacky rejoined them. "Economy class."

"Oh, we had a special Japanese architect come and design for a small space. The main thing is to have everything within reach and easy to keep clean."

"If it's too small for your guests it's useless," Vallerie snapped.

"I'll be sure to give your feedback to the management," Mel chirruped with a sweet smile, reminding Aunty Lee of Cherril when her partner was in stewardess mode.

Jacky was less customer-sensitive. "We call them our restrooms rather than toilets. They all have flowers, not just artificial air fresheners—I make a point of that. There's no reason to separate the essential and the beautiful. I helped to design the lighting and the tiling myself. And in our hotels the gents' are all designed with as much attention as the ladies'."

Aunty Lee thought of something. She got her phone out and fumbled with the buttons, finally handing it to Jacky. "Can you find my photos? Somewhere there I have a shelfie of me and Josephine. I want to show you something—"

Vallerie looked up sharply at the mention of Josephine's name, but Aunty Lee did not give her a chance to speak.

"Show me—yes. That's right. Jacky, tell me, have you seen any of these people here in your hotel?"

Though Vallerie had made her distaste for the flamboyant Jacky very clear by keeping her distance, rolling her eyes, and twisting her mouth, even she drew closer as Jacky squinted at Aunty Lee's phone gallery.

"Well you, obviously. The others, not really. Wait—he looks familiar." Jacky took the phone from Aunty Lee and swiped the screen larger. "Yes, I'm sure I've seen him before." He giggled. "In the loo, actually. I was thinking just my luck. Alone in the loo with a guy like that and it had to be the hotel loo. *Tùzi bù chī wō biān cǎo.*"

"Rabbits don't eat the grass around their homes," Mel translated, seeing Aunty Lee was baffled by Jacky's sudden switch to Mandarin. "Means 'don't shit where you eat'; in this case, no messing with guests."

"What's Mr. Handsome's name?"

"Brian Wong," Aunty Lee said absently. She had taken her phone back and was sending Salim a quick text. This was just one of the things she thought he would be interested in. And in return, she asked him to do her a small favor and join them at the hotel.

18
Café

Cherril was surprised how smoothly the café and kitchen were running, even without Aunty Lee keeping an eye on everything. The systems and routines set up by her boss were in place and worked, and the momentum carried them on. In fact it was almost easier without Aunty Lee sitting in the busiest areas (leg raised on a stool when there were no customers), keeping an eye on things and almost tripping you up when she wanted a closer look at what you were doing. And of course there was always Nina. Nina, who always knew what needed to be done and did it before anyone noticed. Of course there was that mountain of over-ripe mangoes in the cold room that everyone was pointedly not noticing . . .

If she were ever to branch out on her own in the food business, Cherril wondered whether Nina might be persuaded to join her . . . but of course she would not worry about that until and unless she could not persuade Aunty Lee to expand.

And Cherril had to admit Selina was a real help during the mealtime rush. Though she gave nonstop instructions about organizing things that were already organized, she could get down to work when she had to. In fact there was less tension when Aunty Lee was not there, because Selina now talked to Aunty Lee as though she were a not very bright child, as though her fall had damaged her head rather than her ankle. This always provoked Aunty Lee into choruses of "Don't so silly lah, Silly-Nah." Entertained as she was, Cherril realized she had unconsciously been acting the same way toward Aunty Lee. It was too easy to treat the physically weak as though they were stupid.

Now in the afternoon bog between the last lunch customers and the first afternoon tea people, Selina had gone to run errands and Cherril had the place to herself. Later, teatime would merge into people buying food to take home for dinner and that would be the real work of the day. Many places simply closed down between the last lunch order and six so the staff could have a break and clean up. But at Aunty Lee's Delights they cleaned up between customers anyway and there was little more to do.

Of course she could have left things to Nina and the two temporary helpers. But Cherril preferred to spend slow afternoons in the shop rather than back at the Peters house. Mycroft would be at the office and his father seldom left his study. And while Anne Peters was charming and properly kind to her son's wife, she was not exactly someone whom

Cherril was comfortable sitting and chatting with. Despite the comfort and luxury of the self-contained little cabin built on the grounds of the Peterses' bungalow, Cherril Lim-Peters was lonely there. It would be different once children arrived, she reminded herself. If children ever came, but she tried not to think about that.

For now she had the café. And there was Nina, always quietly practical, coming out with a stack of takeaway boxes to be folded. She put them in front of Cherril, who said as she started on them, "I don't like to get involved, but I don't like seeing Josephine with that guy."

Nina looked at her. Cherril looked back, expectant.

"You don't want to get involved then don't get involved *lor*."

"It's already too late. She asked me to help her—actually she more or less forced me to help her, but that's just the way Josephine is. She makes you feel it's easier to just do whatever she wants. But I know that if things go wrong she's going to turn around and blame me."

"Maybe things won't go wrong." Nina pulled out the bags of fresh vegetables that had gone straight into the walk-in chiller without sorting that morning. That was kitchen life; there was never enough time in the mornings and always something to do in the afternoons.

"It's not going to work, right? It's not bad enough that he's been married before. He can't have very good memories of what happened to his family in Singapore. The minute everything goes wrong between them he's going to blame her and Singapore," Cherril burst out. "And Josephine—when she gets angry it's scary!"

Nina spread out a few sheets of newspaper and started sorting the *kangkong* and removing the few wilted leaves. The water spinach had been standing in a bucket of water and most of it was well hydrated. It would be crisp and juicy when stir-fried that evening.

"Plus they come from totally different backgrounds. It's difficult enough marrying a man with so much baggage, let alone one that comes from a totally different background!"

"You're not being fair to your friend, Madame Cherril."

"I only want to help." What she really wanted was a way to distance herself from the disaster she could see coming. She did not want to be dragged into another of Josephine's dramas.

Nina rinsed a basket of red chilies and started slicing them into thin rings. These would be put into the freezer and served as "fresh"-cut chilies in soy sauce. Some of them would be cut into thicker rings with most of the seeds and all the fiber removed. Since it was the soft, pale fibers that gave chilies most of their heat, these would be for people who liked the sweet warmth of chili peppers without too much fire. There was no point in telling people the best chilies were those spicy enough to burn a layer of skin off your tongue. Some people preferred as little excitement as possible in their lives and on their plates.

Cherril pulled out another chopping block to help.

"Gloves are in the drawer." Nina was already wearing disposable latex examination gloves. These were fine enough that you could still feel what you were doing, unlike the thicker washing-up gloves.

"That's okay. I'll wash my hands after."

"You wash your hands ten times and rub your eyes, your eyes will still be pain and turn red and Aunty Lee will scold me."

"I won't rub my eyes. And I won't tell Aunty Lee."

"Wear gloves or don't touch!"

Cherril took the gloves. She did not think she needed them but there was no point antagonizing Nina for nothing.

"Why would anybody marry somebody so different?"

Nina looked at Cherril suspiciously, but her boss's new partner was clearly following her own train of thought. Cherril had never been a top student, but she was good at solving problems because once she latched on to something she held on till it gave way or she was shaken off. The disadvantage, of course, was she missed anything going on outside her focus of interest. But Nina was glad of that right then since the same issues were very much on her mind. But unlike Cherril, the more important something was to Nina, the less likely she was to discuss it.

"You did, madame."

"Me?"

Nina nodded, her eyes on her hands, which were still busy.

"That's not true. Me and Mycroft?"

"Different race, different religion, different background." Singaporeans were conditioned to believe it was impolite to mention such things, as though they did not notice them. Of course this just increased the size of the elephant in the room. But Nina was not a Singaporean. And Cherril, touchy as she was about the social differences between her and My-croft's birth families, could tell Nina meant no offense.

"We both grew up here. Neither of us has been married before. Neither of us got divorced from a crazy person who was threatening to sue the new partner before getting herself murdered. It's a big, big difference."

"I'm not saying it is the same. I am only saying that if people want to do something, they will not listen to anything you say. Plus they will get angry with you for saying it."

Cherril thought back to her own marriage. It was different for her and Mycroft of course. She had had concerns initially (much as she wanted to be with him), but once she decided to commit she had not had any doubt it was going to work out for them. She would not have gone into it if she had had any doubts. But she had also thought that they would have moved on to the next stage of marriage by now.

"It's going to be difficult for your children too." It was as though Nina had picked up Aunty Lee's ability to follow other people's thoughts.

"Not in Singapore. There are more and more mixed kids in Singapore these days. As long as they know who they are, it should be all right. But this Mike lives in England and has kids in school there and everything. Josephine's always wanted to get out of Singapore, but I don't think she knows what it's going to be like. A new country as well as a new man and his kids. And kids can be difficult even if they're your own. Think what it's going to be like handling those two with half-crazy genes. That's not fair to Josephine."

"Does Josephine want children?"

"Of course!" Cherril's voice rang out in the room louder than she intended. Nina looked at her as though she had just answered an important question. "I mean, who doesn't, right? Hey, are there any mangoes left? I've been thinking of trying something with them."

"More than enough!" Nina was successfully diverted. "But no room in the fridge *lah*. Anything you make got to put in the freezer."

Some of the mangoes were already going soft. But that just meant they would be nectar sweet and easy to pulp in a blender.

Josephine was not as busy as she would have liked people to think. Her artistic floral arrangements had been a big hit. But the same fickle fashion that had drawn people to her designs had soon pulled them elsewhere. Now she was not even covering the costs of running the little shop space she rented. It would be time to move on soon, to make herself over yet again. She was quite looking forward to this.

Josephine DelaVega examined herself in the mirror and, as was happening more and more frequently these days, wondered about plastic surgery. Though she had not gone under the knife, this daughter of two secondary school teachers had reinvented herself, enhancing or removing facets of herself to suit the image and lifestyle she desired. All in all things had worked out quite well in her life so far. Even the pregnancy had not been a complete accident.

She had thought it would prompt Mike to get over his reservations about marrying again. Mike was the kind of man who had to be pushed into recognizing what he wanted to do. Josephine could see his late wife had taken full advantage of that.

Remembering Allison drew Josephine's thoughts to Vallerie, Allison's sister.

Allison had been the elder of the siblings. This made Vallerie, like Josephine herself, a younger sister. Growing up, Josephine had dealt with this by taking the opposite path to whatever her sister, Margaret, had done. And she did not regret it. Though she envied Maggie's happy married-with-three-children life, Josephine would have hated to live her life as a dentist, married to another dentist, spending their waking hours looking up people's nostrils to finance a mortgage and their children's education. And besides, now there was Mike. No, Vallerie didn't matter. Josephine would do what she could for the woman, just enough to show Mike how generous she was, and sooner or later Vallerie would go back to America or wherever, and Allison's ashes would go with her in a jar or be scattered in the sea or whatever, and Mike and Josephine would live happily ever after.

The stupid woman had gotten so worked up at the suggestion she join Josephine and Mike for a drink before they all had dinner together at Aunty Lee's Delights. "No way in hell" would Vallerie sit down at a table with Mike. She was convinced Mike had killed Allison and would never rest till she had proved it—

"Nobody warned me he was coming for dinner. That busybody old cow was trying to set me up, wasn't she? You're all in it together. Well, I'm not standing for it!"

"Fine. So don't meet Mike."

"I told the police that if it wasn't him, somebody killed Allison to stop her from taking you to court. I told them you and your devil boyfriend murdered her between you. They're going to be watching you!"

Josephine recognized the malicious triumph of a child on Vallerie's pudgy face.

"Don't think that just because she's dead it's going to stop."

Josephine had hoped being nice to Vallerie now would pay off in the future. Someday when she and Mike had settled down it might be useful to have one more aunt to take his children off their hands. But Josephine was finding it really difficult to be nice to Vallerie.

She smoothed fungicide over some large sunflower stems, hands encased in thin latex gloves to protect them. Josephine paused in the act of cabling the flowers to their stand, remembering the look on Vallerie's face. The woman's intense, focused, *knowing* hatred so startled Josephine that for a moment she had imagined the dead Allison glaring at her through her sister's eyes. Then it was gone and the bloated and bleary-eyed Vallerie was back with her childish spitefulness. Had Josephine imagined that look?

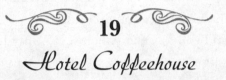

19
Hotel Coffeehouse

When the clearly busy Jacky finally disappeared to attend to the calls he had been ignoring, leaving them alone to wait for Salim's arrival, Aunty Lee suggested they do that in the hotel coffeehouse.

"I need to sit my old bones down. And I always like to check out the competition. And if that nice policeman comes to talk to us here, you can tell him about anything that's missing from your things while we are still in the hotel."

Vallerie agreed, though it was unclear whether it was the hotel tea or sitting down that appealed to her. And once in the Orchid coffeehouse, Vallerie agreed to have something hot to drink (just to calm her down) and something to eat (just to keep her strength up). Aunty Lee knew that feeding people often made them more open to cooperating than starving them did. It was a physiological fact that a comfort-

ably full stomach signaled that if it was safe to eat with someone, it was likely safe to talk to him or her. By the time Vallerie
had finished a hot honey-lemon infusion and buttered waffles with imported genuine Canadian (though packaged in
Japan) maple syrup, and was considering a chocolate mousse
pie, she seemed willing enough to talk.

"So, you and your sister were close?" Aunty Lee started innocently enough.

Vallerie nodded. She could hardly say "I couldn't stand
my sister." All Aunty Lee wanted was to get the conversation
going. Listening and watching how people responded to questions told her more about them than the answers they gave.
Her late husband had joked that his Rosie functioned like a
human detector kit when it came to people's food prejudices,
and perhaps also other prejudices beyond food. Though of
course it was trickier with people she did not know, and even
more so with foreigners like Vallerie.

"So close even though you lived so far apart?" Aunty Lee
asked. "That's so good."

"Like I've said over a hundred times, we had no one else."
But Vallerie seemed willing enough to repeat it a hundred
and one times. She pointed out the mousse pie (with a salty
almond pretzel crust) to the hovering waiter and sat back to
continue. "We were the only ones left in the family. Doesn't
make any difference whether we were close or not. We had
to watch out for each other, because there wasn't anyone
else. Nobody else gave a damn for either of us. Of course it
didn't help that we were living so far apart. If I had stayed in
England I could have been nearer to Allison. I could have

done more for her, just been there, you know? After all, it was where we grew up, where everything was familiar. But oh no. I preferred to stay far away from her and home, even knowing what she was going through. But it's too late now, isn't it?"

Guilt showed up in strange ways and for strange reasons. Aunty Lee wondered if that was why Vallerie was focused on the wrongs done to her dead sister—wrongs done by herself as well as everyone else. She ordered a second chamomile tea for herself. "At least you accompanied her to Singapore when she needed you."

"Fat lot of good I did her. And I didn't even stay in the room with her—I just left her alone there for someone to come and kill her! I'm not letting it go. I'm going to make sure everybody knows what happened to Allison!" Vallerie's words were angry but she did not get up to leave, so Aunty Lee let her go on talking. "All those people who said those terrible things about her. I want them to know this is all their fault. Oh, I should have stayed in the room with her!"

"But you never know, right?" Aunty Lee said comfortingly. "If you had stayed then both of you might be dead now!"

By the time Inspector Salim arrived, the efficient (and apparently multilingual) Jacky had already gathered the details—and people—Aunty Lee had asked for, from the Mandarin-speaking ex–front desk staff to his Malay- and Tamil-speaking cleaning and security personnel.

And when Salim requested the floor plans of the hotel, Jacky promptly handed him a photocopied set in a clear binder.

"Very good," the officer said, clearly impressed. Jacky beamed and blushed.

If Cherril ever expanded operations to the extent that they needed to hire a restaurant or business manager—or if for some reason she ever lost Nina—Aunty Lee thought she could do worse than come back here and look for Jacky.

"There are two suitcases and they say they just packed everything they could into both of them and then put everything else in plastic bags," Jacky said. "I told them to but only after your officers said it was all right." He stopped and looked at Salim. "Did you want to test for DNA and fingerprints and things like that?"

It was the result of too many crime scene investigation shows on television, Salim thought. These days everyone who watched American television was a forensic expert.

"It's all right. The crime scene tech team has already gone over everything."

"Ah, that's all right then."

"Mrs. Rosie Lee and Miss Vallerie Love are in the coffeehouse. If you would like to join them there I can send down the staff members that Mrs. Lee wants to talk to?"

"Perfect, if I can have a coffee," Salim said with a smile that almost melted Jacky.

Vallerie, however, was less pleased to see Salim and hear his first question.

"Look, you have no business judging us. People like you segregate women and make them cover their heads and treat them like ignorant animals. How dare you ask how long we were staying here? What business is it of yours? Your job is to find my poor sister's killer, not sit around asking me stupid questions!" Vallerie flared up. The way she looked at Salim made Aunty Lee think she had been looking for an excuse to deliver the tirade. "You people don't like to see white women traveling alone in the East. That's why you're trying to intimidate me, admit it. You're covering up for whoever killed my poor sister by instead coming in here and harassing me with stupid questions!"

Salim was used to people who turned on the police under pressure. As far as he was concerned it was far better for them to vent their rage on a police officer than on an innocent passerby or helpless family member. What he found interesting was how an apparently innocent question had triggered Vallerie's outburst. The woman was clearly uncomfortable about something. Aunty Lee's bright, interested eyes showed she had noticed that too, but all she said was, "*Hiyah,* Salim. If you want to know how long Vallerie and her sister have been in Singapore, why not just ask the hotel—or check their passports!"

"We'll do that." They had already done that, of course. He had wanted to know what Vallerie would say. "And you said Allison was not feeling well that day she arranged to meet with the former Animal ReHomers? Did she see a doctor?"

Vallerie had been adrenaline-poised to tear down any defenses, apologies, or justifications—ready and looking forward to a fight. But the police officer sounded as though he hadn't realized she was attacking. Social conditioning made her match his tone automatically.

"Allison wasn't really feeling unwell. She just got scared and upset by the attack on the vet clinic."

"Your sister had been feeling sick for some time, right? The room cleaner said she didn't clean the room because someone wasn't feeling well."

"Oh, that was because she didn't want to go out in the heat. And she had to stay with our things because we didn't want the hotel people poking around and stealing our valuables while we weren't in the room."

Aunty Lee opened her mouth to defend Singapore hotel cleaners but caught herself in time. It took almost as much effort for Salim to hold back a grin on seeing this. "Your sister, Allison, spent some time in Singapore years ago, didn't she?"

"I already told you that. That's why she knows what it's like here. That was when she was still married to that jerk. He got posted to a bank here and she came out to look after him and the children. Sacrificed her own career to support his and he just dumped her. She wasn't even getting support from him, you know."

"This is Mr. Mike Fitzgerald?"

"That jerk, yes. Who killed her and who you fools still haven't arrested. If not for him and his stupid job, Allison wouldn't even have been in Singapore and all that fuss about a stupid dog would never have come up. You guys are bringing him in, aren't you? He should be made to face what he did to her. You should go and check up on him. And that stupid Brian Wong. If not for him Allison would still be happily married and none of this would have happened!"

"Brian Wong? Allison blamed him for breaking up her marriage?" Salim's electronic tablet came to life on the table as he made a quick notation with his stylus. He sensed an almost electric sizzle of attention from Aunty Lee, who quickly turned away to examine the water feature (probably placed to disguise a former smoking corner rather than for good feng shui) behind Vallerie with utmost attention.

"He was the one that tried to lead her on and everything. Anyway, he's one of your important people now so nothing's going to touch him, right?"

"What makes you say Brian Wong was leading your sister on? On to what?"

Vallerie spoke through a mouthful of chocolate. "How would I know? You should ask him yourself. Men are all the same. Look at that hopeless husband of hers. If Mike Fitzgerald hadn't dragged her out here Allison would be alive and happily married and not lying dead in this godforsaken country!"

One of the cleaners, a young dark-skinned man whom Aunty Lee had glimpsed earlier with a vacuum cleaner, approached their table shyly. Vallerie saw him and started to shriek. The startled man backed away, looking more terrified than Vallerie. He got entangled with the drinks trolley and a second cleaner—older and female—coming toward them with Jacky. Aunty Lee only just managed not to smack Vallerie. Whether or not slapping helped calm people having hysterics, it would have felt most satisfying to smack Vallerie Love right then.

"Sorry," Aunty Lee said, rising to her feet and trying to

shout reassuringly to the two cleaners. "My friend is a bit upset. Her sister just died. Please, come and join us. Yes, please do come and sit down."

"Those cleaners! Always sneaking around and trying to get into rooms to spy on paying guests!"

Neither of them came up to the table. But when Jacky unobtrusively brought chairs for them they sat down on either side of him a little distance away. Aunty Lee appreciated a manager who did his own fetching and carrying and took care of his staff.

"Yes, I know," the man replied to Aunty Lee. He spoke with a South Indian accent but Aunty Lee could understand him without any trouble. "Her sister is very nice. I am very sad she is dead. I did not know which sister died. I get the sisters mixed up, even though one is fat and one is thin." The woman nodded several times as he spoke but said nothing.

"You met the other sister?" Aunty Lee asked.

"The other sister stayed more in the room. But sometimes when I am cleaning she open the door and say hello. She is always very sleepy. And then one time she asked me to help her to move the cupboard because her phone charger got fall down behind. And then after that she asked me around here where to go to eat cheap cheap, where to go and buy things cheap cheap. Once I saw her downstairs, she asked me to help her to carry her shopping bags inside. Because one of the bags the plastic got tear. So I give her another one, she is very happy."

"What did she buy?"

"Just tourist things. Postcards. Good luck beads."

"What did she do with them?" Aunty Lee had not seen anything of the sort in the storage room.

The cleaner shrugged, suddenly cautious. "I don't know. I never take one."

The man looked acutely uncomfortable, avoiding looking at Vallerie, who had at least quieted down. Aunty Lee had a sudden glimpse of the wretched life of a foreign hotel cleaner. He was probably working there illegally. And that meant he was probably being paid far less than a local or legal "foreign talent" would have cost the hotel. And he obviously bore the brunt of any lost (or misplaced) items from any of the rooms he cleaned. Still, she sensed there was something more from the intensity with which he avoided Vallerie's stare.

"But you took something else, didn't you? Were you the ones who cleaned the room and packed the bags?"

The woman cleaner moaned softly and started crying, muttering something in a dialect that Aunty Lee did not understand. The younger male cleaner looked as though he was about to cry himself.

"What did you take?" It was a different Jacky who spoke now, with all the weight of authority in his voice. The woman next to him moaned more loudly. Without understanding a word, Aunty Lee could tell she was trying to take the blame on herself. Without taking his eyes off the young man, Jacky put a hand over the woman's, which were clasped tightly in her lap. It was unclear whether this was meant to comfort or quiet her, but she subsided into nodding to herself.

"Food. She says when people leave, sometimes there is biscuits and bread in the room. So we take back and share."

"And did the lady tourists leave any food?"

The lady tourists had thrown out cakes, they agreed. Good cakes. Sometimes people threw away things they did not want to carry back while they were still good. They finally admitted to eating the cakes with hanging heads and shamed faces, expecting to be shouted at and fired. Instead Aunty Lee asked them how they felt. Had they eaten them all? What were they like? Yes, they had eaten them all. They were very good. Not fresh, not like at home, but good. No, they did not get sick.

"They stole my food?" Vallerie burst out incredulously. "Did you hear that? They sneaked into my room and stole my food!" But none of them, not even the two cleaners, paid any attention to her.

"Did you take a box of moon cakes?" Aunty Lee asked quietly. She held up the plastic lid liner. "Round brown cakes. Hard outside, soft inside."

It took a while for him to understand, but the male cleaner admitted they took and shared a box of two (originally four) moon cakes from the room after the police released the room and they were asked to pack up the sisters' things.

"I took the box," the woman said. "It was very pretty. I was going to use it to keep things. I will give it back to you. I will buy you another one. Please not be angry. Please not take us to police."

"I don't care about the stupid box," Vallerie said. "What else did you take?" But it seemed as though Aunty Lee had suddenly grown deaf to her.

"I will replace the moon cakes and anything else that was taken," Jacky said. "I take responsibility for this. They were told to clear the room and dispose of perishables, so if they disposed of something you wanted the hotel is responsible." But Aunty Lee was deaf to him too.

Looking at the still weeping woman she said, "I just want to see the box. Can you show us the box?"

"Is it still here?" Jacky clearly did not understand Aunty Lee's moon cake fixation, but was willing to go along with it. The woman nodded.

"Back room."

"Go and fetch it. Raju, go with her. Oh, come on." He went with them. Aunty Lee suspected he was going to deliver a few reassuring words. But she had other things on her mind.

It was a bonus for Aunty Lee that the old woman cleaner still had the box. The pretty box she had folded along its lines. She had planned to send it home to her young granddaughter. The girl liked bright, pretty things, the old woman said. Aunty Lee felt bad taking the carefully preserved box from her, but the woman clearly wanted it off her hands now.

"Her sister, the dead one, wanted to post some things back home," the man said. "She ask me where to post. I tell her where I go to send money and things back to my family. I don't know whether she went or not."

"What did she want to post?"

"Pineapple tarts, I think. Good ones, from Bengawan Solo."

"Nonsense," said Vallerie.

"Was Allison's body tested for poison? Drugs? Did your people find anything?" Aunty Lee asked Salim after Jacky and the cleaners left.

"It was quite obvious how she was killed. Besides there's no point running tests unless you know what you are looking for." Salim did not add that such tests were extensive, expensive, and up to the forensic pathologist rather than him.

"*Hiyah,* what's the point of looking when you know what you are looking for? You should try to find things that you don't know are there! Sleeping medicine and things like that. But anyway—" She turned her attention back to Vallerie, who had fallen silent and was looking both miffed and confused.

"Why don't you go back to the lobby," Aunty Lee suggested. "Pick out everything you want now and we'll bring it back with us. The other things we'll ask them to store until you can arrange to send them home."

"I want it all, of course. I'm not going to leave any of my things here with these people. We must bring everything back today."

Aunty Lee and her walking stick went to make arrangements with Jacky. She also tried to pass him ten dollars each for the cleaners. She knew how difficult it was for them to face talking to the police.

Jacky refused the money. "I already took care of that. That lady was always complaining. When she was staying here she asked what can she eat here that is cheap and not too spicy, and my front desk girl recommended the cheese *prata* next door. You know the shop I mean, right? Same recipe as the old *prata* house his grandfather used to run in Pasir Panjang."

"Of course, it's famous."

"Exactly! And you would think that as a tourist visiting she would want to try something local. I mean, of course it's terrible that her sister got killed, but this was before that happened. She threatened to sue us for trying to give her food poisoning. As though looking at food can give you food poisoning!"

Aunty Lee agreed. The Singaporean need to eat was not only an indulgence as many thought. It was a survival mechanism, the one need that everyone truly had in common, regardless of race, language, or religion. And having more money or more power did not necessarily mean you ate better. Often, in fact, too much money and power cut into the time you had for appreciating good food and left you at the mercy of those who put more money into music and mood lighting than quality ingredients.

"But *aiyoh*, she was so offended that I suggested she eat *prata*. She said that she tried it once and it made her sick for more than a week. I don't know what kind of *prata* she was eating. It is like saying, 'I tried eating bread once and it made me sick for one week,' right? Depends on the bread and what you put on it, right?"

"That must have been the other sister, the one who got killed. She used to live in Singapore."

"No, it was the fat one, the one here today. The skinny one that got killed, she wanted to try new things. But that was only when they first arrived. After that I didn't see her again."

Aunty Lee was thoughtful. She stopped to make a quick phone call before going back to collect Vallerie.

20
Routines

Routine toxicology screenings even in Singapore's most advanced morgues were sorely limited by the need to justify expenses. Even when activated, the normal screening checked only for the most common toxins, such as opiates and alcohol. Only if certain poisons were suspected could the specific analyses requested be individually conducted.

"Routine testing can miss some poisons," Commissioner Raja admitted.

"So if I want to kill somebody I should use those poisons?" Aunty Lee had been suspected of an accidental poisoning just the year before, but she only brought this up as a last resort. "Instead of my *buah keluak*?"

Commissioner Raja knew when he was beaten. "I'll get additional tests done on Allison Love's body. Everything they can think of. Even though death was clearly caused by asphyxiation by strangling with postmortem battering. Satisfied?"

"Get the results first then say satisfied or not." Aunty Lee did not tell him she had already brought up the issue with Salim. It never hurt to have the big boss on your side, but it was those on the ground level who got the job done.

But as she put down the phone Aunty Lee was satisfied that she had done all she could—at least where Commissioner Raja was concerned.

Indeed, everyone seemed satisfied. The Victoria Crest Hotel agreed to waive costs. Aunty Lee suspected Jacky was glad to get Vallerie officially off the premises, plus he seemed to think the future might bring unofficial tours for ghoulish-minded locals. And Aunty Lee was happy to have Vallerie continue staying in the guest room at 88 Binjai Park. After all, that was what guest rooms were for.

Vallerie spent the rest of that day closeted in her bedroom with all her things. But the next morning she joined Aunty Lee and Nina at the café, apparently in high spirits and full of advice: "You really should upgrade your menu. These supposedly exotic dishes are all very well, but what people want is plain good-quality food!"

Aunty Lee, leaning pointedly on her stick, hobbled to a corner table to rub stains off menu covers, leaving Nina to listen to Vallerie's advice.

Nina was better than Aunty Lee at taking food advice. Almost every Singaporean was a self-pronounced expert on food, but Nina Balignasay considered herself an expert on taking advice, whether or not she followed it. This was a skill a foreign domestic worker in Singapore needed to survive. As Vallerie expounded on the merits of fried doughnuts, the entrance bell jangled. It was Anne Peters, looking through the half-open door. She gave Cherril at the other side of the room a quick wave, but it was Aunty Lee in her corner she addressed: "I won't come in. I have Tammy with me. We've come for her food, but don't bring it out yet. Do you have time for a quick chat?"

"Always!"

Dirty menus abandoned, Aunty Lee limped outside to join Anne Peters and Tammy, her large but still puppy-natured dog. Nina escaped from Vallerie to pack the takeaway bags for Anne Peters and Tammy. Like many other neighbors, Anne often stopped by to pick up something (almost home cooked) for lunch or dinner, but the meals for Tammy were a new innovation. Anne Peters had passed Aunty Lee some healthy dog recipes (no salt, no seasonings, no taste as far as Aunty Lee could see—but Tammy seemed to be thriving on them), and Aunty Lee preferred experimenting with dog food over factories.

"You shouldn't be allowed to cook dog food on the same premises as human food. That's so unhygienic!" Aunty Lee heard Vallerie saying. She closed the front door firmly behind her. There were drawbacks to bringing your investigative work home.

Anne was looking pleased with herself. "I have a surprise for you. Connie DelaVega is coming by to join us. We were talking about the Singapore Symphony Orchestra fundraiser and I mentioned you've met her daughter's fiancé and can probably tell her more about him. She said you already spoke to her, but that was before you met the man."

"I don't know how much I can tell her," Aunty Lee demurred, but she was very pleased. She had thought of calling Connie herself but had been unable to come up with an excuse to. In the old days, people just made a cake or harvested a papaya or a few branches of rambutans and dropped in. She had seen much more of her friends in those days before phones, tablets, and computers connected everybody all the time and kept them isolated. Aunty Lee missed those days. "How is Connie?"

"Concerned, of course. But she sounds well."

They sat at one of the folding tables on the front walkway to wait for Constance DelaVega. Tammy was the most sweet tempered of dogs, a big light brown "Singapore Special" mutt mix with large paws and ears that suggested Labrador somewhere in her ancestry. But Singapore's Environmental Public Health Act prohibited live animals from being taken into eateries, and after some uncomfortable encounters with the National Environment Agency the previous year and especially with Selina present, Aunty Lee was strictly obeying the rules.

"I tried making some chicken and pork liver meatballs for Tammy this time," Aunty Lee said. "No salt, no soy sauce like you said. Sure to be no taste. I don't even know will she eat them."

"She'll eat them all right." Anne watched the interest with which Tammy nosed her friend. Tammy knew that a visit to Aunty Lee's Delights usually resulted in food treats and would have been happy if they spent all their time there. But she jumped round and stiffened to alert pose with a warning bark as a taxi drew up. Constance DelaVega waved at them before turning back to pay the driver. Tammy gave another sharp bark. Then, at a soft word from Anne, sat down with her ears alert, a low growl rumbling in her throat till the slim older woman got out of the taxi and walked up the two steps from the road to join them on the walkway. It reminded Aunty Lee that Tammy's approval could not be taken for granted. She was one of the few favored to receive it.

Constance DelaVega looked considerably older than Aunty Lee remembered, although her hair was still black and her makeup still in place. Connie Fernandez had once been considered a belle and a beauty, even more celebrated in her time than her daughter was now.

"This is a very nice place!" Connie said, once greetings had been exchanged.

"This can't be your first time here?"

"I think it must be! Of course I've been to your house—that's straight on up the road on the right side, right? And Anne's place is up the road on the left—but that was years ago. Are there tables inside also or is it one of those takeaway places?"

"Most of the tables are inside. We're sitting outside because of Tammy," Anne explained. Aunty Lee had noticed Connie draw back slightly from Tammy's cautious sniff. Josephine had not gotten her love of animals from her mother.

"I'm slightly allergic," Connie explained. She sat on a folding chair that Nina materialized to place for her. "Thank you for seeing me on such short notice. When Anne told me you had actually met this Mike Fitzgerald, I told her I had to come and pick your brain!"

Aunty Lee darted a quick look at Anne, who was looking politely detached. She was impressed by how quickly her friend had managed to set up this meeting—and to convince Connie she was doing her a favor.

"I don't know how much I can tell you," she said. "I only met him once and he was on his best behavior. What has Josie told you about him?"

"She doesn't tell us anything!" Connie said.

"Have you asked her what she sees in him?"

"I know why already. I watched that girl grow up, always reading her fairy tales and then her romances. 'Someday my prince will come,' that kind of thing. In books like that, the princess is just growing hair or sleeping or whatever until the *ang moh* prince comes along and marries her. That was fine with us. We wanted Josie to marry somebody who would look after her. But in real life, instead of showing up with a sword on a white horse, the man shows up with a dead wife and two kids. Now I don't know—does she think she is going to be Maria in *The Sound of Music*, running around on the mountains singing songs with children and ending up in America?"

"You don't think he's right for Josie because of his dead wife and two children?"

"I never said that. Rosie, you also married a man with a dead wife and two children, what."

"The best thing I ever did in my whole life," Aunty Lee agreed. "The only thing I regret is not marrying him sooner."

Josephine's mother nodded. "I want to believe that is what Josie will say one day. We are friends so I want you to help watch out for her, that's all. She thinks that just because she is grown up she doesn't need looking after, but that is not true." Glancing into the shop window as she spoke, Connie jerked violently backward, almost upsetting her chair. Vallerie was standing just inside the window glaring at her. Aunty Lee steadied Connie's chair and gestured to Vallerie to come out and join them.

"Vallerie! Come and meet Josephine's mother?"

At Aunty Lee's invitation Vallerie turned abruptly, bumping into Nina. Nina followed Vallerie as she headed toward the back of the café. She would have to give Nina a little bonus, Aunty Lee thought. Babysitting difficult adults was so much harder than babysitting difficult children.

"Is that the dead wife's sister? The one that is staying with you?"

Aunty Lee nodded. "I put her in Mathilda's old room. Vallerie was so upset and she didn't want to stay alone in a hotel and doesn't know anybody else here. The room is full of Mathilda's old books. I can open up a secondhand bookshop with all the books she has in there!"

"It's so sad that bookshops don't survive in Singapore," Anne observed. She spoke artlessly, but Aunty Lee saw she was keeping an eye out for Vallerie's return. "Mycroft was just saying that another of his favorite bookshops is turning into a nail spa. You know he was actually thinking about buying over that shop space at Holland Village so that the bookshop could stay there without increasing rent? I told him that if he bought over that shop space I would run a nail spa there myself!"

"I was telling Josie she should do something like that," Connie said as Aunty Lee's admiration for Anne Peters grew. "You know the problem with her flower business is you have to have all the flowers there and fresh all the time because they don't last. So if nobody buys them they are all wasted, money down the drain. And she has to keep ordering and paying her suppliers or else they won't give her the best flowers when she needs them. At least if she opens a nail spa, nail polish lasts for so much longer. And I could go down and help her. I don't know anything about arranging flowers."

"I thought her business was doing so well? That article in the Life! Section a few months ago said some very nice things . . ."

"Everybody says very nice things, but people just aren't buying enough flowers. Here, the only way to make money selling flowers is if you sell them outside the temples for people to buy as offerings!"

Aunty Lee reflected that she should have wondered earlier about how Josephine's business was doing. She knew only too well how unpredictable small businesses could be . . . she would have to set Nina on that.

"You're not driving anymore?" Anne Peters was asking Constance. "Are your eyes giving you trouble?"

"Driving is not a problem. I don't like finding places to

park and tearing those tiny coupons. I asked the taxi to come back and get me in one hour's time."

So Constance had set a clear limit to the time she was spending with them. Anne Peters realized this at the same time as Aunty Lee; their friend had not come for a friendly catch-up. They were silent as Nina came out and served tea, delicately trimmed whole meal sandwiches, and a selection of little jellies. Aunty Lee sniffed—mango jellies, she thought in surprised pleasure. "But how—"

"Mrs. Cherril made," Nina said. "She use *konnyaku* powder and your mangoes."

"They look so pretty, what a treat!" Anne said.

"You should be careful of those funny Japanese powders, Rosie," Constance DelaVega said reprovingly. "And if you don't mind me saying, you shouldn't have that dead woman's sister staying with you. One sister was crazy and this one looks a bit funny in the head also. Now you are having trouble getting around. What if she comes and hits you on the head with a hammer in the middle of the night? The police should not have got you to host the dead woman's sister with your broken leg."

"Nonsense, it's only a sprain, not broken." Aunty Lee tapped her brace with her stick. "Exercise gets the blood circulating, meeting new people gets the brain exercising, and the Ministry of Health is always saying we should exercise more, right?"

Anne Peters suspected Aunty Lee's doctors would recommend physiotherapy or gentle outdoor walking rather than limping with a cane in between chairs and tables filled with cold drinks and hot soups. But it would be no use saying so and she turned instead to Constance. "Did Josephine ask you to come and tell Rosie to throw the dead woman's sister out on the street?"

"Of course not. I didn't even mention I was coming here. Josie would get angry if she thought I was here asking you about Mike Fitzgerald—" Constance looked suddenly apprehensive, and her friends quickly shook their heads to indicate that her daughter would not hear about it from them. "She mentioned she was here and saw Rosie and the sister who was staying with you. Rosie, I'm telling you it's not a good idea getting yourself mixed up with people like that."

"People like what?" They had not noticed Vallerie come out. "What are you saying about me? I know you are talking about me. I saw the way you were staring at me."

Eyes down on the table, Constance DelaVega shook her head genteelly with a small, prim smile. She was ignoring Vallerie with the polite indifference she would have applied to a pavement dog turd, Aunty Lee thought. She suddenly felt sorry for Josephine.

"You're spying on me for that bitch Josephine that's trying to get her claws into Mike aren't you, old woman? Don't think I'm so stupid! You Singaporeans may have killed my sister but you are not as smart as you think!"

"Don't get so worked up," Anne Peters said before Constance could respond. "Besides, how do you know Allison was murdered by a Singaporean?"

Vallerie looked surprised and then pressed her lips together. "She's stalking and harassing me. You saw her watching me just now. I'm going to report this. You've all been threatening me ever since I got here. I am a British citizen. You can't do anything to me here."

Anne Peters stood up and quietly said something into Vallerie's ear that the younger woman clearly didn't like. For a moment Aunty Lee thought Vallerie was going to hit the older woman and tightened her grip on her glass, ready to throw it at her. Then Vallerie turned and slammed back into the café, considerably more noisily than she had come out.

"You better sit back down," Anne said with a shaky laugh, and Aunty Lee realized she was also on her feet. She was torn between going after Vallerie and comforting Constance, who looked frozen in a paralysis of politeness.

"You can't have that creature in your house." Constance was coldly precise. "I knew your late husband. ML would not approve."

For a moment Aunty Lee felt like a scolded schoolgirl. She also felt like sticking out her tongue. Fortunately Anne Peters was saying, "Her sister just got murdered. It's probably the shock."

This seemed to remind Constance of where she was and whom she was talking to. Dropping some of her icy manner, she smiled and said, "We are all old and helpless now. All we can do is stand by and watch these young people make the same mistakes we made. Over and over again it happens. We didn't listen to our parents and they don't listen to us." Her fingers, twisting the straps of her handbag, were white and liver-spotted but still lovely.

"Connie and I will walk back to my house," Anne Peters decided. "Rosie, come and join us?" But Aunty Lee could tell she was in Constance DelaVega's bad books until she kicked Vallerie out as instructed. And she had no intention of doing that just because some woman dared suggest her late husband would disapprove. She was impressed by Anne Peters.

"I'll send her taxi up the road when it comes. What did you say to Vallerie just before she stormed off?"

"I just said, 'Don't use your sister's death as an excuse not to go on with your own life.'" Anne smiled. "That's what I did for a long time. I wanted to make whoever hurt my daughter suffer. And then I realized there was no point."

"That woman staying with you is a troublemaker," Constance said with absolute certainty in her thin voice. "Some people are just born troublemakers. You look at them and think they are harmless, and you don't find out what they are really like until it is too late."

Aunty Lee watched the two old women walking slowly, arm in arm, away from the row of shops. All things considered, they were fortunate to live in Singapore, where safety and stability almost made up for the overcontrol that made them possible. At her age, Aunty Lee appreciated safety, stability, and clean tap water, but she could tell the next generation wanted more. Never having known chaos and instability, Josephine and Cherril did not know to fear it. And if they recklessly hurt themselves and others, weren't their parents to blame for overprotecting them?

Back in the café, Vallerie was lying in wait for Aunty Lee. "What are you scheming?"

"I'm very fond of Constance DelaVega," Aunty Lee said evenly. "I've known her daughter since she was a little girl. Josephine's been hurt before, getting involved with the wrong kind of man. I don't want her to be hurt by the wrong kind of man again." She spoke calmly, ignoring the other woman's question. Vallerie remained tense for a moment, watching for a response. Aunty Lee also waited.

"Mike Fitzgerald is definitely the wrong kind of man," Vallerie finally said. "For anybody."

She was clearly stressed, Aunty Lee saw, but not too stressed to have finished the plateful of little mango jellies.

Much later, when Mark and Selina were getting ready to leave, Mark stopped and stood quietly beside Aunty Lee.

"Is something wrong? Can I help?"

"Help with what? I don't have anything to do," Aunty Lee said. Hearing herself, she realized with a frisson of horror how coldly miserable she sounded, almost like Constance in fact. How long before what was automatic became a habit and then part of her personality? Fortunately Mark was too sensitive or insensitive to remark on this. "You have to eat," he pointed out.

"No, I don't," Aunty Lee said. "The doctor's always saying I should lose some weight. Maybe I should just stop eating and lose all my weight." But she was sounding more cheerful and Mark smiled.

"If you want to lose weight we can go out somewhere and get some fun exercise."

"How can I exercise? I have a twisted ankle!"

"It's not going to be in that thing forever. What would you most want to do if not for the leg?"

"I want to find out who killed that Allison woman. Then people will stop suspecting Cherril and Josephine and Brian and they will stop fighting with each other. And that Vallerie can go home satisfied."

Mark, to do him credit, only blinked. "How would you do that? What would you do that you can't do now?"

Aunty Lee thought about it. There was nothing, really. Except she had always given Nina directions and now Nina was busy running the café and keeping an eye on their temporary assistants. But now, even if Nina had the time, Aunty Lee could not think of any instructions for her.

"We all need routines and rituals to anchor us. You don't have any right now," Mark said. "I learned that in an online course. You need new rituals even if things change for a short period. That's why people enjoy holiday cruises and vacation stays, because they can set up new patterns. At home people follow routines without thinking. But now why not use this time to take the path less traveled?"

"In Singapore, finding a path with less people traveling means you are in the restricted army training area and somebody will shoot you!" Aunty Lee said with mock sulkiness. Mark laughed and planted a kiss on her forehead.

The son of two intelligent parents, Mark was actually very

smart. Aunty Lee suspected he allowed himself to be looked after by Selina because Selina needed someone to look after. Of course there were things that she *had* to do . . . or rather, things she wanted to get other people to do.

"Hurry up!" Selina called. "I'm not feeling very well, my stomach's still acting up. How long are you going to keep me waiting out here?"

Mark grinned and left Aunty Lee feeling better.

21

Lavender Casket Company

The Lavender Casket Company funeral director, Mr. Ping Chan, was on hand to welcome Aunty Lee and Vallerie personally. They were shown directly into his private office, past the tables of efficient assistants making arrangements for the dead that would make the living happiest.

Aunty Lee liked catering funerals almost as much as she enjoyed catering weddings. Funerals were less happy as occasions, of course, but there was far less chance of someone getting cold feet and backing out.

"In cases like this it can be difficult to avoid media attention completely. But we have very good relations with the press, given how much our clients spend on obituaries and memorial notes, so I am sure they will be reasonable. If you agree to let them take one or two tasteful shots of you with one of the wreaths with your sister's photograph on it, I am sure they will agree not to bother you any further," Ping Chan said earnestly, after Aunty Lee explained what they needed.

"No wreaths," Vallerie said. "I said so on the death announcement. No wreaths, no flowers, no big deal."

"But no matter what you put on the announcement people always send something. And it can be a comfort for the family."

"There's no family other than me. And I said Allison would not have wanted any flowers. She never saw the point of having dead flowers around dead people. And anyway, she was allergic."

Mr. Ping Chan changed the subject deftly. He was good at his job, Aunty Lee saw. As Vallerie spoke, he coaxed them both into comfortable chairs facing his desk. Little china cups of hot Chinese tea appeared in front of them, standing on either side of a box of tissues graced by a quilted green satin cover.

"This is a very nice photo but a bit old. Are you sure you don't want to use something a little more recent? You look so much like your sister, Miss Vallerie. Were you twins? It is always hard to lose a sister, but to lose a twin sister must be much, much worse."

"That's ridiculous!" Vallerie snapped. "Use your eyes, man! We don't look anything alike. Everyone always knew Allison was the slim, pretty one. Look at me. Do I look thin to you?"

Aunty Lee was listening with great interest. Polite convention dictated that when a woman asked you whether she looked thin you said yes without stopping to think or look at her. Mr. Ping Chan started to be polite—"Of course you . . ."—but he stopped with a wince at Vallerie's enraged "Bloody pisspot!" Especially as she picked up one of the wooden dolls lined up on his desk and thumped it hard on the surface. Now she stood breathing hard and staring at him as though daring him to say something that would give her an excuse to hit him with the doll. She jerked her arm away when Aunty Lee touched her lightly with two fingers (keeping an eye on the painted wooden doll/blunt instrument). Perhaps following her eyes the funeral director said, "That is a kokeshi doll. They were originally created to remember children lost before or during birth."

"What the hell do you want?" Again Vallerie thumped the dead baby memento on the desk. Ignoring her, Ping Chan's eyes went to Aunty Lee. She was impressed and realized his experience of dealing with emotionally traumatized relatives probably far exceeded her own.

"I was thinking I should plan my own funeral," Aunty Lee said vaguely. "I suppose it's silly. But if I plan everything first—flowers, no flowers, which photo to use—it would be easier for the people who have to make the arrangements, right?"

"Oh, not silly at all!" The funeral director leaped with alacrity back into the familiar subject. "There are many good reasons to preplan a funeral and write a will. It puts you in control of the arrangement and ensures that your wishes will be known and carried out. It allows you to take care of the expenses so as to relieve your family of financial burden. And it means that you can relieve your family of the need to make difficult decisions at a time of deep emotional stress."

Aunty Lee wrinkled her nose to think. "But what if I pay you all the money for my funeral and then your company closes down before I die. Then who is going to bury me? And what happens to the money?"

"You pay us for making the arrangements and recording your wishes. The payment is held by a third-party bank and comes to us only when our services become necessary."

"So even if inflation and price of wood for the coffin goes up, you still stick to the old price that we agreed on, yah?"

"Absolutely, Mrs. Lee. That is a very good observation. Because we absorb all inflation, it is in your interest to buy into our package while you're still young and then live as long as you can to make a profit!" He laughed, and with an eye on Vallerie, who had calmed down enough to drop the doll back on the desk, Aunty Lee laughed too.

"Maybe you can work out a package for me to consider?"

"It would be my pleasure."

However, Vallerie's impatience boiled over.

"That's stupid. You're already too old to make any kind of profit. He's just trying to con you. Just shut up and show us how much you are charging us for my sister's cremation at once!"

"We can speak later," Mr. Ping Chan said to Aunty Lee. "We must take care of our bereaved friends first." He made Aunty Lee feel like a special part of the caring community. Even though she was aware it was just good PR at work, Aunty Lee could not help but feel flattered and honored. Could she apply this to food service? Somehow "we must take care of our desperately starving friends first" didn't sound as classy and nurturing. Perhaps Cherril could come up with a better line.

"Some people leave instructions in their last will and testament," Ping Chan said. "I suppose you have already gone through everything your sister left?"

"Of course!" Vallerie said. "She left me a note. But it was too personal to show anyone else and I destroyed it."

"Perhaps you would like to look at our basic package . . ."

Later, sitting in the lift lobby with printouts of several options, Aunty Lee returned to the note Vallerie had mentioned. "I had a friend who made a new will every time she had to fly on a plane. Is that why Allison wrote you that note about what she wanted?"

"Allison always had very strong intuition," Vallerie said vaguely. "She always had to be prepared for anything because of the kids, you know? Because she knew she couldn't trust that man to watch out for them. And she was right—he's already taken up with that floozy."

Aunty Lee could tell the woman was deliberately provoking her, and part of her wanted to flare up hot and angry in defense of Josephine . . . but she decided she would whip up a really spicy curry once she got back home instead, something that would burn off her frustration.

As though picking up on this, Vallerie said abruptly, "Is there anything to eat around here? I'm hungry."

"There is supposed to be very good *laksa* in the market food center up the road—or if you like there is an ice-cream and waffles place just opened."

"Ice cream," Vallerie Love decided. "It's so bloody hot. But I hope they have real ice cream, none of those sweet corn, red bean, and, God forbid, durian things! Why don't you just close your eyes and pick one plan and be done with it. Just remember I'm not the one paying for it."

"Mike Fitzgerald will be paying for everything. In fact, he will be here in a while," Aunty Lee said. "Since he's paying he has to sign the contract."

Vallerie was already on her feet. "You set me up. Damn you, old fat bitch!"

"It's not a setup. That's why I'm telling you first. Josephine says Mike wants to meet you. After all, he has agreed to pay for your sister's funeral expenses. At least have a cup of tea with him to discuss the arrangements?"

"No, I don't want to see him." Vallerie made for the lift and jabbed at the call button.

"Is she going to walk out to the main road?" Mr. Ping Chan came up behind Aunty Lee. "Should we send someone after her? Or call a taxi?"

"No," said Aunty Lee. Vallerie had money to buy ice cream and would call for help if she needed it. And she wanted to talk to Mike Fitzgerald.

"So this is where the service is going to be. The Lavender Casket Company," Mike Fitzgerald said, looking around. He did not seem surprised to learn Vallerie had left on hearing he was coming. She had been avoiding him since learning he was on the island. Josephine, who arrived with Mike, looked relieved.

"She'll have to meet you at the funeral."

"If she turns up!"

Mike did not have any suggestions of his own but agreed to everything that Aunty Lee and Mr. Ping Chan suggested between them. It was much easier dealing with a bereaved husband than with a bereaved sister, Aunty Lee decided. Nor did he balk at the sum mentioned. If he could be this generous toward an ex-wife who had given him so much trouble, Aunty Lee began to feel better about Josephine ending up with him . . . provided, of course, that the man was not in the habit of being generous only after killing his wives.

"Thank you. It sounds nice. Allison liked things to be nice. She always wanted everything to be perfect. If anything wasn't perfect she would throw it out. I remember she told me she had a tiff with a boyfriend she once had. It was just a misunderstanding. After they sorted it out he wanted to get back together with her, but Allison said no, she didn't want to, because it had been a perfect relationship and after this breakup it wouldn't be perfect anymore. She used to write poetry when we were in school, did you know that? Very deep and depressing things. But she wasn't like that in person at all. She just thought that was how serious poetry was supposed to sound." Mike's eyes were vague, thinking of the young Allison.

"Is there any other family?" Mr. Ping Chan interposed smoothly. "Even if they cannot be present in Singapore, we might mention them in the service and make sure to send them a copy of the service program as a memento." He brandished a bright green folder displaying samples.

"Perhaps there's somewhere we can talk it over," Aunty Lee suggested.

"Of course—please take your time and discuss it. I'll be outside if you have any questions."

Josephine took the folder and pointed out one, then another to Mike, who said, "Nice, very nice," with unseeing eyes.

"Her parents are both dead, I understand," Aunty Lee prompted.

"Yes. About ten—no, twelve years ago. Very tragic or very romantic, depending how you look at it. Mrs. Love had some kind of cancer. In her throat and spreading everywhere by the time they found it. Mr. Love just quit his job and they lived on his savings while he nursed her. Then the day after she died he went home and killed himself. OD'd on his wife's painkillers and sleeping pills. I heard he just swallowed everything that was left. It was a huge mess of course with the bills and everything, but my parents and the other neighbors all chipped in and helped sort it all out. We had been married just over a year at the time, and we were living in London, but Allie went back to help see to things. She was so mad at her old dad for taking the coward's way out, but I remember my own dad saying the old man had been on duty nonstop around the clock twenty-four hours a day, three hundred and sixty-five days a year, and he was probably just tired. And my mum saying he loved her so much, he didn't want to live without her. Romantic in a way. But anyway, the entire old neighborhood and the council chipped in to help. It was still that sort of place where they remembered growing up during the war and didn't trust Germans and Communists, let alone Chinese dollars and Indian satellites. You can imagine what a shock it was for Allie, growing up there and then ending up in Singapore!

"Allie was also upset because she always thought she would get her parents' old house, but it had to be sold to pay off the mortgage and medical bills. She'd always said she hated it, called it slummy, but when she left me she had nowhere to go. She tried to sue the council and bailiffs for selling it without her permission and cheating her, but it didn't come to anything."

"Poor woman," Aunty Lee said. "Losing your childhood home can be terrible. Especially so soon after losing your parents."

Mike laughed wryly. "Allie once said she was glad her mum was dead because she couldn't stand being around her, her mum had criticized her too much. And our Gemma said— she was about ten years old—that Allie criticized people too much too. And Allie got so furious, she was shouting and crying about how Gemma twisted her words and attacked her . . ." His words trailed away. "It was crazy. That's when I first realized something was wrong. Allie was screaming at Gemma that no one would ever want to marry a stupid fat bitch like her. Gemma, our beautiful baby girl . . ." His face twisted in pain. Josephine rolled her eyes, but discreetly.

The Love sisters used the same insults, Aunty Lee thought.

"The children." Mike ran a hand through his hair. "I'm thinking of flying them over for the funeral, but I don't know. It's a long way for them to come alone. I'll talk to my sister."

"They are staying with your sister?"

"Yes. With my sister Rosalie's family. She has two of her own so it's easier for them to fit in. And my other sister, Jeanette, doesn't have kids, but she and her partner take all four of them out on weekends."

Aunty Lee thought she saw why Allison had been cross with Vallerie for not having anything to do with her children. She would have been calculating how much more time Mike's sisters (one married, one not) spent with her children than her own sister did.

"I gave Allison everything she asked for in the divorce settlement. But I had it put into a trust for her. So she would always have enough to live on but she couldn't do anything stupid with the capital. I even set up a board of trustees that I wasn't part of. It was all to protect her—and to protect my children from having to support her. Because she couldn't be trusted.

"I tried to stand by her, of course I did. The big mess in Singapore, I honestly didn't see what all the fuss was about. If it were up to me I would have kept Lola. But Allie had the dog humanely put down. If that was against the law in Singapore, well, then the vet should have explained it to her. I was getting flak from my boss, from the department head, saying clients were not happy to have me handling their cases . . . they told me, 'You don't just barge into other countries and tell them they aren't running things the right way.' Allie always tried to help people do better. That's all she wanted to do, you know. But frankly I was glad to leave. But it didn't stop there."

"Oh?"

"Tell Aunty Lee about the other animals," Josephine prompted. "After you got back to England."

"There's no proof Allie had anything to do with any of them."

"Just tell her. So she knows what you were putting up with. Vallerie's been telling her horrible stories about you—hasn't she?"

Aunty Lee waited expectantly.

Apparently other animals had died inexplicably after the Fitzgeralds returned to England: A neighbor's dog that barked in the night was found dead. So was the cat Gemma brought home. And after Allison had a tiff with the chairman of their Actively Involved Parents group, both his dogs died.

Aunty Lee shook her head. "Poor woman."

Mike looked surprised, then gratified.

Josephine looked peevishly at Aunty Lee. "You wouldn't say that if it was your dog she poisoned!"

"Look, there was no proof—" Mike started to say, but a manicured fingernail digging into his arm stopped him. Aunty Lee felt a stab of disquiet. But why? So many women controlled what their husbands were allowed to say.

"So do you know if the police have come up with anything new?" Josephine leaned forward to ask Aunty Lee. "How long can they afford to keep Mike under suspicion without any proof? Have you got any idea what the police are doing now?"

"I'm trying to get them to help me track down a moon cake box," Aunty Lee said.

"A moon cake box?"

"Like the one that was in Allison's room, but Vallerie is sure neither she nor her sister bought it."

"And you think that box of moon cakes had something to do with Allison's death? That's absurd! That's so freaking crazy!" Josephine laughed harshly.

Mike looked at Josephine in surprise, but Aunty Lee shook her head. "I'm just curious where it came from. The cleaners took the moon cake box because it was pretty and they thought it was going to be thrown away, and Vallerie got so angry with them. I thought if I can find out where it came from, I'll buy a box of moon cakes and give it to them. But also . . ."

"Also?"

"Selina hasn't been feeling very well. She has been having stomach trouble and thinks it's food poisoning. I know it's not from my food and I want to make sure it's not from the moon cakes people gave her. Nowadays so many places use ready-made lotus and red bean paste filling. If there is something wrong with one batch, it can affect so many places!"

"Unless someone's trying to poison her," Mike joked. No one laughed.

Back at Aunty Lee's Delights, Aunty Lee filled Nina and Cherril in on everything that had happened at the Lavender Casket Company. Vallerie was at the kitchen counter arranging platters of sweet, colorful *kuehs*. Her spurt of independence, or perhaps finally having fixed a date for her sister's funeral service, seemed to have done her good, and she was humming softly to herself.

"She took a taxi back and came in to ask me to pay the driver," Cherril told Aunty Lee.

Aunty Lee watched Vallerie thoughtfully. "The problem is we all think we are writing our own recipes, but we are also ingredients in other people's recipes. We just have to find out who the dish is for."

Cherril also looked at Vallerie. "There's something about her that gives me the creeps. If she doesn't want to see Mike or Josephine, why is she staying around? Why all the song and dance about getting Mike to take care of things and then refusing to see him?"

Aunty Lee thought she knew where Vallerie was coming from. "I think she wants Mike to take care of Allison's funeral so she can believe he still cares for her. And this way Mike can tell the children that in spite of the divorce he took care of their mother at the end. One day he may be glad of that. So Vallerie may be doing him a favor."

Her young partner studied Aunty Lee. Seeing possible good outcomes was a choice, not hopeless naïveté, she realized.

"That's true," Cherril said.

Whether or not they believed this, they both felt better for having said it.

22

Different Realities

The terrible nausea seemed to be easing up. Exhausted, he felt tightness in the muscles of his face and neck, and there was a raw, metallic taste in his painfully dry mouth. And someone shaking him—

"Damn you, wake up. What's your password?"

"It hurts—"

"Your computer. What's your password?"

"J-O-S-1-9-8-2."

Brian kept his eyes closed as he answered. He knew he was lying on the dark green leather couch in his study, that there was someone there with him, that something very important was happening, but he couldn't focus on what it was. He felt his arms and legs stiffening and jerking, and flashes of light shot across the insides of his eyelids. He tried to open his eyes but it was too much effort.

Was he really at home? A strong smell of what seemed to be chemical cleaner distracted him. He knew there was something very important he had to do—he had to explain why they had to go to the police right away. They could go to the Bukit Tinggi Neighborhood Police Post where Inspector Salim would understand. They had no alternative now that Aunty Lee had told the police that he had been at Allison's hotel the day she died. If only Aunty Lee had talked to him first he could have given her the explanation they had prepared . . . though he could not remember what it was now. And he could not understand why Josephine had made things worse. She had also gone to the police and said, "We weren't together all of that day. I didn't think much of it until I heard Brian told the police that we had been together all morning till we got to the café. It's not a big deal, I just want to get it right." He had thought Josephine liked him, but she had just gotten him deeper into trouble. Why? Had she been afraid of ending up as his alibi for murder? But Josephine had liked him, hadn't she? Hadn't Josephine spent so much time volunteering with the Animal ReHomers all those years ago because she had liked him?

But it had been all those years ago. Even if Josephine had liked him then, he hadn't been good enough for her. She deserved so much more than he could give her as a poor animal rights organizer. His throat hurt and he tried to swallow, but he could not remember how to. Brian had tried to become someone worthy of Josephine DelaVega. He had built up a business, made a name for himself, and years later when they met again he had dared to hope he had a chance, that it had all been worthwhile. Had it all been worthwhile?

Brian tried to shake his head but the movement sent a painful shudder down his whole body. For some reason the puppy that had started the whole business came into his mind. Lola had been a gentle, playful, and good-natured little dog. The animal psychiatrist who screened her had described her as sociable and good with children. There had been no signs of the aggression Allison complained about.

"Your printer's out of ink," an annoyed voice said. "Where are your printer cartridges? Don't you keep spares, dammit?"

Brian moaned softly. He felt as though he was sinking underwater. It was an effort to breathe and he could no longer feel his arms and legs. He heard drawers being pulled open and slammed shut, the sound of things falling. He tried to surface but sank back in.

He felt the puppy Lola nuzzling him and then she was there with her little wet snub nose and goofy, trusting grin. Sorry, Brian wanted to say to her, sorry. I really thought they would give you a good home. And Allison was there too, looking at him as though she blamed him, but Brian was not sorry she was dead. Then Josephine was leaning over him, looking at him. I love you, Brian tried to say. I did all this for you. But Josephine was not listening to him. He tried to reach out to her but it was no use. He was sinking and suffocating and could not remember how to breathe. Something had gone wrong, very wrong.

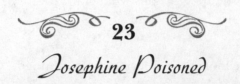

23
Josephine Poisoned

Not unusually for a weekday evening in the suburbs, Aunty Lee's Delights was empty of customers by nine thirty that night. Vallerie joined Aunty Lee and Nina, who had seated themselves at one of the larger tables with a stack of napkins to be folded.

"It's quite a nice place you have here when people aren't barging in and out," Vallerie observed.

"People barging in and out and paying," Nina said. But aware of Vallerie's nonpaying status, she said it to be heard only by Aunty Lee.

"The police asked again if I want to get in touch with anybody in America. Why would I? They don't have any idea what's been going on here. I can't go to them for support. Anyway, it won't make any difference to them that Allison's dead or that that's what those evil animal activists wanted all along!"

"They didn't even want that dog to die, of course they wouldn't want your sister to die," Aunty Lee pointed out.

"That blasted dog! That's what started everything! I hate dogs!"

"All dogs?"

Aunty Lee looked at Vallerie, who continued: "Can you believe back in England the stupid girl starts saying she wants a puppy again and that fool Mike says why not—my sister, Allison, said no way in hell. No way she was having another animal under her roof."

"Can I get you some tea?" Aunty Lee offered. "I mean, would you like Nina to get you some tea?" She was not trying to stop Vallerie from talking—far from it. But when people got too angry it could be difficult to understand what they were saying. Aunty Lee appreciated the emotional impact, of course. But you needed to have facts, like protein, in a dish to make it worth savoring. And there was something in what Vallerie had just said that sounded slightly off to her, like a spot of soft rot on a cucumber. What was it? "My sister, Allison, said no way"? Why should that be strange? Aunty Lee was irritated when Cherril, who had been checking updates on her mobile, interrupted to ask if she could have a private word with her. Cherril's "private words" were usually about cost comparisons and outsourcing the soothingly repetitive kitchen tasks that Aunty Lee found so therapeutic.

"Here is private, what," Aunty Lee said. "What do you want to tell me?" Cherril might not want to discuss her business plans in front of Vallerie, which would put them off for a little while.

But then Cherril had been looking stressed and miserable for the last few days. There had been so much excitement going on that Aunty Lee had not tried to figure out what was wrong . . . surely all that, along with Vallerie's unhappy presence, was enough to make anyone with less stamina than Aunty Lee feel down!

However . . . "It's important," Cherril insisted. And what Cherril told her made Aunty Lee decide the napkins could wait till tomorrow. She and Cherril would bring a tray—"Just cover with cling film"—of leftovers and *kuehs* to the police station immediately. Late as it was, there was a good chance Inspector Salim would still be there, studying in the privacy of his office. If they were less lucky there would be someone on duty who would be glad enough of their food offering to call him for them.

Salim was still working in his office but willing enough to see them, and the sergeant on duty let them in.

"Brian was waiting in the hotel lobby when he called me to say they would be late. Josephine had gone to the ladies'. Allison had called and asked them to pick her up from her hotel for the meeting. He was hoping Allison had changed her mind or realized how hopeless it was and wanted to yell at them so as not to lose face before withdrawing her suit. But when they went to the hotel she wasn't in the room, and the guy at the hotel said Allison had already left. He was certain because he had called the taxi for her himself."

Salim stared at Cherril. "Why didn't he say something earlier? Why didn't you?"

"Smart men can still be stupid boys inside," Aunty Lee said. "But if he is telling the truth now, that means both Brian and Josephine were at the hotel when Allison was killed. They might have seen something."

"Or he might have killed her," Salim said. "Brian Wong could have killed her while Josephine was in the ladies', then pretended to have been in the lobby all along. Women can take so long in the loo. Plenty of time to go up, commit a murder, and come back down."

"You wonder why Brian didn't want to say anything sooner?" Cherril asked crossly. "He probably knew you would suspect him like this!"

"But you say he wants to say something now?"

"He said he talked to Josie and they agreed they wanted me to tell Aunty Lee and see what she suggests."

Salim looked at Aunty Lee, who smiled sweetly at him though she seemed disturbed.

"You know I have to talk to Brian and Josephine about this. But first, has either of them said anything to you? On or off the record?"

"No. You know I would have told you. As soon as Cherril told me I straightaway told her she must come here and tell you." Aunty Lee still did not believe that Brian and Josephine could have had anything to do with Allison Love's death—or the death of the young vet.

"When are you going to talk to them? Do you have to tell them that we told you? Will you tell us what they say?"

Inspector Salim touched his intercom and instructed, "Get me Josephine DelaVega on the phone."

But Inspector Salim did not get to talk to Josephine that night.

Aunty Lee called him in great excitement. "Josephine's been poisoned! She's in observation at NUH and they think she is going to be all right. They wanted to pump out her stomach but she said no need. Connie—her mother—just told me. She said Mike told her it was the moon cake because it's the only thing she ate that he didn't. Luckily she stopped eating when it tasted funny. They sent the leftover cake for testing but no results yet."

Josephine was under observation at the National University Hospital. Just before it was time to go to her parents' house for dinner, Mike had found her curled up on the bathroom floor moaning in pain. Josephine told him she had vomited and was all right, but Mike was not taking any risks. He called her parents and rushed her to the nearest hospital.

Commissioner Raja and Aunty Lee found Connie and Jojo DelaVega with Mike Fitzgerald in the corridor outside Josephine's hospital room.

"More questions?" Mike Fitzgerald said. The tension was clear in his voice and he looked as though he would have liked to be anywhere in the world other than Singapore. It was natural, Aunty Lee thought, given that Singapore had accused him of murdering his ex-wife and might yet accuse him of poisoning his current girlfriend. At least Josephine's parents looked as though they had decided to do their best to accept him. Losing a daughter to an *ang moh* husband was nothing compared to the threat of losing her altogether. Mike looked as though he had not shaved in some time, though Aunty Lee knew that with Caucasian men it was difficult to tell. "Josie's all right, thank god. But I really don't think she's up to answering any more questions," Mike said in response to the question Commissioner Raja was starting to ask. He added, "The hospital took the rest of that damn cake for testing."

"We just want to make sure she is all right," Aunty Lee said. "Raja is my dinner date. We were just getting ready to go out for dinner when we got the news. He drove me over here because I wanted to make sure she was all right." She looked around them at the open door of the room. "Is Josephine awake?"

"I'm awake . . ." Josephine called weakly from inside the room. "Aunty Lee, is that you? Please come in. I just told my parents to go out and get some dinner. Tell them you'll stay with me while they go and eat."

Aunty Lee made her way into the room without waiting for a second invitation. Josephine, propped up in the hospital bed with a saline drip in her arm, looked tired but not dangerously so.

"The doctor said it was lucky that I thought the cake tasted funny and didn't eat more of it. I probably already vomited most of it up before it could affect me. They pumped out my stomach just in case, just to be on the safe side."

"Moon cakes?" Aunty Lee's attention was caught.

Josephine said the box of moon cakes had been left on a

table in her shop and she assumed a satisfied client or delivery person in a hurry had left it. There were many food gifts being sent out before the Mid-Autumn Festival, so she didn't think much of it. "I didn't have time for lunch, so I decided to taste it. It tasted a bit funny but I thought it was just some fancy flavoring. Then I started to feel sick. I told Mike to call my parents to cancel dinner but he told them he was bringing me to hospital."

In Singapore in September moon cakes were everywhere. Most would say it was impossible to trace the supplier of a particular moon cake. But Aunty Lee remembered the box in the hotel room and wondered.

"At least that proves Josie didn't have anything to do with Allison's death!" Mike Fitzgerald said. "They're after her too. Are we just supposed to wait around while somebody picks us off one by one?"

Commissioner Raja started to say something, but as Aunty Lee held up an imperious hand he remembered he was there as a chaperone rather than as a police officer and held his tongue.

"You think this is linked to what happened to your wife, Allison," Aunty Lee said. "And the vet."

"Of course it is. What else could it be?"

"What exactly happened when you were in Singapore? Can you think of anybody else who was close to Allison and might have got involved?"

"My bosses laughed about it at first and told me to shut up and lie low. They said it would blow over. Boy, were they wrong. Allison couldn't shut up. She defended herself, which only fanned the flames. She got very angry with me for not being more upset; in fact she accused me of being behind the attacks, of being in league with the web vigilantes. She wasn't well. That was all part of her breakdown; I can totally see that now. She thought everybody was against her. She even blew up at Nick for saying he had liked the dog. She slapped him so hard I was afraid she might have snapped his neck. And then she tried to . . . but luckily Mrs. Ameeta—she's a retiree who lives next door to us in the UK—she called me at work and I got back in time . . . But no, no one else was involved. She refused to talk to anyone else.

"But we hadn't talked for some time, just through the kids, you know what I mean? I don't even know how much she knew about me and Josephine." He smiled and took Josephine's hand. "If Allison suspected that I cared about you she would have gone crazy. So I'm guessing she didn't know."

It might have been someone out to hurt Mike Fitzgerald who had killed Allison and tried to poison Josephine, Aunty Lee thought. But why would that person have attacked the vet?

"What happened that day when your neighbor Mrs. Ameeta phoned you at work?" Aunty Lee already felt a kinship with the woman. Nosy old aunties from all over the world had to stick together and follow up on each other's stories.

"Good thing she called me. Allison had locked the children up in one of the bedrooms and was trying to set the house on fire. She had stacked up newspapers and started burning them outside the room but it didn't spread. It totally destroyed the flooring and the walls in the corridor and it cost me a bundle to fix it up, but that's one thing about old brick houses: they're not so easy to burn down. And because she locked them in, the door blocked the fire from getting into the room, thank god. And Gemma had the sense to open the window for air and to stop Nick from jumping out. When I got back Allison was in the kitchen trying to start up a fire there as well. Luckily we're not on gas or she would have Sylvia Plath'ed them. I tell you, reading poetry doesn't do anybody any good. It just makes the crazy ones crazier. And Mrs. Ameeta called the cops after calling me, so they turned up around the same time as I did and they got the fire rescue people in and put out everything—another bloody mess. I swear the foam stuff made a greater mess of things than the fire did. The kids were okay, which was the main thing. I owe Mrs. Ameeta big time, I tell you. Big time. Allison couldn't start up a proper fire to save her life, but who knows what she would have tried next. The police wanted to take Allison in, of course. And she started screaming that the police were against her and were assaulting her in her own home . . . One of the policemen asked if she was on medication. Nick said, 'Don't hurt Mom,' but Gemma wasn't having any of that. She said, straight out and in front of everybody, 'You tried to kill us, I hate you.' After that is it any wonder I wouldn't give her time alone with the kids? Mrs. Ameeta watches the two of them after school when I'm at work. She gives them their tea and calls the police if Allison shows up and throws things at her house." He turned to Josephine. "That's why I had to keep us a secret. I didn't want her starting on you too. And the fastest way of making her do that would have been to let her know I cared about you."

Josephine had been looking shocked, but that last sentence melted her. She put her hand on his arm and smiled at him.

To Aunty Lee's surprise she found herself liking Mike Fitzgerald. It was difficult to judge people who survived great natural disasters, and Allison certainly sounded like a great natural disaster.

"Why didn't she move on with her life? What was she living on?"

Josephine took Mike's hand in both of hers protectively. Allison might be dead, but her hatred still echoed. Josephine's parents, who had come in to stand on the other side of the bed, joined hands, and her father laid a gentle hand on the corner of his daughter's bed as though to cover it with his protection.

"I was still giving her an allowance. She hadn't been able to get a job since Singapore. She went for some interviews, but then every time they got to the subject of previous employment, Allison would go off on a rant and then it was 'there's the door, don't call us, we'll call you.' It was like she didn't want to move on, you know? That puppy killer thing was the first time she had been in any kind of spotlight. The problem here was that everybody was looking at her. Then back in England she couldn't get used to nobody looking. Being notorious was the closest she'd come to being famous.

It was like a drug rush almost. I think that's why she kept harping on it.

"Anyway, I was paying all her bills. Her rent, her car, the medical bills—though she wasn't turning up at the consultations. She was supposed to go for a full psychiatric consultation and follow-ups. It was one of the conditions of her getting off with a fine. And of course I didn't press any charges and I persuaded Mrs. Ameeta not to either."

It showed a different side of the man from what Aunty Lee had been seeing. But if Allison Love had been his burden even after their divorce, it just gave him more reason to murder her. And of course it wasn't just Mike who had reason to want Allison Love dead—Josephine DelaVega had a very good reason too. Even if Mike could afford to wait for Allison to settle down, Josephine and her baby did not have that luxury.

"If someone wanted to send out moon cakes to her clients, where would she order them from?" Aunty Lee asked as soon as she got home. There was no sign of Vallerie, and Nina had been preparing vegetables in front of the television while waiting for her.

Nina did not pause in her tailing of bean sprouts. "Clients she wants to impress or to say thank you to?"

"Both I suppose. Without spending too much. She's doing well but she's not one of those big banks sending out gold pieces inside moon cake boxes." Aunty Lee sat down on the sofa and swung her legs up.

"Madame, you sit down now very hard to get up later! You should shower and go to sleep! Traditional or snow skin or crazy new recipes?"

"She didn't say they were special, so I think they must have been traditional."

"Probably somewhere like Bao's New Moons, where they personalize and deliver and don't charge too much. And Belinda Bao is a friend of Josephine's, right?"

"That's what I thought." Aunty Lee was pleased with the confirmation as well as with how far Nina had come. When Nina first arrived in Singapore she had not liked moon cakes, finding them far too heavy for her taste. Since then she had become quite a connoisseur.

Aunty Lee herself did not order moon cakes to send to friends and clients. She always baked a few herself, just to keep her hand in. She only made the traditional sort with salted egg yolks and lotus paste because they were the ones she had learned to make when ML Lee teased her for not knowing how to make a basic Chinese cake. Aunty Lee had always loved a culinary challenge. She would get in touch with Belinda Bao. It was too late to try that night, and anyway there was no hurry.

24

Changing Portraits and Perspectives

"Miss Vallerie not awake yet?" Nina was back from the wet market. She appreciated the convenience of Singapore's twenty-four-hour supermarkets but, like Aunty Lee, her first loyalty was to food that appeared according to daily as well as yearly rhythms.

"She hasn't come downstairs yet."

"I put the *chee cheong fun* I bought for you on the marble table outside. And there's some sweet bean curd and fresh *youtiao*. You should eat while it is still hot. Shall I call Miss Vallerie?"

If she could be persuaded to try it, Aunty Lee knew Vallerie would enjoy the smooth, silky sheets of *chee cheong fun*— rice paste rolled around juicy fillings of shrimp and scallops and steamed. And she would definitely enjoy the deep-fried crispy *youtiao,* or dough fritters, even if she rejected the delicate, sweetened tofu pudding.

"I'm sure she will be down soon," Aunty Lee said. She did not feel up to facing Vallerie yet. On hearing Josephine had been poisoned, Vallerie had abruptly declared her intention of leaving Singapore immediately, not even waiting for her sister's funeral and cremation. She had asked Aunty Lee to book her a ticket to London as soon as possible, without even a pretense of offering to pay. Perhaps she felt Singapore owed her board, lodging, and travel costs for her sister's death. Or, Aunty Lee thought more likely, Vallerie simply chose not to think about it. From what Josephine and Mike said, Allison had shared this blindness to her own responsibilities. Not for the first time, Aunty Lee wondered about the parents and environment that had produced these sisters. Or had coming east out of their comfort zone brought out this side of them? But Vallerie had moved away from England on her own years ago . . .

"Why London?" Aunty Lee wondered aloud. "Why would she go to London now?"

"Why not London?" Nina came in with a bucket of clams and other things on her mind. She wanted to get her boss and guest fed so she could start on the work for the day at the café. "You buy me free ticket to London I also want to go. See? I found stingray and *lala* today." *Lala,* or thin-shelled clams, were a seasonal treat that didn't last long, so finding them in the market automatically made them a special.

Aunty Lee was distracted by the prospect. "We can steam with golden mushroom and lemongrass, or just fry with salt and pepper and garlic. Better put on the website so people know that today we have."

"Already put on the website, madame!" Nina's Internet prowess might make Selina uncomfortable, but her menu updates boosted customer flow to Aunty Lee's Delights.

"I remember as children we would go wading on the mud-flats at low tide with our little spades and pails digging for these. We called them baby bamboo clams. And my father would do a cookout and throw them onto the grill next to his steak and *satay,* and we would grab them off once they opened . . ."

"Before cooking, the *lala* must scrub clean properly." Nina was already getting down to it with a fierce-looking brush. "Then we can leave them to soak in salt water until time to cook for lunch. And we can cook some with your chili sauce, madame."

"*Sambal lala!*" Aunty Lee said. "*Lala* with my ginger and yellow bean sauce. Special seafood noodles with *lala* and — did you get fresh prawns and scallops, Nina?"

"Of course got, madame." Nina sounded offended to be asked.

At the café that day, Vallerie eschewed the clams but agree-ably arranged cubes of colored cake and agar-agar on large, round, woven wicker trays lined with parchment, eating any that she deemed too large, too small, or lopsided. She did not look up as Aunty Lee limped around the table to look at her handiwork, though Aunty Lee could tell the woman was aware of her; her exaggerated focus on the dessert tray gave that away. It was beautiful, the bright colors of the *kuehs* contrasting with the translucent jellied agars. The woman had an artist's eye for color.

"It looks beautiful," Aunty Lee said. "Good job."

Vallerie looked surprised, but she automatically dismissed the compliment. "They're just stupid cakes. Fattening."

"Once imported ingredients like sugar, butter, and white flour were expensive so cakes and desserts like this were a luxury, only made for special occasions, to show people had money. Nowadays people can afford the ingredients but they cannot afford the time. Making *kueh* like that is a dying art nowadays. Did you make your own cakes in California?"

Vallerie looked blank for a moment. "Of course not. There are professionals there. And they make beautiful cakes, gâteaux and things. It's not just homemade stuff like here!"

After lunch, when Salim's dropping in prompted Vallerie to go back to the house for a nap, Aunty Lee asked the young inspector to look up Vallerie Love's connections in America. All along they had only been trying to find connections to Allison in Singapore and England, and all they came up with was that she had filed complaints against her neighbors, school boards, and temporary employers.

"The sister? Why?"

"Vallerie Love talks a lot about her sister but nothing about herself," Aunty Lee said. "I think we should find out more about her."

"Ah." Salim thought he understood. "She is ready to go

home and you want to make sure there is somebody there who will look after her."

Sometimes Aunty Lee thought the young man was too nice to be a good policeman. Surely you had to have a more suspicious mind and sharper nose to do a good job. But then that was why there were people like herself to sniff around and make sure all the nice people blindly following set recipes didn't get thrown off by bad ingredients. Because Aunty Lee did not trust suppliers without checking out their sources, especially when the products smelled a little funny . . .

"I just want to get in touch with someone, anybody, who might know Vallerie. She's lived in America for how many years—about thirteen years at least? She must have made some friends there."

"That's true. You think Miss Vallerie is going to go home soon?"

"She says she wants to go as soon as possible. She doesn't want to attend her sister's funeral if the husband is going to be there—and he is. And you people—the police—aren't keeping her here, right?"

"Oh no. We told her she is free to go as long as we can reach her."

"I was thinking, sometimes the best way to find out what somebody is like is to see what kind of friends they have. I asked Jacky about numbers called from their hotel room, but they didn't make any."

"Once people buy local SIM cards no need to use expensive hotel phones," Nina said. "But Miss Vallerie used the

phone in the house, right? Can check on Madame Silly's machine. The one that records who is using your phone line."

Nina had learned over the years that the strangest of
Aunty Lee's hypotheses sometimes came true. But more im-
portantly where she was concerned, if Aunty Lee was trying
to do long-distance detecting, she was less likely to be trying
to climb up ladders with a damaged ankle.

"Selina is monitoring your calls?" Salim wondered why
Aunty Lee did not seem more horrified.

"That Silly-Nah means well," Aunty Lee said generously.
"She set up the machine to monitor calls because she said I
don't know who is Nina talking to when I am not there. But
she doesn't know how to get the information out of the machine, only Nina knows how to, so it's okay. Nina, later you
try to get any numbers that weren't called by you or by me,
okay?"

Some of Aunty Lee's wilder suppositions were not worth
contradicting. Besides, Nina was curious about what the
friends in L.A. had to say about Vallerie too.

"Now is not busy, I can go back and look—" But before
Nina had finished and before Salim had managed to find
an excuse to walk Nina back to the house (one drawback of
living in one of the safest estates in one of the safest cities
in the world), Anne Peters pushed open the door and half
stepped, half fell through it.

The look on her friend's face brought Aunty Lee back two
years to when Marianne Peters had died, and for a moment
she froze, unable to go to her.

"My dog is very sick. Tammy is very sick. They say she may not make it!"

Tracing calls was forgotten as Aunty Lee sat with a sobbing Anne Peters. Tammy was still alive, but barely, and staying over at a Mount Pleasant vet clinic with a drip in her. Anne had brought her to the twenty-four-hour emergency clinic the previous night and come straight to the café when they told her to go home and leave Tammy to them. Even Josephine's poisoning (which Aunty Lee was not convinced hadn't been accidental or imagined) was dwarfed by this state of emergency.

"I don't know what happened. Tammy was fine all day. Then after dinner she started vomiting and there was blood oozing out of her hind end. The vet said she may have eaten rat poison or something. All they can do is try to rehydrate her and keep her going until she gets stronger. I should have watched her better! Rosie, I can't bear to lose her too!"

Neither of them noticed as Salim answered a call, stepped outside for better reception or privacy, and came back in. Nina hurried over when she saw him go over to where the two older women still sat.

"Not now, Salim," Nina said. Then she saw something in his face. "What is it?"

"Brian Wong is dead."

"What? How?"

"He killed himself."

"No!" Aunty Lee shook her head.

Even Anne looked up, shocked. "Are you sure?"

"He left a message on his computer before doing it. Confessing that he killed Allison Love and Samantha Kang."

"Why would Brian commit suicide?" Aunty Lee asked even as her mind darted around various possibilities. Had Brian killed Allison in an attempt to frame Mike? Had the two dead women known something about him that he had killed them to conceal? Had he been so hopelessly in love with Josephine all these years he would rather die than see her married to Mike Fitzgerald? Even if any of those reasons was true . . .

"Why would he kill himself now?"

"Mike Fitzgerald is not a suspect in Brian Wong's death," Salim continued without answering the question. "He has been released without charge."

Brian's suicide note, written on his computer and sent to Inspector Salim, filled in details that Josephine's account had left out. The vet, Samantha Kang, had sent him a note the day after Allison's murder. She said she had to talk to him, urgently, about someone suspicious she had seen. He guessed Dr. Kang had seen him in the hotel and was intending to blackmail him. He killed her to prevent her from talking.

"The fire at the vet clinic happened the morning that Allison was killed," Aunty Lee said. "Samantha Kang couldn't have been at the hotel that day. She was at the clinic, rescuing animals from the fire, and then they would have taken her to the hospital, right?"

"Guilty conscience," Nina said.

The dead vet must have been talking about somebody she saw at the clinic during or before the fire, Aunty Lee thought. That would have been uppermost in her mind. But if Brian had been at Allison's hotel, then whom had Dr. Samantha Kang seen?

"The left side a bit down. No, that's too much. Yes—yes, that's right. Now come down carefully."

Nina descended and folded the stepladder as Aunty Lee studied the casual photograph of ML in a light blue polo shirt. Here he had been caught off guard, squinting against the sun as he turned from opening the car door. It brought her back to a time when cars were already air-conditioned but car doors still had to be opened with keys. Mark's wife would have something to say when she saw it; she always dropped snide comments when Aunty Lee changed pictures around in her house or café. This time it would probably be something like "The frame probably cost more than the picture!" or "I'm sure Pa would prefer a more dignified picture."

They thought she rotated ML's photos because there were too many of them to put up all at once. Several times Mark, prompted by Selina, had suggested Aunty Lee just pick and stick to her favorite portrait shots of his father rather than keep switching them around. "Selina says it makes her dizzy. Why not just put up the studio portraits with all of us in them?"

But though all photos of the late ML Lee were favorites of Aunty Lee's, she particularly liked those that captured him in unposed moments—those moments she would have taken for granted if he had been in front of her, because we seldom notice or appreciate what we see every day. And that was the reason Aunty Lee switched ML's pictures around. When she missed her late husband most, looking at his photographs helped her see him anew. And after the shocking news of Brian's suicide she needed him more than ever.

"You should really think about moving somewhere more convenient," Nina said, picking up the ladder. She had returned from the café to find the folding ladder out and her already limping boss looking guilty. If Aunty Lee had managed to get the ladder out of the storeroom more quickly, she might have finished before Nina got back. "Somewhere smaller. Where can hang pictures lower. And got railings for old people!"

"Maybe."

They both knew Aunty Lee was never likely to move.

Rosie Lee had lived in other houses before this one. Before single-family high-rise apartments became more common than extended family dwellings, most had taken for granted the presence of multiple relatives who came to Singapore to work or study or simply because they had nowhere else to go. And she had not felt reluctant to leave the houses run by her grandmother or mother. Indeed, each previous departure had signaled a new stage in her life and been eagerly looked forward to. She had outgrown all her previous homes before she left them. Until now the move had always been toward, rather than away from, something. Perhaps you had to lose somebody in a house before you felt truly attached to it.

Aunty Lee looked at the photo she had just taken down. Much as she liked it, she did not feel as close to ML when he was standing in formal wear next to Inche Yusof bin Ishak, the first president of the Republic of Singapore, and surrounded by foreign dignitaries. Now, as she caught her reflection in the glass front of the portrait, she was the one who looked like a shadowy ghost. As a ghost, she thought she could still pass for a wife of about the same age as the late ML Lee had been in this photo. Would the day come when she looked into this dear face, more familiar to her than her own, and see a much younger stranger? The thought upset her.

"Let me just sort out this mess with Jojo and Connie's girl," Aunty Lee whispered. "Then I'll be ready to join you." But now as she stared into the reflection of her eyes she already looked old—old, useless, helpless, and unwanted. Even Nina, who had not returned from putting away the stepladder and was probably trying to get the latest news from Salim on the phone, would be better off without having to look after her. And if she died now, if there was some unimaginable existence beyond, would her ML recognize her in the old woman she had become? And anyway, wouldn't he prefer to be with his first wife who had died young? Her reflection was looking too upset. The rational part of Aunty Lee's mind warned, Snap out of this before you make yourself miserable for nothing! But then a strong, calm thought came into her head in ML's voice: *Here we neither marry nor are given in marriage. Here we are like angels in heaven.* It was so clear that for a moment she thought someone had spoken.

"But I don't know what angels are like," Aunty Lee said softly.

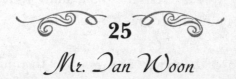

25
Mr. Ian Woon

"Mr. Ian Woon speaking."

The name sounded Chinese but the voice was West Coast American. Aunty Lee wondered whether the speaker was very young or very insecure, to introduce himself with a "Mister" when answering the phone. Then again, it might just be an American custom she was not familiar with.

"My name is Mrs. Rosie Lee. I am phoning from Singapore so no small talk please, this is costing me a lot of money. Are you the lawyer that Allison Love talked to in Long Beach, California?"

"I cannot discuss my clients—"

"Allison Love is dead," Aunty Lee said bluntly. "So we want to find everybody who might have known her and tell them."

There was a pause. Then, tentatively, "Is this some kind of

joke? Because it's not funny. You can get into serious trouble for making jokes like that."

"What's your fax number?"

"Beg your pardon?"

"Do you have a fax? Or an e-mail address? Yes, then give me your fax number, Mr. Ian Woon!"

Nina faxed over the newspaper report of the murder. Aunty Lee fixed herself a drink of sour plum tea and dialed the number again. This time Mr. Ian Woon answered on the first ring. "Mrs. Lee? This is terrible. You have my condolences. I believe Allison went to Singapore with her sister, Vallerie. Is Vallerie Love still in Singapore? Is she all right?"

"You know Vallerie Love?"

"It was Vallerie Love who brought her sister, Allison, to us. She said Allison was visiting and needed a lawyer. At the time I thought she was just humoring her, but now it's almost as though she had a premonition of some sort."

"So you knew that Allison was coming to Singapore to file a lawsuit?" Aunty Lee was not sure how premonition came into this.

"Allison Love mentioned she was going to Singapore to sort things out with her ex-husband. But she didn't elaborate on that. At least not with me. I remember she was very eager to get her will done in a hurry," the lawyer said. "Do you have Skype, Mrs. Lee? There's someone else you should talk to but I'll have to call you back in about an hour." He paused. "Should we be sending this information to the police?"

Aunty Lee decided to make things easy for Mr. Ian Woon

by having Salim come by the café at the time of the call. Salim assumed it was Vallerie who had called her late sister's lawyer and seemed pleased. It was only Aunty Lee's efforts to help that he labeled "interference," Aunty Lee thought. She would bring it up when there weren't so many other interesting things going on.

"Thank you for speaking to me, Mr. Woon," Salim said after identifying himself. Fortunately Selina had taken Vallerie out for a pedicure and foot rub, so Nina had linked the Mac-Book to the television mounted on the wall beside the cold room door. This way Aunty Lee and Salim could sit side by side at the counter and Nina was on hand to fix any computer connection issues.

Aunty Lee had warned Salim of the importance of using the "Mister" when addressing the American lawyer without understanding why. But the two people who showed up on-screen soon explained it.

Aunty Lee had imagined Mr. Ian Woon as a small Chinese man, compensating for goodness knew what imagined inadequacy of height, race, or prowess by lording it over his clients. Instead Ian Woon as seen on-screen was a broad-faced, broad-shouldered man whose fair skin and light brown hair suggested mixed rather than pure Asian ancestry. And the woman beside him—

"I'm Mrs. Yen Woon," said the woman on the screen. Smaller than her husband, she looked pure Chinese but also spoke like a West Coast American. "My parents named me Yen Ling but everybody calls me Yen. If you think this is confusing you should see our family reunions. My sisters are Yen Mei and Yen Seng, and all their partners, friends, and in-laws call them Yen too!" She laughed. "Of course my marrying an 'Ian' didn't help matters!"

Beside her Mr. Ian Woon grinned, content to let his wife talk.

"We're both lawyers and we work together when I'm not on maternity leave."

"You got new baby?" Aunty Lee interrupted here. As far as she was concerned, babies were always worth talking about. The dead would stay dead, but babies changed so quickly. "Boy or girl?"

"Girl, thank goodness. After three boys I was getting seriously outnumbered here!"

"Wah! You got three boys already, ah? I thought young people these days all don't want to have so many children?"

But even as Salim was wondering how he could steer the conversation back to his murder inquiry, Mrs. Yen Woon said, "Vallerie Love brought her sister in to consult my husband. But after one meeting with her he asked me to take over."

"Why was that?" Inspector Salim asked.

"My wife is an expert on wills and successions," Ian Woon said.

"So is my husband, actually," his wife said. "But I'm less intimidated by loud women."

Aunty Lee thought of Vallerie. The sisters must have been quite alike.

"I got that Allison was having some problems with her marriage. The first thing she said was that she'd left her husband, Mike, with the kids to give him a taste of what it was like looking after them all day and night. She wanted to set us right too, expecting everybody to have heard about the ruckus in Singapore. She said she had had to put down a vicious dog that had been sent to her for fostering. No one had warned her that the dog was dangerous, and she had two children and a maid in the house to worry about. If she had sent the dog back it would have spent the rest of its life in a cage, and she couldn't stand the thought of that so she had it put down. All that was no different from what she would have done in the UK and she had no regrets. She would have done the same thing over again, she kept saying. But there was a vicious woman in Singapore who was after her husband and stirred up trouble, just to be vindictive. According to her this woman started up a whole online bullying thing, and she was talking about Chinese triads and the Yakuza and how they had barely managed to get out with their lives . . . I'd always thought Singapore was a pretty safe place to live. So safe it sounds boring, no offense. I didn't know whether to believe her or not, but that wasn't the point, was it? So we just listened and let her talk." Yen Woon lowered her voice. "I got the feeling Vallie thought Allison had demonized Singapore in her mind and seeing it for real might snap her out of it. Plus her sister had turned up without warning and she was afraid she might stay for good. Every time Vallie asked when she was leaving Allison would cry and say people were hateful to her . . . I think Vallie just needed to find a way to get her out of her place!"

It was much how Vallerie seemed to have settled at her house, Aunty Lee thought.

"Vallerie Love is here in Singapore now." Inspector Salim concealed his dislike of the woman. Very often you under-stood people better once you saw their friends, and these friends of Vallerie's seemed like pleasant people. "She came over with her sister. It was a great shock for her, of course. She hasn't been able to tell us much about Allison."

"Aunty Vallie is still in Singapore?" A young boy came on-screen, standing behind his mother and leaning against her shoulder so their faces were side by side. "How is she? Can she talk to us? Can you given her a message from us?"

There were advantages to having so many crime shows on television, Salim thought. People assumed that giving the police information to help them with investigations was just part of the routine.

The child was hushed by his father as his mother explained they had thought something was wrong with Vallerie when she stopped Skyping them. They had tried calling the hotel but she had not been in, and Allison told them Vallerie was all right, only the phone and Internet connections in Singa-pore were very unreliable (Aunty Lee was very offended on behalf of Singapore's Internet providers but held her tongue).

"Aunty Vallie said she would buy me manga!" the boy pro-tested. "But I just wanted to tell her thanks for the pineapple tarts!" He shot a reproachful look at his parents, who had forgotten their manners.

Aunty Lee pounced on this. "Pineapple tarts? Bengawan Solo?"

"Yes, I think so," Mrs. Yen Woon said. "Anyway they were delicious—and all gone now."

"Tell Aunty Vallie to send some more!" another child piped up.

"He's a cop, Marko, not a message service, yadada?" But Ian's tone was affectionate. Two younger children joined their brother in front of the camera now, one climbing into his mother's lap. "Are you recording our mum?" the eldest asked. "Do you need to use her testimony in court? You can fly her over to Singapore if you need her, you know. We can all testify if you like."

"I'll keep that in mind, thanks," Salim said agreeably. The affection this family clearly had for Vallerie Love made him think he had misjudged her as being racist. "Any other messages?"

"Just tell her we said hello."

There was a chorus of groans to this and "You can do better than that!" and "Tell her to climb the Merlion!"

"Tell her we're here for her. There'll always be a bed for her over at our place, okay?" Yen Woon said. "Just remind her she's not alone."

"Tell Aunty Vallie if she comes back to babysit I will brush my own teeth," the hitherto silent toddler announced from his mother's lap.

"And we'll get back to yoga" from Yen.

Yoga? Vallerie Love? Aunty Lee sniffed around the idea as though it was a possibly ripe durian.

"Vallerie did yoga?"

"Oh yes. And she loved it. We took yoga classes together. It was great! She used it to de-stress from her crazy sister—oh sorry. I forgot."

None of this fit with the image of Vallerie Aunty Lee had seen so far. Of course she must have been shocked by her sister's murder and shock did strange things to people. But scrambling a chicken egg did not turn it into a duck egg. The essential nature of eggs—and people—did not change.

"Vallerie is fat," Aunty Lee said plainly. "If fat people like her can do yoga, then I also can do yoga, right?"

"Oh, I'm so glad you asked!" Exaggerated groans from Mr. Ian Woon and the little Woons worried Aunty Lee a little. As far as she was concerned, fanaticism was a form of madness, whether it took the form of devotion to God or to exercise.

"First of all, everybody can do yoga. Real yoga, I mean. I'm not talking about the jumping around in hot rooms sweating to get skinny sort. But if you do real yoga and you get balanced, you'll find you lose weight without even trying. You may not get skinny, but your body will get balanced, toned, and healthy. Yes, dear Vallie was overweight when she first got here. She had all kinds of eating issues from her childhood and then both her parents dying. But once she settled here things just fell into place. When the student is ready the teacher appears and all that, you know? And Vallie was ready."

"And you haven't heard from her at all?"

"No. I left several messages on her phone and I know she'll get back to me when she can. If not, I'll see her back stateside."

It was almost impossible to offend someone who did not take offense, Aunty Lee thought. "Just one more thing. It may sound crazy but can you get something for me and send it over? Salim will give you the address."

Salim said what Aunty Lee was thinking: "They don't talk about her like she's a fat person."

"Maybe that's because they're Americans," Aunty Lee mused.

There were still times Aunty Lee forgot ML was dead. The next morning, in the drowsy swamp between dream sleep and waking, she found herself earnestly telling ML that talking on Skype was not much better than talking on the phone, just better than nothing . . . and feeling irritated because instead of listening he said, "Remember, there's always a bill, Rosie. Always check the bill." As awareness dawned, she tried to cling to her husband and his sweet presence in her dream. But as always happened, she surfaced into the new day. ML Lee was dead and had been for some time. And Brian Wong was newly dead.

"Nina, can you find out for me how much the Skype calls cost?"

"Madame, the bill will come end of the month like usual."

"But can you find out earlier? And can you find out from the bill the numbers that were called from here?"

"Madame, you want the number for Mr. Ian Woon I have got it, I can give it to you."

"I just want a printout of all the numbers, not just last night. Please?"

Nina shrugged as she put Aunty Lee's two soft-cooked eggs and *kaya* toast in front of her. It was a breakfast familiar from her childhood, and Aunty Lee was not sorry to be on her own to enjoy it while looking out on the dwarf coconut trees, the mango tree, and the rambutan tree in the garden. All these had been here since before ML died, indeed before the first Mrs. Lee died. She was the only one around to enjoy them now. And she enjoyed the lingering scent of night jasmine from the bushes, the soft warm eggs with their burst of rich yolk, the crisp toast, and the gently nourishing rays of morning sun. No matter how much you lost, feeling the loss reminded you that you were still alive.

"Someone else has been using the connection from here to make Skype calls." Nina returned faster than she had left. "Must be Miss Vallerie. But she is always saying she has got no family to contact, right?" She looked up at the second-floor window but there was no sign of Vallerie, who seldom appeared till ten at the earliest.

"Can you tell—was she making overseas or local calls?"

"Better than that, I can call back."

Feeling guilty (though it was her house and her computer after all), Aunty Lee moved herself into ML's study and seated herself in front of the computer that Nina had set up for her. Without asking, Nina locked the study door before joining her.

"I have a right to use my own computer, you know."

"Yes, madame. But Miss Vallerie likes to shout and cry, very difficult to listen if she wakes up. You press there—call.

No, you must use the mouse. This is not touchscreen like your iPad."

It took some time for the connection to be linked. Then the camera came on and there was a lot of fumbling.

Then a woman's voice said, "Christ, do you bloody know what time it is?" to the accompaniment of a child screaming protest. "It's Mummy! I want to talk to Mummy!"

"No, dear. Your mum's not there."

A boy's face loomed large on the screen. "I want to talk to Mummy!" it shrieked. "Mummy's calling to talk to me!"

"Mike, is that you? I wish you'd warn me before calling." A woman's face appeared on the screen. "Mike?" She did not seem able to see them.

Mike's sister? Aunty Lee wondered. She heard another child's voice in the background: "You're not supposed to tell anybody Mum called. Especially not Dad!"

"I don't care. I want to talk to Mum. I don't want to go to the dentist tomorrow! I want to run away like Mum!"

And the connection was broken.

"They couldn't see us?"

"No. I switch off camera," Nina said. "Enough? Satisfied?"

Aunty Lee was relieved. "I need to think."

Nina switched off the computer and left her there, returning silently to place a bowl of pu-erh tea on the desk. Fermented pu-erh was Aunty Lee's favorite thinking tea.

"I will go to the shop first. I put Miss Vallerie's breakfast in the dining room." Her boss nodded, barely hearing her. Nina felt hopeful. Whether Aunty Lee thought their guest a murderer or merely a liar about using her computer, her preoccupation with Vallerie's secret calls suggested the woman's stay would be drawing to an end.

For Aunty Lee the process of reverse engineering a dish or perfecting a recipe was often more important than the final dish.

The same ingredients went into a rich, hot, savory soup and a delicately chilled meat jelly. Pigs' head or calves' foot jelly, for example. But there was such a difference in texture depending on whether the dish was heated or chilled. And people felt so differently when you offered them a cow's feet or head instead of a steak cut out of its side. Was that because they preferred not to be reminded their crown roast or tenderloin had come from an animal?

The theme that was running through Aunty Lee's head just then was how people saw themselves and their situation. It was all a matter of perspective. And what seemed the same situation could have very different effects on the people affected. Like the story told of two boys born poor; one stayed poor and turned to crime because he never had a chance, while the other worked up to become a rich philanthropist helping the poor because he knew what it was to be poor.

But Aunty Lee took the story further. If the poor boys had been brothers, they would also have influenced each other. The one who stayed poor might have done badly because in addition to all the other factors, he was full of resentment that his brother who was doing well was not helping him more. And the more he was eaten up with resentment at his brother, the poorer he got, to emphasize the unfairness of his brother not helping him. And what if they had been sisters instead of brothers?

"From what those Woons in America said about Vallerie, I can understand her coming to Singapore with her sister. But I still can't understand why Vallerie changed so much after getting here."

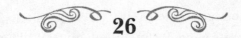

26

Belinda Bao: Chill to Set

Belinda Bao's autumn special moon cake boxes matched the one that had been sent to Josephine. The one containing the moon cake that had poisoned her. They also matched the box that had been found in the Love sisters' hotel room.

"Yes, these are the ones that Brian Wong ordered this year," Belinda Bao said. She was a fair, plump young woman with pink cheeks and a pink streak in her dyed blond hair.

"Brian bought a box of moon cakes from you? Are you sure?" This particular ingredient did not fit into the recipe Aunty Lee was concocting for this murder.

"Oh yes. Brian orders at least ten boxes every year. This year it was fifteen boxes. We have a delivery service, but Brian liked to deliver them himself. He says—said—everybody else gives clients and family members hampers at Chinese New Year, so to stand out, he did it at the Moon Cake Festival."

Belinda smiled. Then as the sides of her mouth pulled down-
ward the rest of her face crumpled and she started to cry.
"He was such a sweet guy. I think I was a little in love with
him. In a fairy-tale prince kind of way, you know?"

"Sorry, sorry," Aunty Lee said soothingly. "Good people
like Brian, they go to their reward."

"People are saying Brian killed himself. They're saying
that he confessed to killing a whole lot of people and then
killed himself, but I don't believe it! I mean, when I saw him
he was so funny and sweet and normal.

"Oh, I forgot—" Belinda wiped her face on a white towel
she pulled out of her apron. "Brian took sixteen boxes this
year. He ordered fifteen and picked them up, no problem.
Then the next morning he called me, said he very urgently
needed one more box and he would come round and pick it
up. So it was sixteen in the end."

"What day?"

"Saturday."

"Ah." The recipe was coming together at last, Aunty Lee
thought. She still did not know how it would turn out, but she
had just managed to pick up a vital ingredient.

"Toxicology tests were not performed previously as the cause
of death was obvious. But samples had been taken during
the autopsy, so when a request was made for further tests . . ."
Here Commissioner Raja gave Aunty Lee a small, wry smile.

Aunty Lee was almost bouncing on her seat in her anxiety
to hear the results. "What? What? What?"

"Results show Allison Love was drugged before she was strangled with the cables and hit in the face."

"Ah . . ." Aunty Lee nodded. Finally things were beginning to fall into place. And perhaps it wasn't too late.

"Allison Fitzgerald was taking off-label antipsychotics as sedatives, for her insomnia and to calm herself. She was also taking sleeping pills. It seems most likely that she took a dose, felt it wasn't working fast enough or simply forgot, took another dose, and another, until she passed out." He stopped, but Aunty Lee sensed he had more to say. Indeed, she would have been disappointed if he did not.

"It's also possible that her sister gave her the medicine. Maybe just to calm her down. We know that Allison Love could be difficult, and Vallerie might have given her too much by accident."

Or not even by accident. Given what Aunty Lee had heard about Allison Love, the need to calm her down or put her to sleep for a while must have been very strong, even if the people at the hotel had seen a different side of her. But the way Vallerie handled difficult situations troubled Aunty Lee. She was someone who flared up in a burst of anger and almost went crazy. People like her attacked other drivers in road rage or threw noodles on stewardesses in sky rage or killed their partners in crimes of passion. Such a person would have shouted at her sister rather than feeding her calming pills. And the way Vallerie talked about her sister and kept score of all the wrongs done to the dead Allison was almost worshipful.

"What if Vallerie killed Allison?" Aunty Lee asked. "And Josephine and Brian found out so she tried to kill them and frame them."

Aunty Lee had no reason to dislike Vallerie, who was her guest, a victim, a helpless stranger in a strange land. But even less did she want to believe Brian Wong had been responsible.

Commissioner Raja did not answer immediately. This may have been because he was engrossed in his menu. After her excursion to Holland Village to see Belinda Bao, Aunty Lee had asked him to meet her at a restaurant there, which she had wanted to visit for some time because of its name. "Original Sin" sounded more like a den of iniquity than the classy vegetarian restaurant it turned out to be, and its name blended nicely with the theme of sibling murder running through Aunty Lee's mind. If Cain could kill Abel, why could Vallerie not have killed Allison?

Commissioner Raja might have been reflecting. Or it might have been because he thought it safer not to answer.

"You're thinking I just don't want to believe Brian Wong killed those women even if he confessed. That's not true. I just can't believe he could have tried to poison Josephine."

"All I was thinking is that the spanakopita looks interesting. Look here, Rosie. There was a time when Allison Fitzgerald had thousands of Singaporeans, not to mention people from Malaysia, Thailand, Indonesia, Japan, Taiwan, and as far away as Finland and Norway sending her hate mail. It was cyberbullying. And Josephine, Cherril, and your Saint Brian were responsible for that. It's not acceptable." He held up a hand to forestall the protest that was bubbling out of Aunty Lee. "This started with them. They were responsible." He turned both hands palms down on the table as though to signal the matter closed.

"It must be tough for you, having the sister staying with you for so long." Commissioner Raja threw this out as an unspoken offer: *Do you need help getting her out of your house?* In a choice between loneliness and strangers, Raja Kumar would pick loneliness every time.

"It's not too bad," Aunty Lee said. Aunty Lee herself would have picked strangers. Being Aunty Lee, they would not remain strangers for long. "She's eating better and feeling better. I don't know what she was eating before coming here, but now she is eating less processed local foods and her headaches and allergies don't seem so bad. But she still has difficulty sleeping." Aunty Lee had not been sure whether the insomnia that sometimes drove Vallerie to walk around the house at night was caused by guilt, fear, or some underlying medical condition. But then she had seemed much more relaxed after news of Brian's confession and suicide, so it seemed fear had been the cause . . . though she had become surprisingly agitated when Aunty Lee pointed out that the dead vet could not have been at the hotel to see Brian because of the fire . . .

It was well after lunchtime when Commissioner Raja dropped Aunty Lee back at the café and there were no customers in. If Aunty Lee had not been her own landlord (as well as landlord of several other shops along the row), the absence of customers might have bothered her. As it was, she happily went to sit by the café's front corner window. This was the table Cherril, Josephine, and Brian had been sitting at the Saturday it had all started. Aunty Lee did not want to believe any of them had killed a woman in cold blood. But someone had—two women, in fact.

The reason cold dishes were complicated was the multiple cooking methods involved. All the individual ingredients had to be prepared in all their individual ways and carved from bones or excised from shells. Then professional cutting skills were needed as the morsels were trimmed into shapes that looked appealing when suspended in the gel. And at the very end, serving skills made all the difference. Any flaws around the rim could be disguised with decorative bits and the gravy—tested for seasoning—poured over. Unlike a stew or a stir-fry, which were open to receiving whatever was in your fridge, a cold, savory mold called for design, execution, and presentation.

It was the same thing with creating the perfect revenge.

27

Dinner Climax

The next evening Aunty Lee arranged a special dinner at her house. It was to celebrate the end of the suspicions against Mike and introduce him to Josephine's family and friends on neutral territory, she said when she invited the young woman to bring Mike, warning her that not only would her parents be coming—along with Cherril, Mycroft, and Anne Peters— but that Vallerie was not expecting them. Otherwise her guest would probably leave the house in order to avoid them.

"But I think it's a good idea for her and Mike to be in the same room at least once before Vallerie leaves." Mike seemed keen, so Josephine agreed. She didn't see any point to it, but it would be just one evening.

Commissioner Raja and Inspector Salim were also present, but not in uniform, which left it unclear whether they were there officially. Salim had disappeared into the kitchen, possibly to help Nina, but it was also possible he was keeping an eye on the back door.

Mike Fitzgerald and Josephine were the last to arrive. As soon as Nina showed them into the dining room, Vallerie immediately got up to leave.

"Oh no, wait—don't go," Aunty Lee said.

"You can't bully me into staying. Tell the servant to bring my dinner upstairs."

The "servant" stood quietly in front of the dining room door, effectively barring Vallerie's exit. She sent a little smile in the direction of Salim, who had moved casually to the sliding glass doors leading to the patio, now closed because of the air-conditioning, once Josephine and Mike were inside, effectively blocking it as well. This had not been planned; they had instinctively moved into the best positions to survey the people already around the table.

The long, polished table was set for dinner and Commissioner Raja was seated at one end with Aunty Lee on the other. Anne Peters was next to Commissioner Raja, with Mycroft and Cherril beside her, followed by Joseph and Constance DelaVega, who were seated by Aunty Lee. Mark was by the sideboard with his bottles of wine, and Selina, who had been sitting by Vallerie, also rose to her feet. She had not known Josephine was coming either.

Mike stepped forward, eyes on Vallerie. "Hey, I'm sorry about what happened to Allison. But I had nothing to do with that, honest."

"Please sit down," Commissioner Raja said, managing to direct his words at everyone standing.

"Why, are you going to give a speech?" Vallerie remained standing. "Save it for my sister's funeral!"

"But not for Allison Love's funeral," said Aunty Lee. Vallerie had looked really terrified, afraid for her life, on first seeing Mike Fitzgerald, but now she looked both smug and puzzled. "Vallerie Love is dead in a freezer in the morgue of the Singapore General Hospital."

"What?" Josephine was startled out of the mask she had been wearing since coming in. She stared at the large woman. "But if Vallerie is dead, then who—"

"This is Allison Love, formerly Allison Fitzgerald. Allison has been pretending to be her sister, Vallerie," Salim interjected, carefully not looking at Commissioner Raja. "The fingerprints of the corpse did not match the fingerprints of Allison Fitzgerald processed five years ago when she was taken in for biting and scratching a police officer. No charges were pressed but her prints remain on file. Aunty Lee suggested we compare the fingerprints of her houseguest on a water glass she supplied, and it was a match."

"Allie?" Mike looked uncertain. "I thought—I told the children that you—" He started toward her but Josephine's grip on his arm yanked him back to her side.

"Mike, you coward, you never backed me up."

Mike stared, openmouthed.

"You idiot, you fool. I never wanted a divorce."

"You did. You left—"

"I wanted to teach you a lesson. I wanted you to see how much you needed me. Instead, you stupid idiot, you ungrateful bastard, you went running to that skinny bitch. I knew she was after you!"

"You knew?"

The woman's snort of disdain prompted Aunty Lee to fill in what she had learned. "Thanks to Skyping with your son, you knew that your husband was seeing Josephine. You knew Josephine had been to visit them in England. And you wanted to catch them together in Singapore and confront them."

"You killed your own sister?" Mike asked.

"You think you're so clever." Allison Love turned to stare at Aunty Lee with loathing. "Well, you're not. Of course I didn't kill my stupid sister."

Hatred could make people forget their own pain just as love could, Aunty Lee thought.

"I hated my stupid sister but I never killed her. Why would I? And whoever killed her thinking she was me is going to be after me now, thanks to you. If I get killed now it's going to be all your fault!" Hearing her own words she looked wildly around the room and wailed. "He's going to kill me now! Him and his bitch slut! What difference does it make whether he killed me or killed my sister? I was only protecting myself. I thought that if he thought he already killed me he wouldn't come after me again and I would be safe! I only pretended to be my sister because I was scared of him. I was always scared of him. You can ask anyone. Ask my kids, my son will tell you."

Josephine stared, stone-faced. Mike looked baffled.

"We had a lovely time but we really have to be going," Constance DelaVega murmured icily. She half-rose from her seat and tapped at her husband's shoulder, but Joseph DelaVega, looking between Aunty Lee, his daughter, and his daughter's boyfriend's ex-wife, ignored or possibly didn't notice her. Constance sat back down, her mouth in a tight line. Observing her, Aunty Lee thought how much Josephine took after her mother.

"I didn't want that poor animal to live the rest of its life in a cage, that's all. I was thinking of it. And you viciously destroyed my life and killed my sister because of it," Allison said to Josephine.

"We should go." Josephine echoed her mother's words. Like her father, Mike Fitzgerald did not move. "Look, you've got her. You know she's Allison Love. Why don't you just arrest her and take her away?"

"Vallerie was the fat sister while you were growing up, but she blossomed after she made a new life for herself in California. She was teaching yoga and working with herbal cures and she had made new friends. When you went to see her in Long Beach she wasn't the 'fat sister' anymore. You were." Aunty Lee spoke to Allison's back, but the woman nodded. "Maybe it was being mistaken for Vallerie that gave you the idea. Everyone knew Allison was the slim, smart sister. Vallerie was the fat, stupid younger sister."

"It started as a joke," Allison said. "People kept getting us mixed up. People who used to know us, who knew Vall was the fat sister. They automatically assumed I was Vall. So I said let's turn the joke back on them. Vall thought it was a huge joke. She could be so stupid but she was a good sport." Her voice cracked as her face crumpled. "Oh, Vallie!" It was the first honest statement about her sister this woman had made, Aunty Lee thought. But she had other points to make.

"You wanted revenge on the veterinary clinic so you threw a glass bottle of kerosene with a lighted candle into it. And you invented the threats against yourself to make it look as though the Animal ReHomers were targeting you. I'm guessing you drugged your sister when she objected. Did she wonder what you were doing with kerosene? Where did you buy it—the provision shop behind the hotel?" Salim gave a small nod, confirming this was so.

"Did you see the vet who put your dog down at the clinic on the day of the fire? Was that what made you think of her as soon as you heard a vet had been killed?"

Allison looked surprised, then confused. "I might have. Someone called out my name, but more like a question than knowing it was me. I ignored her. After all, what could she do about it? There was smoke and noise and animals all over the place, and the fire engine was blocked from the car park by the construction lorry. She can't have been sure it was me. Even if she was, what could she say—that she had seen me there? She couldn't prove that I had done anything! So I just left."

"After Allison went back to England she killed animals by feeding them rat poison when she got angry with them or their owners. She boasted to her husband about it, didn't she, Mike?" Josephine said. "She killed the vet just like she killed her sister."

"Tammy?" Anne Peters whispered. "Did she poison my Tammy?" Cherril put an arm around her mother-in-law's thin shoulders.

Allison didn't bother to contradict her, not turning as Aunty Lee rose to her feet behind her, leaning both hands on the table for support.

"After drugging Vallerie, Allison went down to the reception to call a taxi to bring her to Aunty Lee's Delights for the meeting. She had to go down because she couldn't communicate with the Mandarin-speaking receptionists over the phone. Downstairs she learned that someone had dropped off a box of moon cakes for them, which had been brought up to the room. Her sister was in a drugged sleep and Allison had disconnected the phone, so just to check she returned to her room and found her sister dead, strangled by the cable ties. She knew at once whoever it was had meant to kill her. She had to think fast."

Allison took over the narrative. "I dashed back up because I was furious at Vall. I had made her promise not to tell anyone we were coming to Singapore, but if someone was sending her moon cakes, I knew that she must have broken her promise. I found Vallerie dead, her face all black and her lips swollen with bubbles and something tight around her neck. I knew at once I was the real target. I took the fire extinguisher from outside the room and smashed it in her face—if the killer wanted to kill 'Allison' then I would become 'Vallerie' and let

'Allison' be dead. I thought that was the safest thing for me to do. But I didn't kill her. You have to believe me. She was already dead or I wouldn't have hit her. That was just to make sure people thought she was me."

"I believe you," Aunty Lee said. "There were too many clues pointing to you. That's why I had to find out where the moon cakes came from. That's why I knew you didn't kill your sister, Vallerie." Even Allison turned to stare at her.

"But someone tried to poison Josie," Constance DelaVega said. "That poisoned moon cake that Brian sent to her shop. She almost died! They tested the cake and found the same poison that Brian used to kill himself!"

"That's what made me suspicious," Aunty Lee said. "Josie, why did you eat so little of the moon cake? I thought you like moon cake."

"It tasted funny." Josephine did not look at her parents or Mike. She could have been alone with Aunty Lee the way she smiled with persuasive, girlish charm at the older woman. "I do like moon cake, but when I took a mouthful it tasted funny so of course I stopped. Luckily for me."

"The poison in the moon cake is tasteless." Aunty Lee did not smile back. "You wouldn't know it was poisoned by tasting. You wouldn't know unless you injected the poison in the moon cake yourself after you cut out that piece. You must have used one of the syringes you use to inject preservatives into your flowers. Of course there was nothing wrong with the mouthful you ate. You were pretending, to frighten Mike into raising the alarm and rushing you to hospital.

"Brian wanted everything sorted out to make everybody

happy. He did all he could to help Josephine end up with Mike," Aunty Lee said softly. "That's why he went to Allison's hotel with you. Did he think you were going to apologize to Allison and defuse the situation and thereby the lawsuit? Then when the hotel receptionist refused to tell you which room Allison was in, you asked him for one of the boxes of moon cakes in his car so that you could watch which room they were brought to. He had just picked up the special moon cakes he ordered for clients. That's why he had to go back to Belinda Bao's shop to get a replacement box the next day."

"That's ridiculous," Josephine said. "I wasn't at the hotel."

"You strangled Vallerie thinking she was Allison. You were convinced that as long as the woman was alive she would never leave you and Mike in peace.

"Brian waited for you downstairs—one of the hotel staff remembers him. Did you tell him Allison refused to see you, or that she had already left? In any case you told him not to mention you two had gone to the hotel in case it made Allison think you were worried.

"But news of Allison's death probably made Brian uncomfortable. And when you learned we were looking for the source of the moon cakes found in the room, which would lead us to Brian, you decided to silence him. He didn't suspect you, did he? But you didn't want to leave any trails that would lead to you. And all the facts in Brian's suicide note were true. Because you were the one who wrote that suicide note after poisoning Brian."

"If only Vallie had woken up, she would have told you she wasn't me," Allison said. There was real pain in her voice, but she was more calm and focused since the first time she set foot in the café.

"She did. She woke up and said she wasn't Allison, but I knew she was lying," Josephine said. "It was years ago but I recognized her at once. You're all lying and trying to trick me! She was the only bloody woman in the room, of course it was her!"

Cherril rose, almost unaware she was moving, to stand at Aunty Lee's side. "I thought you were worried about the lawsuit. I thought that's why you didn't fuss about her being late. You're usually so impatient. You said you had a 'nervous stomach' because of meeting Allison. Brian accepted that because he always accepted everything you said. That's what you told him when he waited for you in the hotel, isn't it? Then you probably told him you felt silly or embarrassed or something like that and asked him not to say anything to me, which would be just like you, and he would have swallowed it. You just wanted him on the premises to be another suspect, but he turned out more useful as an alibi. Until he started telling you that you should both come clean about what had happened at the hotel. He told me he had something to tell me, but he had to sort it out with you first."

Josephine snorted, perhaps at Brian's perfidy in talking to Cherril, but Cherril was not finished yet. "You poisoned Brian and pretended to be poisoned yourself. But why did you kill Samantha Kang? She would never have tried to blackmail you like you wrote in that e-mail. Sam Kang would have given you money if she thought you needed it!"

Josephine did not answer.

Aunty Lee thumped the table in her excitement. "That day of the fire at the clinic. I think the vet, Samantha Kang, saw Allison there. She may not have recognized her and only remembered who she was later. I suspect Dr. Kang texted you saying she had seen someone suspicious and needed to talk to you . . . She was talking about Allison, but your guilty conscience made you think Dr. Kang saw you at the hotel and wanted to blackmail you. You told her to meet you at Holland Village—near your shop and near her clinic. You went to the toilet together, and you had the cable ties and gloves you use for your floral arrangements—the same cable ties and gloves you used to kill the woman you thought was Allison Love. You pulled the cable ties tight around Samantha Kang's throat and pushed her back into the stall to die."

Josephine rolled her eyes. "You're making up crazy stories. At your age it's probably dementia. Anyway, you can't prove anything. Or do you have a medium that can talk to ghosts?"

"Technology is better than mediums," Aunty Lee said firmly. "Holland Village shops all got surveillance cameras inside and outside. Now they know who they are looking for—should not be too hard for the police to prove you were there at that time!"

Commissioner Raja's eyes moved to Salim, who nodded. "We've already got the film. Thank goodness for shoplifters." He left the room, texting on his phone.

"The poor woman was no real threat to you. Even if she had seen you, you could have given her some excuse—you're good at lying—and she would have believed you. But you also killed her to draw suspicion away from Mike. That's why you killed her the same way you killed Vallerie, at a time when you knew Mike had an alibi. Because there was always the risk that the police might look into the people who had the most reason to want Allison Love dead—her ex-husband and his pregnant girlfriend."

"Pregnant?" Mike Fitzgerald looked between his ex-wife and pregnant lover with an expression that was a blend of horror and incredulity.

"Look, Mikey, I did it for you, for us. Because I wanted our life together to be free from all Allison's craziness."

"You're just like Allison—you're worse! Allison killed animals but not people."

"I wouldn't have had to if you hadn't kept dragging your feet about getting married! This is all your fault!"

"I think Mike was changing his mind about marrying you, Josephine," Aunty Lee said quietly. She turned to Mike Fitzgerald. "As you got to know her better she started to remind you of Allison, didn't she?"

Mike hesitated, and then nodded. "I thought it was me. Imagining things. But yes. I'm sorry."

"Of course he's going to marry her!" Constance DelaVega's thin voice shrilled. "Our Josie is not the kind of girl you can pick up and throw away! He must join the church and marry her."

Distracted eyes turned to her till Commissioner Raja suddenly shouted, "Watch out!"

Josephine had grabbed the carving knife off the sideboard, and now she lunged at Mike, leaving a bloody streak on the arm he threw up to protect his face. The table wedged Commissioner Raja in, and Mycroft was entangled by Selina clinging to both him and Mark, screaming. SS Panchal appeared at the kitchen door on Commissioner Raja's shout, but was on the other side of the room, with Salim even farther away outside as Josephine raised the bloody knife again.

"The samples! The samples!" Aunty Lee shouted, flailing at Josephine with her walking stick, giving Mike a chance to retreat against the wall. Nina rolled the open containers across the floor toward Aunty Lee, who whacked and spun them around with her stick as Josephine, knife raised, moved in on Mike for the kill—but skidded and fell. She got back on her feet, charged at him again, but her feet twisted and shot out from under her and she fell again. This time she stayed down.

"Be careful, ah," Aunty Lee warned. "There's oil on the floor."

"Oil?" Salim stopped SS Panchal abruptly, thinking of biological attack. "What kind of oil?"

"Soybean oil, canola oil, sustainable palm oil," SS Panchal said, sniffing, "And some sesame oil."

Aunty Lee looked at the policewoman with new respect, "There's some more around the back door. I thought she would try to run away. I didn't think she would attack, I'm sorry, she's going to make your police car all oily. I give you some newspapers for her to sit on. The *Straits Times* is very good for covering up messy business."

Josephine's eyes were fixed on Mike. "You bastard. I'm going to kill your baby."

Mike stared. He looked as though he was having trouble following all that had just happened, Aunty Lee thought. The greatest victim here was the unborn child who seemed no more than a bargaining chip to its mother.

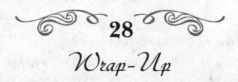

28
Wrap-Up

Allison Love was charged with cruelty to animals for poisoning Tammy and would be subject to a fine of up to S$10,000, a jail term of up to a year, or both. She should also have been charged for firebombing the vet clinic but the case was dropped for lack of evidence.

Josephine DelaVega was arrested in connection with the murders of Vallerie Love, Samantha Kang, and Brian Wong. Her parents claimed first that she was being framed, then that she had been manipulated into it by Mike Fitzgerald and Allison Love as part of a complex revenge for the online bullying and harassment they held her responsible for. They had already applied to be made legal guardians of their unborn grandchild.

Mike Fitzgerald went home to be with his children in

London, but would return to Singapore for the trials of his ex-wife and ex-lover.

Nina posted a "Closed for Private Party" announcement on the website and put a sign on the front door, and Aunty Lee threw a *pohpiah* party to celebrate everything getting sorted out and getting her ankle out of its cast.

"We will all wrap up our own food to celebrate Salim wrapping up the case and me unwrapping my foot," she said.

Nina rolled her eyes but said nothing. Aunty Lee's hot *pohpiah* filling was delicious and needed no excuse. There were fresh prawns, crabmeat, shredded omelet, spring onions, and garlic to go with it. It was the ideal spread for a hostess who wanted to enjoy her own party because all the work could be done in advance and during the meal everyone rolled their own dinners according to their taste.

And there were even little dog *pohpiahs* (filled with bacon and pork hash) for Tammy, who was fully recovered and had been smuggled in for the celebration.

"*Pohpiah* and my super new invention: Chilled Revenge. Because Mark said revenge tastes better cold."

"Where is Mark?" Mycroft asked. "Not coming tonight? I hope Selina's not still feeling bad. For a while I was afraid someone poisoned her and my Cherry might be next!" He grinned at Cherril, who smiled back wanly.

"Mark is not coming," Aunty Lee said with a huge, beaming smile. "So many things to cook, I almost forgot. Selina went to see the doctor but she is not poisoned, she is going to have a baby! My first grandbaby! Tonight they are at Selina's parents' house."

This led to a round of toasts to the absent couple and laughter that they were spending the evening interviewing various pregnancy fitness coaches and pregnancy diet counselors, but talk soon returned to Josephine and Allison, whether it was worse to kill humans than dogs, and how two apparently nice, normal young women could have turned to violence.

"It all started with the puppy killer case," Aunty Lee said. "Like Raja said, Allison—who we knew as 'Vallerie'—was traumatized by the online mob rage directed against her after the incident with the puppy. Allison had always thought of herself as a super organizer and controller, and it was a shock for her to discover she couldn't control what people thought of her. Like many insecure people she was a big bully in small ways—taking it out on the people and animals around her.

"Josephine was also changed by what happened. With the Internet community cheering her on, Josephine felt famous and powerful. More dangerously, she enjoyed the self-righteousness of having unleashed well-deserved vengeance. The problem is that feeling is addictive, as you can see from witch hunters and Anti Pink Dot gay bashers. When the excitement was over and Allison left Singapore, Josephine was forgotten. Her flower-arranging service was not very successful, but it explains her familiarity with the cable ties and latex gloves she used as the murder weapons. She saw herself more as a vigilante than a murderer. I don't think she would have put it so plainly even to herself, but that is what it was.

"In fact, Josephine and Allison were very alike. It struck me that they made very similar comments about a gay man working in the hotel—"

"I know you showed Jacky that photo of Josie and Brian," Cherril pointed out. "He only recognized Brian."

"Jacky said he didn't remember seeing Josephine," Aunty Lee corrected. "That threw me off too. Then I realized that was because dear Jacky doesn't pay much attention to women. A big mistake, Jacky! Poor Brian. Of course he went to the hotel with Josephine, but I'm sure he didn't know what she did there."

"Poor Josie. You know I used to wish I was like her?" Josephine had always been the confident, beautiful one. Cherril had envied Josephine's confidence even more than her beauty. Josephine had never cared whether other people would accept her or what they would think of her.

"Of course. But you grew beyond it and she didn't. That's the problem with hitting your peak too early. You stay at the stage you feel most successful. You don't try out new things. You don't grow anymore. You are like the bean sprouts that are grown in the dark. Your body stays white and you never grow green leaves to survive on your own. And you are only good for crisp eating—you will never become a plant.

"Allison wasn't thinking logically. The lawsuit was a straw she grabbed at and gave her an excuse to come back to Singapore to get revenge on the people who had ruined her here. I wondered why she wasn't rushing to get out of Singapore as fast as possible, given she was always saying how much she hated Singapore. I think she came to believe that if her ex-husband, Mike, was imprisoned or hanged for murdering 'Allison,' then her kids and her London apartment would be hers again. She really didn't know where else to go or what to do with herself. For all that she bossed her husband around, he had always taken care of all the practical details. And that was also why the people she resented most in her life were not just you animal people but her ex-husband and her sister."

"Why? What did they do to her?"

"They were successful and they were happy—without her. To add insult to injury, Mike Fitzgerald was planning on getting married again. And to the woman she blamed for what had happened in Singapore. While staying with her sister, Vallerie, in America, Allison learned from her children that their father was going to Singapore. She assumed it was to announce his engagement to Josephine. She got Vallerie to come with her—and records show Vallerie paid for their tickets. But when the real Vallerie found the kerosene that Allison bought to set fire to the clinic, she was horrified. Allison drugged Vallerie with her sleeping medication, and it was Vallerie who was asleep in the hotel room when Josephine came up. It was Vallerie who Josephine killed."

Aunty Lee continued: "Allison was fine until the Internet explosion against her. There may always have been that side to her personality, but if not for the wave of Internet hatred, it might never have surfaced. In a way, Josephine and the web activists had created the monster in Allison. Or awoken it anyway. Because there is probably some such monster inside each of us."

When Aunty Lee disappeared with Nina to prepare to present her special dish, Cherril drew Mycroft aside.

"I have to talk to you."

"You want to talk now?" Mycroft asked. He looked around the room. "We can go back home to talk."

"No." Cherril also looked around the room. She did not want to bring this back to the beautifully laid out Peters house. That would always be Mycroft's home more than hers. But they belonged equally in this familiar, cozy café. Most had finished eating by now. Only a few diehard eaters were still going strong. Anne Peters was tempting or perhaps challenging SS Panchal to swallow just one more *pohpiah* that she was folding specially for her . . . one filled with little more than her favorite prawns and crabmeat and lashings of chili, garlic, and sweet sauce. Once immediate hunger was satisfied, people could choose to eat what gave them the most pleasure rather than what would fill them up fastest. And that was when their true tastes were revealed. Cherril felt a stab of jealousy. It was not fair. She had a home and a husband and—

"Well?" said her husband.

"What if we never have children?"

"Then we'll get a dog."

"Mykie, I'm serious."

"Two dogs then. So they can keep each other company when we're not around. And if we want to travel they can look after Mother and Tammy. What sort of dogs, do you think?"

Cherril was almost distracted. It was tempting to think

they could just have dogs instead and never have this discussion, but she had just seen firsthand the damage secrets could wreak on a marriage. But how to begin? Aunty Lee always said, when dealing with prickly subjects (crabs in her case), "Just throw it into the pot first. Afterward you can slowly see which parts you can use."

"I almost had a baby. Long ago, right after school. But it died—I don't even know if it was a boy or girl—soon after I found out I was pregnant. I think maybe that's why we're not having children now. Maybe I can't have any more babies." She expected him to be angry, to accuse her of lying and keeping things from him.

"Sweetheart, what happened?"

"I don't want to talk about it. Not yet."

"All right. But what happened to the baby?"

"I don't know. The doctor said sometimes it happens and nobody knows why. I don't know whether it was my fault and he didn't want to tell me. I was only seventeen then."

"Good lord."

But Mycroft did not seem angry, at least not with her. "Why should that mean you can't have another baby now?"

The answer came out of her mouth automatically: "Because I don't deserve to have one."

"Do you want us to have a baby?"

"Oh yes, of course. But it's been so long and there's still nothing."

"Then we'll go and find out what's wrong. But if you got pregnant before then the problem is more likely to be with me. Would you leave me if that's the case?"

"Of course not!"

"We'll figure it out together, okay? Trust me this time."

"Okay."

Watching from across the room, Aunty Lee saw Mycroft put an arm around his little wife and give her a big hug. Cherril buried her face in his shoulder and the awful tension that had been growing in her was finally gone. Well, thought Aunty Lee, now Cherril had let go of whatever had been bothering her, and very likely Anne Peters would soon have the grandchildren she was so looking forward to!

Aunty Lee's Chilled Revenge was a *tom yam*–flavored spicy seafood jelly made in her largest lotus flower mold and turned out onto a bed of watercress and surrounded by chunks of pineapple. Suspended in the cold blossom's savory pale yellow gel were chunks of crabmeat, prawns, scallops, and red, green, and orange filaments of sweet peppers, baby asparagus, and carrots. It was beautiful, Cherril thought. But then everything looked beautiful to her tonight.

"Because people say revenge is best served cold," Aunty Lee explained. "Same with jelly. First must be boiled very hot until the gelatin melts, like Allison's hot anger. But having hot anger inside for so long made her go a bit crazy. Josephine covered up her anger at Allison—not for killing the dog but for treating her like a stupid local girl. Josephine was full of things she had never forgiven her parents and friends for. And holding so many nuggets of revenge inside her made her cold and dead inside."

Aunty Lee gestured at her chilled creation with satisfaction. "Sometimes getting successful results isn't a matter of stirring and applying heat all the time. Sometimes you have to step back and sit down and let things get cold enough for their true nature to show."

The jelly was a success. The *pohpiahs* were a success. And Aunty Lee's ankle was sufficiently healed that she had walked without support all evening without noticing.

"Go to bed first, Nina. I'm just going to sit here awhile." Aunty Lee settled herself by the open doors to the breakfast patio.

"I just put everything in the fridge first."

The sweet scent of night jasmine wafted gently in with the night sounds of Singapore. No matter where you were on the island there was the hum of traffic in the background, with occasional vehicles closer at hand. And the lights too—it was never completely dark here. But this was Aunty Lee's kind of peace. A small photo of ML stood on the low coffee table beside her and she picked it up and ran a finger over the worked silver frame. She had done this many times before. The finger was worn and roughened now and the frame was scratched, but the half figure in the frame remained buoyantly unchanged, laughing into the sun shining on him.

"Your son is having a baby," Aunty Lee whispered. For a moment a miserable loneliness threatened to overwhelm her. How she wished ML could have seen his first grandchild to carry the Lee name.

Nina appeared with a small glass of Yomeishu health tonic. "Nah. To help you sleep. Otherwise too tired, too excited, you cannot sleep." She paused. "You may have to order more mangoes."

"Really? You mean all the mangoes I bought . . ."

"All finished already. People are already ordering more mango *konnyaku* jellies."

Aunty Lee sipped her tonic wine and allowed herself to be tired. Her twisted ankle had taught her to allow other people to do things for her, and now she was going to allow herself to take things easy when she had to. That was what was really important—along with knowing others needed you, you had to know what you yourself needed. And, of course, she had discovered online bulk shopping.

"We don't have to stop at mangoes," she told Nina. "Durians are coming into season soon."

Acknowledgments

So many people helped (and put up with me) during the writing of this book. In particular I want to thank my agent Priya Doraswamy; my super editor Rachel Kahan; all my fellow Singaporeans (right up to ministerial level!) who spoke up for Tammy, the 7 month old puppy who was adopted then euthanized; and all the great people at William Morrow/HarperCollins who did the real work of creating this book: Trish Daly, Joanne Minutillo, Lucy Gibson, Alaina Waagner, Katherine Turro, Serena Wang, Jennifer Hart, Liate Stehlik, and David Wolfson.

Insights,
Interviews
& More . . .

Meet Ovidia Yu

Kar-Wai Wesley

OVIDIA YU is one of Singapore's best-known and most acclaimed writers. Since dropping out of medical school to write for theater, she has had more than thirty plays produced in Singapore, Malaysia, Australia, the United Kingdom, and the United States, including the Edinburgh Fringe First Award–winning play, "The Woman in a Tree on the Hill."

She is the author of *Aunty Lee's Delights* and *Aunty Lee's Deadly Specials*, and a number of other mysteries that have been published in Singapore and India. Ovidia Yu received a Fulbright Fellowship to attend the University of Iowa's International Writers Program, and has been a writing fellow at the National University of Singapore. She speaks frequently at literary festivals and writers' conferences throughout Asia.

Despite her writing career, when she is recognized in Singapore it is usually because of her stint as a regular celebrity guest on Singapore's version of the American television game show, "Pyramid." ∽

Reading Group Guide

1. At the start of the novel we learn that the victim, Allison Love, had been run out of town by animal activists. Was their outrage warranted? What does Allison (and furry Lola's) story say about social media and its powers? Are we meant to sympathize with Allison or the activists?

2. The narrator tells us: "[Inspector Salim] was aware his country's strength came from its ability to attract the best and brightest of foreign talent. Like he had learned as a boy breeding guppies, for the best colors you had to constantly add specimens caught in different canals to vary the gene pool." Do you think this is an accurate description of Aunty Lee's Singapore? Are there pros and cons to its highly diverse society?

3. "As a foreign domestic worker, Nina was exposed to a lot more of the hidden underside of people. Nina had observed that people were generally worse than they appeared socially. . . ." Do you agree? Which characters have a hidden underside? How are those undersides revealed?

4. Josephine de la Vega, a former Miss Singapore who feels increasingly washed up, has pinned her hopes on marrying expat Mike as a way to get out of a country where she increasingly feels trapped. Is she right to feel that way? Why does

marriage seem like the only possible out to her?

5. "Life would be so much simpler if people said what they thought," Aunty Lee reflects. True or untrue? Does Aunty Lee herself always say what she thinks?

6. Do you agree with Cherril's decision to keep her abortion a secret, despite, as Aunty Lee points out, that it was perfectly legal? Was her mother-in-law right to hire a detective to discover Cherril's secrets before she married the family's only son?

7. How does Aunty Lee get to the truth about Vallerie's identity? How did the infamous Allison Love manage to hide in plain sight for so long in a place where she was so infamous?

8. Who is Aunty Lee thinking of when she reflects: "The reason cold dishes were complicated was the multiple cooking methods involved. . . . A cold, savory mold called for design, execution and presentation. It was the same thing with creating the perfect revenge."

Cherril's Mango Konnyaku Jellies

KONNYAKU is a traditional Japanese high fiber health food that has recently taken Singapore by storm, especially as a substitute for gelatin in jelly desserts. Konnyaku jelly molds come in a range of designs, from sheets of 8 mini-molds each (this recipe fills 2 sheets) to large animal or cartoon character shaped molds.

Ingredients:

2 cups of ripe mango cubes
10g packet of Konnyaku powder
Water

Instructions:

Distribute half the mango cubes in the jelly molds.

Blend the other half of the mango to a puree and add enough water to make up 1 liter. (Instructions on the packet will probably tell you to add sugar, but it's not necessary if you are using mango puree.)

Heat the mango-water mixture in a pan and stir in the konnyaku powder.

Bring to a gentle boil, stirring till the konnyaku has completely dissolved (about 5 minutes) then turn off the flame.

Ladle the thick liquid over the fruit in the molds.

Chill in the fridge for at least 3 hours before unmolding. ∾

Homebaked Mooncakes

TRADITIONAL MOONCAKES consist of a "moon," usually represented by a salted duck egg yolk, surrounded by a sweet filling encased in a decorated pastry shell. Most Singaporeans leave mooncake making to professionals but others, like Aunty Lee, love a hands-on challenge, especially when it comes to a tradition of several hundred years!

Note on molds: Mooncakes molds come in two sizes, regular and small. There are some really lovely traditional hand carved wooden molds as well as modern plastic plunger molds. But for hundreds of years mooncakes were shaped into rounds or squares and decorated by hand (legend has it, with secret messages) so you can do the same.

Ingredients for 8 regular-sized mooncakes:

Filling:

2 12-oz. cans of lotus seeds cooked in
    water
¾ cup of sugar (or more to taste)
Pinch of salt
6 tablespoons of peanut oil (lard is
    traditional if you can get it and don't
    mind the smell)
8 salted duck egg yolks (Be sure
    you buy salted duck eggs and not
    fertilized duck eggs, which are a
    delicacy elsewhere in Asia but would
    be unsuitable and possibly shocking
    here. Remove whites, rinse yolks, ▶

Homebaked Mooncakes *(continued)*

coat yolks with peanut oil, and steam for about 10 minutes over low heat. If translucent, the yolks are still raw. They should be yellow gold and crumbly.)

Pastry:

1 cup of flour
Pinch of salt
Pinch of bicarbonate of soda (baking soda)
¼ cup of golden syrup
½ teaspoon of Lye water (This alkali solution is what puts springy chewiness in egg noodles and Japanese ramen. You can make a baking soda substitute—boil 1 teaspoon of baking soda in 4 cups of water for 5 minutes and use when cool.)
2 tablespoons of peanut oil
Flour for dusting surfaces and molds
Egg wash (one egg beaten with 2 tablespoons of water) for glazing

Pastry:

Sift the flour, salt, and baking soda into a bowl. Make a well in the center.

Whisk together the golden syrup, Lye water, and peanut oil in a separate bowl (the mixture will not be homogenous). Pour slowly, stirring the liquids into the flour, forming a dough. Gently knead this until it comes together in a lump. Cover and set aside to rest for two hours.

Lotus Filling:

Drain the canned lotus seeds and place them in a food processor with sugar and a tablespoon or two of water and blend until smooth.

Transfer to a pan and stir over medium heat until the puree thickens.

Add the peanut oil and continue stirring until the lotus puree forms a glossy dough that leaves the side of the pan. This should take about 5 minutes.

Remove from heat and set aside.

Compiling

Preheat your oven to 350 degrees.

Gently knead the rested dough mixture. Divide into 8 balls and place on a floured tray.

Roll the lotus paste into a long tube and cut into 8 pieces.

Press each egg yolk on a cushion of lotus paste and form a ball around it.

Roll and flatten (or flatten with your palm, village style!) a lump of dough and wrap it around a ball of lotus paste (thinner skins are considered more elegant, but thicker skins are easier to work with), and press the edges together until the filling is sealed in. Some people prefer to roll out two small balls of dough, wrapping one around the filling and the second over it in the opposite direction.

Dust your mold with flour and press the ball of dough in firmly.

If you are using a plastic plunger ▶

Homebaked Mooncakes *(continued)*

mold, press the handle (over a floured surface) and release your mooncake.

If you are using a traditional wooden mold, flip it over and tap to release your mooncake (it may take several taps).

If you are molding your mooncakes by hand, the traditional shapes are rounds and squares, but there are also house-shaped and fish-shaped mooncakes, so set your imagination free!

Place your mooncakes on a parchment-lined baking sheet.

When you're finished forming the mooncakes, bake in your preheated oven for 8 minutes.

Remove the mooncakes from the oven and glaze the tops and sides with egg wash.

Return the mooncakes to the oven for another 10 minutes or until golden brown on top and fragrant.

Now comes the hardest part. You have to wait two days for your mooncakes to reach their prime! After your mooncakes cool completely, store them for at least two days in an airtight container to "return oil" from filling to skin. This will make the skins shiny and soft and the fillings less oily. ∾

Aunty Lee's Guide to All Things Singapore

Her favorite places to check out for food, shopping, and everything in between!

Aunty Lee's Favorite Food Spots in Singapore

Food courts and hawker centers are the best introduction to Singaporean food because they offer the widest variety of foods. As a general guideline, food courts are mostly air-conditioned while hawker centers are not.

Best Place for First-Time Visitors:

The Food Republic on Level 3 of VivoCity

The decor here evokes the good old-fashioned hawker streets with wooden stools and tables, but with air conditioning, clean toilets, and clearly marked prices. And it is handy if you're going across to Sentosa. Aunty Lee recommends their thunder tea rice, butterfly fritters, and egg pratas . . . and the *kueh tutu* (coconut and peanut).

Best Place for Breakfast or Lunch:

Tiong Bahru Market is the best place for an authentic heartland breakfast or lunch. It's best not to risk trying to have dinner there as most of the stalls close once they are sold out for the day, which usually happens by mid-afternoon. Aunty Lee likes the *chwee kueh* there—*chwee kuehs* are tiny savory rice cakes served with a topping of preserved radish and eaten with chili sauce. ▶

Aunty Lee's Guide to All Things Singapore
(continued)

Best Spot for Locals:

Lau Pa Sat (meaning "old market") is what the locals call Telok Ayer Market. Unlike Tiong Bahru Market, you don't want to get here too early. The stalls inside the pavilion are open all day but every evening around 7 P.M. the road outside is closed off for the satay stalls to set up. Lau Pa Sat dates back to the time of Singapore's founder, Sir Stamford Raffles. Aunty Lee recommends the barbecued prawns and octopus.

Aunty Lee's Favorite Shopping and Spots in Singapore

1. **Kampong Buangkok.** Singapore's last "kampong" or village. This is what Singapore looked like when Aunty Lee was growing up, with zinc roofs and red mailboxes and open doors. It makes Aunty Lee nostalgic for the calm and quiet (except for birdsong and insect buzz) of old Singapore. But she doesn't visit often because despite their openness these are people's private homes and lives.

2. **Indri Collection In People's Park Complex.** They have a large collection of ready-made Peranakan embroidered *kebayas* and batik sarong skirts (and batik shirts for men). Indri is really more a stall than a shop and doesn't have a unit number. It's on Level 1 of

the People's Park Complex, just off the central atrium and next to the Security Guard counter. (And if you make it there, Aunty Lee suggests you take a take a quick detour to the basement food court of People's Park Complex to try their noodles.)

3. **Arab Street.** One of Singapore's oldest and most beautiful mosques is found here. Sultan Mosque was built in 1826 by Sultan Hussein Shah of Johor. If you wish to enter the mosque, and are not appropriately dressed, robes are provided. Arab Street is a rich bazaar-style mix of cafés and shops dating from the 1950s selling textiles, carpets, and souvenirs. Aunty Lee also recommends Haji Lane around the corner, where pre-war shophouses showcase the latest up-and-coming fashion designers.

4. **The German Girl Shrine and Chck Jawa on Pulau Ubin.** Pulau Ubin is Singapore's second largest offshore island, but completely different from Sentosa. The German Girl shrine, also known as the Barbie Doll shrine, is a yellow hut beneath an Assam tree. Legend has it that it commemorates a German girl who fell to her death in a granite quarry during World War I and some believe she brings good luck. ▶

Chek Jawa is Singapore's only surviving multi-ecosystem site—sandy beach, rocky beach, seagrass lagoon, coral rubble, mangroves, and coastal forest—and protected from development till 2012. Now, in 2016, its time may be running out.

5. **And finally, the Mustafa Centre in Little India (Syed Alwi Road).** This is a huge department store that sells everything from refrigerators, jewelry, tea towels, and mobile phones to plasters and painkillers. In operation since 1971, it is open twenty-four hours a day, every day (including Chinese New Year) and also has a foreign currency exchange. Aunty Lee suggests you take a look around Little India while you are there and explore the ayurvedic medicine shops, fortune tellers, henna tattoo artists . . . and of course sample the roti prata, thosai, dhal, and kebabs!

Aunty Lee's Top 5 Food Favorites

1. **Katong laksa** with homemade barley water. Fierce debate rages in Singapore over the most "authentic" *katong laksa*. It consists of rice noodles served in a rich, spicy gravy with fish cake, prawns, and cockles and garnished with laksa leaf.

2. **Kaya toast** with soft eggs. A delicious sweet coconut jam.

Kaya toast and eggs are a standard breakfast set available all day at most "kopi-tiams" or corner coffee shops.

3. **Fish head curry.** The head of a red snapper stewed in a sweet and sour tamarind curry with okra and eggplant and ginger flower buds. This is best eaten with fingers off banana leaves but also tastes good with cutlery.

4. **Kueh lapis.** Multi-layered, multi-colored, traditional steamed cakes made of glutinous rice flour, coconut, and sugar. *Kueh lapis legit* is made of layers of rich batter, each spread over the previous layer and grilled separately, creating the brown lines in the buttery cake.

5. **Tau suan.** A sweet hot dessert soup made of split mung beans and flavored with pandan (screw pine) leaves. Though widely available at dessert stalls, this is a favorite comfort food . . . and full of protein and soluble fiber, it's healthy as well as delicious! ∽